A Devil is Waiting

ALSO BY JACK HIGGINS
FROM CLIPPER LARGE PRINT

The Judas Gate

A Devil is Waiting

Jack Higgins

W F HOWES LTD

This large print edition published in 2016 by
W F Howes Ltd
Unit 5, St George's House, Rearsby Business Park,
Gaddesby Lane, Rearsby, Leicester LE7 4YH

1 3 5 7 9 10 8 6 4 2

First published in the United Kingdom in 2012
by HarperCollins*Publishers*

A CIP catalogue record for this book is available
from the British Library

ISBN 978 1 51002 386 4

Typeset by Palimpsest Book Production Limited,
Falkirk, Stirlingshire

Printforce ... den Rijn,
The Netherlands

For Tessa-Gaye Coleman
Night & Day,
You Are the One

Where there is a sin
A devil is waiting

—IRISH PROVERB

BROOKLYN

LONDON

CHAPTER 1

It was late afternoon on Garrison Street, Brooklyn, as Daniel Holley sat at the wheel of an old Ford delivery truck, waiting for Dillon. There were parked vehicles, but little evidence of people.

Rain drove in across the East River, clouding his view of the coastal ships tied up to the pier that stretched ahead. A policeman emerged from an alley a few yards away, his uniform coat running with water, cap pulled down over his eyes. He banged on the truck with his nightstick.

Holley wound down the window. 'Can I help you, Officer?'

'I should imagine you could, you daft bastard,' Sean Dillon told him. 'Me being wet to the skin already.'

He scrambled in and Holley said, 'Why the fancy dress? Are we going to a party?'

'Of a sort. You see that decaying warehouse down there with the sign saying "Murphy & Son – Import-Export"?'

'How could I miss it? What about it?' Holley took out an old silver case, extracted two cigarettes,

3

lit them with a Zippo, and passed one over. 'Get your lips round that, you're shaking like a leaf. What's the gig?'

Dillon took a quick drag. 'God help me, but that's good. Ferguson called me from Washington and told me to check the place out, but not to do anything till I got a call from him.' He glanced at his watch. 'Which I'm expecting just about now.'

'How kind of him to think of us. Brooklyn in weather like this is such a joy,' Holley told him, and at that moment, Dillon's Codex sounded.

He switched to speaker and General Charles Ferguson's voice boomed out. 'You've looked the place over, Dillon?'

'As much as I could. Two cars outside it, that's all. No sign of life.'

'Well, life there undoubtedly is. I made an appointment by telephone for you, Daniel, with Patrick Murphy. Your name is Daniel Grimshaw, and you're representing a Kosovo Muslim religious group seeking arms for defence purposes.'

'And who exactly is Murphy and what's it all about?' Holley asked.

'As you two well know, several dissident groups, all IRA in one way or another, have raised their ugly heads once again. The security services have managed to foil a number of potentially nasty incidents, but luck won't always be on their side. You'll remember the incident in Belfast not long ago when a bomb badly injured three policemen,

4

one of whom lost his left arm. Since then another policeman has been killed by a car bomb.'

'I heard about that,' Dillon said.

'Police officers are having to check under their cars again, just like in the bad old days, and some of them are finding explosive devices. We can't have that. And there's more. Attempts have started again to smuggle arms into Ulster. Last week, a trawler called the *Amity* tried to land a cargo on the County Down coast and was sighted by a Royal Navy gunboat. The crew did a runner and haven't been caught, but I've firm evidence that the cargo of assorted weaponry originated with Murphy & Son.'

'Was your source MI5?'

'Good Lord, no. You know how much the security services hate us. The Prime Minister's private army, getting to do whatever we want, as long as we have the Prime Minister's warrant. At least that's what they think. They just don't appreciate how necessary our services are in today's world—'

Holley cut in. 'Especially when we shoot people for them.'

'You know my attitude on that,' Ferguson said.

'Getting back to Murphy & Son, why not get the FBI to handle them? We are in New York, after all.'

'I'd rather not bother our American cousins. This comes from Northern Ireland, and that's our patch. Part of the UK.'

'I've always thought that was part of the problem,'

Dillon said with a certain irony. 'But never mind. What do you want us to do?'

'Find out who ordered the bloody weapons in the first place, and I don't want to hear any crap about some Irish American with a romantic notion about the gallant struggle for Irish freedom.'

'Lean on them hard?' Holley asked.

'Daniel, they're out to make a buck selling weapons that kill people.' He was impatient now. 'I couldn't care less what happens to them.'

'Wonderful,' Dillon told him. 'You've appointed us to be public executioners.'

'It's a bit late in the day to complain about that,' Ferguson told him. 'For both of you. What do they say in the IRA? Once in, never out?'

'Funny,' Holley said. 'We thought that was your motto. But never mind. We'll probably do your dirty work for you again. We usually do. How do you want them? Alive or dead?'

'We're at war, Daniel. Remember the four bastards who raped your young cousin to death in Belfast? They were all members of a terrorist organization. You shot them dead yourself. Are you telling me you regret what you did?'

'Not for a moment. That's the trouble.'

Dillon said, 'Leave him alone, Charles, he'll do what has to be done. Have you seen the President yet?'

'No, I'm sitting here in the Hay-Adams with Harry Miller, looking out over the terrace at the White House, waiting for the limousine to deliver

6

us to the Oval Office. We've prepared to brief him on the security for his visit to London on Friday, all twenty-four hours of it. As far as I can tell, we've got everything locked down, including his visit to Parliament and the luncheon reception on the terrace.'

'Westminster Bridge to the left, the Embankment on the far side,' Dillon said.

'Yes, you've got experience with the terrace, haven't you?' Ferguson said. 'Anyway, the Gulfstream is standing by, ready and waiting, so the moment I'm free, it's off to New York for this UN reception at the Pierre. I want you two there, too.'

'Any particular reason?'

'I've got someone new joining the team from the Intelligence Corps.'

'Really?' Holley asked. 'What have we got?'

'Captain Sara Gideon, a brilliant linguist. Speaks fluent Pashtu, Arabic, and Iranian. Just what we've been needing.'

'Is that all?' Holley joked.

'Ah, I was forgetting Hebrew.'

Dillon said, 'You haven't gone and recruited an Israeli, have you?'

'That would be illegal, Dillon. No, she's a Londoner. There have been Gideons around since the seventeenth century. I'm sure you've heard of the Gideon Bank. She inherited it. While she pursues her military agenda, her grandfather sits in for her as chairman of the board.'

7

'You mean she's one of those Gideons?' Dillon said. 'So why isn't she married to some obliging millionaire, and what the hell is she doing in the army?'

'Because at nineteen, she was at college in Jerusalem brushing up on her Hebrew before going up to Oxford when her parents visited her and were killed in a Hamas bus bombing.'

'Ah-ha,' Holley said. 'So she chose Sandhurst instead of Oxford.'

'Correct. And in the last nine years has served with the Intelligence Corps in Belfast, Bosnia, Kosovo, Iraq, and two tours in Afghanistan.'

'Jesus, what in the hell is she after?' Dillon said. 'Is she seeking revenge, is she a war junkie, what?'

'Roper's just posted her full history, so you can read it for yourself.'

'I wouldn't miss it for anything,' Dillon said.

'Yes, I'm sure you'll find it instructive, particularly the account of the nasty ambush near Abusan, where she took a bullet in the right thigh which left her with a permanent limp.'

'All right, General, I surrender,' Dillon said. 'I'll keep my big gob shut. I can't wait to meet her in person.'

'What do we do with her until you get to the Pierre?' Holley asked.

'Keep her happy. She was booking in at the Plaza after a flight from Arizona. There's some secret base out there that the RAF are involved in, something to do with pilotless aircraft. She'll be returning to London with us. She's been on the staff of Colonel Hector Grant, our military attaché at the UN, and this will be her final appearance for him, so she'll be in uniform.'

'Does she know what she's getting into with us?'

'I've told Roper to brief her on everything – including you two and your rather murky pasts.'

'You're so kind,' Holley said. 'It's a real privilege to know you.'

'Oh, shut up,' Ferguson told him. 'Miller is very impressed with her, and I'm happy about the whole thing.'

'Well, we're happy if you're happy,' Dillon told him.

'We've got to go now. Why don't you two clear off and do something useful. I'll see you tonight.'

Dillon walked away through the downpour, the nightstick in his right hand. He turned left into an alley and Holley waited for a few moments, then took from his pocket a crumpled Burberry rain hat in which a spring clip held a Colt .25. He eased it onto his head, got out of the truck, and walked quickly through the rain.

Dressed as he was as a beat cop, Dillon didn't need to show any particular caution, tried a door, which opened to his touch, and passed into a decaying kitchen, a broken sink in one corner, cupboards on the peeling walls, and a half-open door that indicated a toilet.

'Holy Mother of God,' he said softly. 'Whatever's going on here, there can't be money in it.'

He opened the far door, discovered a corridor dimly lit by a single lightbulb, and heard voices somewhere ahead. He started forward, still grasping the nightstick in his right hand, his left clutching a Walther PPK with a Carswell silencer in the capacious pocket of his storm coat.

The voices were raised now as if in argument and someone said, 'Well, I think you're a damn liar, so you'd better tell me the truth quickly, mister, or Ivan here will be breaking your right arm. You won't be able to swim very far in the sewer after that, I'm afraid.'

There was no door, just an archway leading to a platform with iron stairs dropping down, and Dillon, peering out, saw a desk and two men confronting Holley, who was glancing wildly about him, or so it seemed. Dillon eased the Walther out of his pocket, stepped out, and started down the stairs.

When Holley had entered the warehouse he had found it dark and gloomy, a sad sort of place and crammed with a lot of rusting machinery. The roof seemed to be leaking, there were chain hoists here and there, and two old vans that had obviously seen better days were parked to one side. There was a light on further ahead, suspended from the ceiling over a desk with a couple of chairs, no sign of people, iron stairs descending from the platform above.

He called out, 'Hello, is anyone there? I've got an appointment with Patrick Murphy.'

'Would that be Mr Grimshaw?' a voice called
– Irish, not American.

The man who stepped into the light was middle-aged, with silver hair, and wore a dark suit over a turtleneck sweater. He produced a pack of cigarettes, shook one out, and lit it with an old lighter.

'Yes, I'm Daniel Grimshaw,' Holley said.

'Then come away in.'

'Thank you.' Holley took a step forward, the rear door of the van on his right opened, and a man stepped out, a Makarov in his hand. He was badly in need of a shave, his dark unruly hair was at almost shoulder length, and he wore a bomber jacket. He moved in behind Holley and rammed the Makarov into his back.

'Do you want me to kill him now?' he asked in Russian, a language Holley understood.

'Let's hear what his game is first,' Murphy told him in the same language.

'Now, that's what I like to hear,' Holley said in Russian. 'A sensible man.'

'So you speak the lingo?' Murphy was suddenly wary. 'Arms for the Kosovans? Are the Serbs turning nasty again this year? Ivan here's on their side, being Russian, but I'll hear what you've got to say.' This was said in English, but now he added in Russian, 'Make sure he's clean.'

Ivan's hands explored Holley thoroughly, particularly between the legs, and Holley said, 'It must be a big one you're looking for.'

Ivan gave him a shove so violent that Holley

11

went staggering, and his Burberry rain hat fell to the floor, disclosing the Colt, which the Russian picked up at once, throwing the hat across to the desk.

'Now can I shoot him?'

Murphy pulled the Colt from the clip in the rain hat and examined it. 'Very nice. I like it.' He left the cap on the desk and slipped the Colt into his pocket.

Ivan said, 'Only a pro would use a shooter like that.'

'I know that, I'm not a fool. Show him where he's going to end up if he doesn't answer a few questions.'

Ivan leaned down, grasped a ring in the floor, and heaved back a trapdoor. There was the sound of running water, the smell of sewage.

Where the hell are you, Dillon? That was the only thought running through Holley's mind. He glanced about him wildly, trying to act like a man in panic.

He said to Murphy, 'What is this? What are you doing? I told you my name is Daniel Grimshaw.'

'Well, I think you're a damn liar, so you'd better tell me the truth quickly, mister, or Ivan here will be breaking your right arm. You won't be able to swim very far in the sewer after that, I'm afraid.'

'You're making a big mistake.'

'It's not my mistake, my friend.' Murphy shook his head and said to Ivan in Russian, 'Break his arm.'

12

Dillon called in the same language, 'I don't think so,' and shot Ivan in his gun hand. Ivan cried out, dropped the Makarov, and slumped to one knee beside the open sewer.

Murphy took the whole thing surprisingly calmly. Remembering that he'd slipped the Colt .25 into his pocket, he watched Holley pick up the Makarov and realized there was still a chance things might go his way.

'I assume I'd be right in supposing that your fortunate arrival isn't coincidental, Officer. I congratulate you on your performance – the NYPD would be proud of you.'

'I used to be an actor,' Dillon said. 'But then I discovered the theatre of the street had more appeal. Audience guaranteed, you see, especially in Belfast.'

Murphy was immediately wary. 'Ah, *that* theatre of the street? So which side did you play for? You couldn't be IRA, not the both of you.'

'Why not?' Dillon asked.

'Well, admittedly you've got an Ulster accent, but your friend here is English.'

'Well, I'd say you're a Dublin man myself,' Dillon told him. 'And admittedly there's some strange people calling themselves IRA these days, and a world of difference between them. We, for example, are the Provo variety, and Mr Holley's sainted mother being from Crossmaglen, the heart of what the British Army described as bandit country, his Yorkshire half doesn't count.'

Murphy was beginning to look distinctly worried. 'What do you want?'

Dillon smiled amiably. 'For a start, let's get that piece of shit on his feet. He's a disgrace to the Russian Federation. Putin wouldn't approve of him at all.'

Holley pulled Ivan up to stand on the edge of the sewage pit. Following Dillon's lead, he said, 'Is this where you want him, Dillon? He might fall in, you know.'

Dillon ignored him and said to Murphy, 'I'm going to put a question to you. If you tell me the truth, I'll let you live. Of course, if you turn out to have lied, I'll have all the fuss of coming back and killing you, and that will annoy me very much, because I'm a busy man.'

Murphy laughed uneasily. 'That's a problem, I can see that, but how will you know?'

'By proving to you I mean business.' He turned to where Ivan stood swaying on the edge of the pit, pulled Holley out of the way, and kicked the Russian's feet out from under him, sending him down with a cry into the fast-flowing sewage, to be swept away.

'There he goes,' Dillon said. 'With any luck, he could end up in the river, but I doubt it.'

Murphy looked horrified. 'What kind of a man are you?'

'The stuff of nightmares, so don't fug with me, Patrick,' Dillon told him. 'Last week a trawler named *Amity* was surprised by the Royal Navy as it attempted to land arms on the County Down coast. Our sources tell us the cargo originated with you. I'm not interested in Irish clubs or whoever raised funds over here. I want to know who ordered the cargo in Northern Ireland. Tell me that and you're home free.'

For a moment, Murphy seemed unable to speak, and Holley said, 'Are you trying to tell us you don't know?'

Murphy seemed to swallow hard. 'No. I know who it is. We do a lot of this kind of work, putting deals together for small African countries, people from the Eastern European bloc. None of the players are big fish. Lots of small agencies put things our way, stuff the big arms dealers won't touch.'

'So cut to the chase,' Dillon told him.

'I got a call from one of them. He said an Irish party was in town looking for assistance.'

'And he turned up here?'

'That's right. Ulster accent, just like you. A quiet sort of man, around sixty-five, strong-looking, good face, greying hair. Used to being in charge, I'd say.'

Dillon said, 'What was his name?'

'I can only tell you what he called himself. Michael Flynn. Had a handling agent in Marseilles. The money was all paid into a holding company who provided the *Amity* with false papers, paid half a dozen thugs off the waterfront to crew it. Nothing you could trace, I promise you. My end

15

came from Marseille by bank draft. It all came to nothing. I never heard from Flynn again, but from what I saw in the newspaper accounts, the Royal Navy only came on the *Amity* by chance. A bit unfortunate, that.'

Holley turned to Dillon. 'Okay?'

'It'll have to be, won't it?'

'You mean I'm in the clear?' Murphy asked.

'So it would appear,' Dillon told him. 'Just try to cultivate a different class of friend in the future. That bastard Ivan was doing you no good at all.'

'That's bloody marvellous.' Murphy hammered a fist on the desk and came round it. 'You kept your word, Mr Dillon, and I'm not used to that, so I'll tell you something else.'

Dillon smiled beautifully and turned to Holley. 'See, Daniel, Patrick wants to unburden himself. Isn't that nice?'

But even he couldn't have expected what came next.

'I was holding out on you on one thing. I actually did find out who Flynn really was. He wasn't particularly nice to me, so I'll tell you.'

Dillon wasn't smiling now. 'And how did you find that out?'

'He called round to see me one evening and discovered his mobile hadn't charged up properly. He was upset about it, because he had a fixed time to call somebody in Northern Ireland. He was agitated, so it was obviously important. He asked if he could use my landline.'

Dillon shook his head. 'And you listened in on an extension.'

Murphy nodded. 'He said it was Jack Kelly from New York, confirming that Operation Amity is a go. Arriving on the night of the eighth, landfall north beach at Dundrum Bay, close to St John's Point.'

'That's County Down,' Dillon said. 'Anything else?'

'I put the phone down. I didn't want to get caught. I had the number checked on my phone bill and found it was to a phonebox in Belfast on the Falls Road.'

Holley said, 'Whoever they are, they're being very careful. That would have been untraceable.' He paused. 'Could Jack Kelly be who I think it is? It's a common enough name in Ireland, God knows.'

'You mean the Jack Kelly we ran up against, working for our old friend Jean Talbot?'

'I know it doesn't seem likely,' Holley began, and Dillon cut in.

'The same Jack Kelly who became an IRA volunteer at eighteen, was involved for over thirty years in the Troubles, and served on the Army Council?'

'And never too happy about the peace process,' Holley said. 'So if it *is* him . . . I wonder what he's up to.'

'That's for Ferguson and Roper to decide.'

'Strange, us having a foot in both camps,' Holley said. 'How do you think that happened?'

'Daniel, me boy, if I was of a religious turn of

17

mind, I'd say God must have a purpose in mind for us, but for the life of me, I can't imagine what it would be.'

'Well, I'm damned if I can,' Holley said. 'Although I should imagine that the general will pay Kelly a call sooner rather than later.'

Dillon turned to Murphy. 'Happy, are you, Patrick, now that you've come clean? I mean, as you did turn out to have lied, you must have thought I might take it the wrong way?'

'Of course not, Mr Dillon,' Murphy said, but there was a gathering alarm on his face.

'Don't worry,' Dillon carried on. 'You've done us a good turn. Although it would help the situation, restore mutual trust, you might say, if you produced my friend's Colt .25. It doesn't seem to be on the spring clip, which I can see quite clearly inside the rain hat on the desk there.'

Murphy managed to look astonished. 'But that's nonsense,' he said, and then moved with lightning speed behind Holley, grabbed him by the collar, and produced the Colt.

'I don't want trouble, I just want out, but if I have to, I'll kill your friend. So just drop that Walther into the sewage, and then we'll walk to the door and I'll get into my car and vanish. Otherwise, your friend's a dead man.'

'Now, we can't have that, can we? Here we go, a perfectly good Walther down the toilet, in a manner of speaking.' Dillon dropped it in.

Murphy pushed Holley towards the entrance,

the Colt against his skull, and as Dillon trailed them, cried, 'Stay back or I'll drop him.'

Holley said to Murphy, 'Hey, take it easy. Just be careful, all right? I hope you're familiar with the Colt .25. If you don't have the plus button on, those hollow-point cartridges'll blow up in your face.'

They were just reaching the door. Murphy loosened his grip, a look of panic on his face, and fumbled at the weapon. Holley kicked out at him, caught him off guard, then ran away and ducked behind one of the old vans. Murphy fired after him reflexively and then, seeing that the Colt worked perfectly well, he realized he'd been had. He turned and ran out through the heavy rain into the courtyard.

Dillon had a replica of Holley's Colt in a holder on his right ankle. He drew it now, ran to the entrance and fired at Murphy, who was trying to open the door of a green Lincoln. Murphy fired back wildly, then turned, ran across the road and up the stone steps leading to the walkway, the East River lapping below it. At the top, he hesitated, unsure of which way to go, turned, and found Dillon closing in, Holley behind.

'No way out, Patrick. So have you told me the truth or not?'

'Damn you,' Murphy called, half-blinded by the heavy rain, and tried to take aim.

Dillon shot him twice in the heart, twisting him around, his third shot driving him over the low rail into the river. He reached the rail in time to see Murphy surface once, then roll over and disappear in the fast-running current.

Holley moved up to join him. 'What was all that about? Sometimes you play games too much, Sean.'

'Sure, and all I wanted was to make sure he was telling the truth. He'd lied at first – isn't that a fact?'

'So is the name really Jack Kelly?'

'We'll see, but for now, it's time for the joys of the Plaza and our first meeting with the intriguing Captain Sara Gideon.'

'Definitely something to look forward to,' Holley said, and followed him down the steps.

At the same time they were driving away in their delivery truck, Patrick Murphy, choking and gasping, was swept under a pier two hundred yards away downstream. He drifted through the pilings, banged into stone steps with a railing, hauled himself out, and paused at the top, where there was a roofed shelter with a bench.

He sat down, shivering with cold, pulled off his soaking jacket, then his shirt. The bullet-proof vest he'd been wearing was the best on the market, even against hollow points. He ripped open the Velcro tabs, tossed the rest down into the river with his shirt, struggled back into his jacket, and walked through the rain to the warehouse.

He expected Dillon and Holley to be long gone

and went straight inside and up to his office. He peeled off his jacket, pulled on an old sweater that was hanging behind the door, then lifted the carpet in the corner, revealing a floor safe, opened it, and removed a linen bag containing his mad money, twenty grand in large bills. He got a suitcase from the cupboard, put the money into it, and sat there thinking about the situation.

He had to get away for a while, the kind of place where he'd be swallowed up by the crowds. Vegas would be good, but he needed to cover his back, just in case he wanted to return to New York. He rang a number and, when a man replied, said, 'I'm afraid I've got a problem, Mr Cagney.'

'And what would that be?'

'You sent me a nice piece of business. The man from Ulster, Michael Flynn.'

'What's happened?'

'I had a client calling himself Grimshaw. He said he was seeking a consignment of weaponry, but the truth was he wanted information about the *Amity* and who'd been behind it.'

'And did you tell him about Michael Flynn?'

'Of course I did. He and another man with him killed Ivan and threatened to do the same to me if I didn't tell them. Anyway, your client's name isn't Flynn, it's Jack Kelly. He got careless using my phone one night.'

'How unfortunate. Have you any idea who these people are?'

'One posed as an NYPD officer, had an Ulster

accent, and was called Dillon. The other was English, named Holley.'

'They seem to have been rather careless with their names.'

'That's because I was supposed to end up dead, which I nearly was. Look, they claimed to be members of the Provisional IRA. I thought your client, Flynn or Kelly or whatever his name is, should know about that.'

Cagney said, 'I appreciate your warning, Patrick. What do you intend to do now?'

'Get the hell out of New York.'

'Where can I contact you?'

'I'll let you know.'

Murphy replaced the phone, grabbed the suit-case, and went out. Within minutes, he was driving the undamaged car, a Ford sedan, out of the courtyard.

Shortly afterwards, Liam Cagney, a prosperous 60-year-old stockbroker by profession and Irish American to the core, was phoning Jack Kelly in Kilmartin, County Down, in Northern Ireland.

'It's Liam, Jack,' he said when the receiver was picked up. 'You've got a problem.'

'And what would that be?'

'Somebody's asked Murphy about the *Amity*. Do the names Dillon and Holley mean anything to you?'

'By God, they do. They're both Provisional IRA renegades now working for Charles Ferguson and British Intelligence. What did Murphy tell them?'

'He told me they killed his man Ivan and almost got him. He also heard you using your real name in a phone call.'

Kelly swore. 'I *knew* that was dangerous, but I had no choice. So he's on the run? I don't like that. You never know what he might do.'

'Don't worry, it's taken care of. He won't be going anywhere.'

'That's good to know. You've served our cause well, Liam, and thanks for the information about Dillon and Holley. If they turn up here, we'll be ready for them. It's time someone sorted those two out. Take care, old friend.'

He was seated behind his desk in his office at Talbot Place, the great country house in County Down, where he was estate manager. He sat there thinking about it, then opened a drawer, took out an encrypted mobile phone, and punched in a number.

There was a delay, and he was about to ring off when a voice said, 'Owen Rashid.'

'This is Kelly, Owen. Sorry to bother you.'

In London, Rashid's flat was huge and luxurious, and as he got rid of his tie, he walked to the windows overlooking Park Lane. 'Is there a problem? Tell me.'

Which Kelly did. When he was finished, he said, 'Sorry about this.'

'Not your fault.' Rashid poured himself a brandy.

'Dillon and Holley. They're bad news, but nothing I can't deal with. My sources will tell me if they try anything.'

'I'm always amazed by what you know, Owen.'

'Not me, Jack, Al Qaeda. In spite of bin Laden's death, it's still a worldwide organization. We have people at every level, from a waiter serving lunch to a talkative senator in New York, to a disgruntled police chief in Pakistan, to a disenchanted government minister in some Arab state who hates corruption – or a humble gardener right here in London's Hyde Park, watching me take my early-morning run and seeing who I'm with. In this wonderful age of the mobile phone, all they have to do is call in.'

'And I'm not sure I like that,' Kelly said.

'No sane person would. Is Mrs Talbot still with you?'

'She flew to London yesterday in the Beach Baron.'

'I'll look her up. As to Dillon, Holley, and Murphy, don't worry, we'll sort it. But it'd be a good idea if you called Abu and reported in.'

'Where is he?' Kelly demanded.

'Waziristan, for all I know. He's a mouthpiece, Jack, passing us our orders and receiving information in return. He could be living in London, but I doubt it.'

'Why do you say that?'

'He knows too much. They wouldn't want to take the chance of him falling into the wrong hands. He'll be sitting there, nice and safe in a mud hut with no running water or flush toilet, but the encrypted phone is all he needs. I would definitely give him a call, if I were you.'

'Okay, I will,' and Kelly switched off.

Owen stood under the awning on the terrace, rain dripping down, late-night Park Lane traffic below and Hyde Park in the darkness. He loved London and always had. Half-Welsh, thanks to the doctor's daughter his father had met at Cambridge University, who had died in childbirth; half-Arab from one of the smaller Oman states.

Rubat had little to commend it except its oil. It didn't have the interminable billions of the other states, but the wealth generated by Rashid Oil was enough to keep the small population happy. Sultan Ibrahim Rashid was chairman, and his nephew, Owen Rashid, was CEO, running the company from the Mayfair office and living in considerable comfort, especially as he'd managed to avoid marriage during his forty-five years.

His one mistake had been to get involved with Al Qaeda. He was not a jihadist and wasn't interested in the religious side of things, but he'd reasoned that it would give him more muscle in the workplace and more power in the business world for Rashid Oil. He had been welcomed with open arms, but then found he had made a devil's bargain, for he had to obey orders like everyone else.

Right now his task was to cultivate Jean Talbot, the chairman of Talbot International. Her son had been under Al Qaeda's thumb – pure blackmail – until he died, and he had started by attending her son's funeral. She had apparently known nothing about the connection, but Jack Kelly had, an old IRA hand who was itching to see some action again.

To meet Jean Talbot, he'd visited the Zion Gallery in Bond Street, where there was an exhibition of her art, and loitered until she'd turned up. A compliment on her famous portrait of her son had led to lunch at the Ivy.

The point of all this had only recently been made clear by his Al Qaeda masters. A single-track railway ran down from Saudi Arabia and ended up in Hazar next door to Rubat. It was called the Bacu. In modern times, it had been convenient to run pipes alongside the railway from the oil wells in southern Arabia, and over years of wheeler-dealing, the Bacu had ended up being owned by Talbot International.

Owen Rashid's primary task was to persuade Jean Talbot to look favourably on the idea of extending the Bacu line through Rubat. The benefit to Yemen, a hotbed of Al Qaeda activity, was obvious: the possibility of instant access to the world's biggest oil fields.

The truth was that he'd come to like Jean immensely, but that was just too bad. He had his orders, so he raised his glass and said, softly, 'To you, Jean. Perhaps you'll paint *my* portrait one day.'

At the same time in New York, Patrick Murphy was leaving his apartment and proceeding along the street to catch a cab. He hadn't packed a suitcase. He'd decided he'd buy new clothes in Vegas, so he was just carrying the suitcase. He didn't hear a thing, was just suddenly conscious of someone behind him and a needle point slicing into his clothes.

'Just turn right into the next doorway.' The voice was very calm.

Murphy did as he was told. 'Please listen. If Cagney's sent you, there's no need for this. I've got money, lots of money. Just take it.'

The knife went right in under the ribs, finding the heart, killing him so quickly that he wasn't even aware of the man picking up his suitcase and walking away, leaving him dead in the doorway.

WASHINGTON

AFGHANISTAN

CHAPTER 2

Aveteran of both Vietnam and the Secret Service, Blake Johnson had served a string of presidents as personal security adviser and was something of a White House institution. He'd known Ferguson and Miller for years.

Now he joined them in the rear of the limousine, closing the window that cut them off from the driver. 'I can't tell you how good it is to see you,' he said. 'Things are pretty rough for all of us these days. I wonder how the Prime Minister would cope if he didn't have you.'

'Oh, he'd manage, I'm sure,' said Ferguson. 'But my team is always ready to handle any situation with the appropriate response.'

'Which usually means general mayhem,' Harry Miller put in. Miller was the Prime Minister's main troubleshooter and an under-secretary of state.

'Well, you should know,' Ferguson told Miller. 'Mayhem is your general job description. When you're not being used to frighten other Members of Parliament to death.'

'A total exaggeration, as usual,' Miller told Blake. 'Anyway, I'm sure the President will be happy with our security arrangements for his brief visit to London. We wish it could be longer, but I know he's expected in Paris and Berlin.'

Ferguson said, 'I'm surprised he can find the time at all with everything going on in the Middle East and Africa.'

'And Al Qaeda threatening worldwide spectaculars in capital cities,' Miller put in. 'In revenge for the death of bin Laden.'

'We can't just sit back and wait for things to happen,' Ferguson said. 'We've got to go in hard, find those responsible for running the show these days, and take them out.'

'Well, I think you'll find that's exactly what the President wants to talk to you about,' Blake said. 'You know he supports action when necessary. But I think you'll find he favours a more conciliatory approach where possible.'

Ferguson frowned. 'What does that mean?'

Miller put a warning hand on Ferguson's knee. 'Let's just see what the President says.'

The general pulled himself together. 'Yes, of course, we must hear what the President has to say.'

In the Oval Office, the President and Blake faced Ferguson and Miller across a large coffee table. Clancy Smith, the President's favourite Secret Service man, stood back, ever watchful.

'London, Paris, Berlin, Brussels – it's going to be quite a stretch in four days,' said the President.

'But I'm really looking forward to London, particularly the luncheon reception at Parliament.'

'It'll be a great day, Mr President,' Ferguson said. 'We've completely overhauled our security system for your visit. Major Miller is the coordinator.'

'Yes, I've read your report. I couldn't leave it in better hands. What I actually wanted to ask you about was your report of the inquiry into the Mirbat ambush in Afghanistan that cost us so many lives. It seems you were right when you supposed that British-born Muslims were fighting in the Taliban ranks.'

'I'm afraid so.'

'That's bad enough in itself, but the fact that the man leading them was a decorated war hero, that he was chairman of one of the most respected arms corporations in the business – it defies belief.'

'Talbot was a wild young man, hungry for war,' Miller said. 'Originally his supplying illegal arms to the Taliban across the border was strictly for kicks, but that led to Al Qaeda blackmailing him.'

'As you can see from our report, he had Dillon's bullet in him when he crashed his plane into the sea off the Irish coast,' Ferguson shrugged. 'An act of suicide to protect the family name.'

'So his mother knew nothing about this Al Qaeda business?'

'No. And she's now chairman of Talbot International simply because she owns most of the shares.'

'And in the world's eyes, he just died in a tragic accident?'

Ferguson said, 'Of course, Al Qaeda knows the truth, but it wouldn't be to their benefit to admit to it. Nobody would believe such a story anyway.'

'And thank God for that, and for the part you and your people played in bringing the affair to a successful conclusion, particularly your Sean Dillon and Daniel Holley. I see the Algerian foreign minister has given Holley a diplomatic passport.'

'The Algerian government is just as disenchanted with Al Qaeda as we are,' said Ferguson. 'That passport makes him a very valuable asset.'

'Who in his youth was a member of the Provisional IRA, as was Sean Dillon. Men who are the product of extreme violence tend perhaps to believe that a violent response is the only way forward.'

'International terrorism is the scourge of our times, Mr President, powered by fanatics who insist on extreme views. It's like a cancer that needs to be cut out to stop it spreading.'

The President said, 'As you know, General, I believe in necessary force. But you can't kill them all. The only way forward is to engage in dialogue with people with extreme views and attempt to reach a compromise. With Osama out of the way, I have great hopes for such an approach.'

'I agree,' Ferguson said. 'But what about those who believe in the purity of violence and are willing to bomb the hell out of anyone who refuses to agree with them? Wouldn't it be better to have people like Dillon and Holley stamp out such a fire before it spreads?'

'Can such actions ever be condoned?' the President asked.

Ferguson said, 'In 1947, a brilliant commando leader named Otto Skorzeny was accused of war crimes because he had sent his men into action behind American lines wearing GI uniforms. Many of these men, when captured, were executed out of hand by the American forces.'

'What's your point?'

'The chief witness for the defence was one of the most brilliant British Secret Service agents operating in occupied France. He admitted he'd been responsible for many operations in which his men had fought and killed German soldiers while wearing German uniforms. He also spoke of his superiors handing out such orders that could only be concluded by assassination. He told the court that if Skorzeny was guilty of a war crime, then he was just as guilty.'

There was a brief silence, and the President said, 'What was the verdict?'

'The case was thrown out of court. Skorzeny was acquitted of all charges.'

There was a long silence, and then the President said bleakly, 'So what *is* the answer?'

'That the kind of war we now face is a nasty business,' Miller said. 'And you can only survive if you play as dirty as the other side. That's what twenty years of army service during the Irish Troubles taught me.'

The President sighed heavily. 'I suppose I could have picked a better time to take up the highest office in the land, but here I am and, by God, I'll see it through.' He stood up and held out his hand. 'Thank you for coming, gentlemen. We'll meet again on Friday.'

Blake insisted on returning them to the hotel personally. In spite of the rain, there were a number of people outside the White House gates, mainly tourists by the look of them.

'I told you how it would be,' Blake said. 'This is America, land of the free. The President has a difficult path to tread. We tried the Guantánamo Bay solution and received hate mail from all over the world. And there are even those who disapprove of the way we handled Osama.'

'We know that, Blake. The trouble is that you can say what you want about universal freedom, individual liberty, the rule of law, but when you get into power, the intelligence services pass confidential dossiers across your desk full of information that proves how bloody awful the threat really is. More 9/11s have been foiled by the skin of our teeth than the public could imagine.'

'And often because the Sean Dillons and Daniel Holleys of this world are prepared to act in the way they do,' Harry Miller said, 'and take responsibility for it in a way other people can't.'

'And thank God for it,' Ferguson said. 'You know, we've been good friends with the French Secret Service for some time now.'

Blake said, 'I'm surprised. I thought you used to be at odds with them?'

'Not any more. Their agents, some of whom have Algerian Muslim roots, infiltrate Al Qaeda training camps in Afghanistan and Pakistan, and the information gained has enabled the French to crush many terrorist cells in France since 9/11. But not only in France.' Ferguson laughed grimly. 'They call our capital city Londonistan – did you know that? From time to time, they pass over information to us of crazy plots to blow up Nelson's Column, Tower Bridge, Harrods. You get the picture?'

'I surely do,' Blake said. 'I suppose in Paris it's the Eiffel Tower.'

'I'd hate to be a Muslim living in Paris,' Miller said. 'I remember how the French reacted in the Algerian War. Nobody would want that.'

'Al Qaeda would,' Ferguson said as the limousine turned in to the hotel. 'It would suit them down to the ground to return to the bad old days, so they could produce a few martyrs who'd been fixed up for sound.'

'Dillon and Holley would seem tame by comparison,' Miller said.

The limousine drove away with Blake and they watched it go. Harry Miller said, 'What do you think?'

'That I'd like a large bourbon on the rocks, but I'll leave it until we're on the Gulfstream. Let's get our things and go,' Ferguson said, and he led the way into the hotel.

When Captain Sara Gideon boarded the plane at Tucson for her flight to New York, she wore combat fatigues. This was America, where patriotism ruled and the military were received with enthusiasm, especially when the wearer was a good-looking young woman with cropped red hair. The shrapnel scar that slanted down from the hairline to just above the left eye made her even more interesting-looking. She was five foot six with high cheekbones in a calmly beautiful face that gave nothing away. It was as if she was saying: This is me, take me or leave me, I don't give a damn. She had a window seat in first-class, and people glanced curiously as a flight attendant approached to offer her a glass of champagne.

'Actually, I think that would be very nice,' Sara Gideon told her.

'Oh Lord, you're English,' the young woman said.

Sara gave her a smile of unexpected charm. 'I'm afraid so. Is that all right? I mean, we're all fighting the same war, aren't we?'

The flight attendant was totally thrown. 'No, no, I didn't mean it like that. My older brother is a Marine, serving in Afghanistan. Sangin Province. I don't suppose you've been there?'

'I have, actually. The British Army was in Sangin for some time before the Marines took over.'

'I'm so glad,' the attendant said. 'Let me get you your drink.'

She went away and Sara stood up, took her shoulder bag out of the locker, removed her laptop, and put it on the seat beside her. She replaced the shoulder bag and sat down as the flight attendant returned and gave her the champagne.

'This Sangin place? It's okay, isn't it? I mean, Ron always says there's not much going on.'

A good man, Ron, lying to his family so they wouldn't worry about him. She'd been through two tours attached to an infantry battalion that suffered two hundred dead and wounded, herself one of them. But how could she tell that to this girl?

She drank her champagne down and handed the glass to her. 'Don't you worry. They've got a great base at Sangin. Showers, a shop, burgers and TV, everything. Ron will be fine, believe me.'

'Oh, thank you so much.' The girl was in tears.

'Now you must excuse me. I've got work to do.'

The attendant departed, and Sara opened her laptop, feeling lousy about having to lie, and started to write her report. At the Arizona military base, location classified, she had been observing the new face of war: pilotless Reaper drones flying in Afghanistan and Pakistan but operated from Arizona, and targeting dozens of Taliban and Al Qaeda leaders.

It took her around two hours to complete. When she finished, she replaced the laptop in her shoulder bag. It had been a hell of an assignment – and where was it all going to end? It was like some mad Hollywood science-fiction movie, and yet it was all true.

Her head was splitting, so she found a couple of pills in her purse, swallowed them with some bottled water, and pushed the button for attention.

The young flight attendant appeared at once. 'Anything I can get you?'

'I'm going to try to sleep a little. I'd appreciate a blanket.'

'Of course.' The girl took one out of the locker and covered her with it as Sara tilted the seat back. 'Sweet dreams.'

And how long since I've had one of those? Sara thought, and closed her eyes.

The dream followed, the same dream, the bad dream about the bad place. It had been a while since she'd had it, but it was here now and she was part of it, and it was so intensely real, like some old war movie, all in black and white, no colour there at all. It was the same strange bizarre experience of being an observer, watching the dream unfold but also taking part in it.

The reality had been simple enough. North from Sangin was a mud fort at a deserted village named Abusan. Deep in Taliban territory, it was used by the BRF – the Brigade Reconnaissance Force – a

British special ops outfit made up of men from many regiments. The sort who would run straight into Taliban fire, guns blazing.

It was all perfectly simple. They'd got a badly wounded Taliban leader at Abusan, a top man who looked as if he might die on them and refused to speak English. No chance of a helicopter pick-up, two down already that week, thanks to new shoulder-held missiles from Iran. Headquarters in its wisdom had decided it was possible for the right vehicle to get through to Abusan under cover of darkness, and further decided that a fluent Pashtu speaker should go in with it, which was where Sara came in.

She reported as ordered, wearing an old sheep-skin coat over combat fatigues, a Glock pistol in her right pocket with a couple of extra magazines, a black-and-white chequered headcloth wrapped around her face, loose ends falling across the shoulders, leaving only her eyes exposed.

The vehicle that picked her up in the compound was an old Sultan armoured reconnaissance car, typical of many such vehicles left behind by the Russians when they had vacated the country. Three banks of seats, a canvas top rolled back over the rear two, and a general-purpose machine gun mounted up front. It was painted in desert camouflage.

The three members of the BRF who met her looked like local tribesmen. Baggy old trousers, ragged sheepskins, and soiled headcloths like her own. They carried AK-47 rifles, were decidedly unshaven, and stank to high heaven.

One of them said, 'Captain Gideon?'

'That's right. Who are you?'

'We dispense with rank in our business, ma'am. I'm the sergeant in charge, but just call me Frank. This rogue on the machine gun is Alec, and Wally handles the wheel and radio. You can use the rear seat. You'll find a box of RPGs to one side, just in case, ma'am.'

'Sara will be fine, Frank,' she told him, and climbed in as the engines started up and the trucks nosed out of the gates in procession.

'Convoy to supply outposts in the Taliban areas,' Frank told her. 'Best done at night. We tag on behind, then branch off about fifteen miles up the road and head for Abusan, cross-country.'

'Sounds fine to me.' As she climbed into the seat, he said, 'Have you done much of this kind of thing before?' Another truck eased up behind them.

'Belfast, Bosnia, Kosovo, Iraq, and this is my second tour in Afghanistan.'

'Forgive me for asking.' He climbed into the second bank of seats. 'Get after them, Wally.' He lit a cigarette and shivered. 'It's cold tonight.'

Which it was – bitter winter, with ice-cold rain in bursts and occasional flurries of wet snow. The canvas roof offered a certain protection, and Sara folded her arms, closed her eyes, and dozed.

She came awake with a start as Frank touched

her shoulder. 'We're leaving the convoy soon and going off to the left.'

She glanced at her watch and was surprised to see that an hour had slipped by since leaving the compound. As she pulled herself together and sat up, a tremendous explosion blew the lead truck apart, the sudden glare lighting up the surrounding countryside.

'Christ almighty,' Frank said. 'The bastards are ambushing us.' As he spoke, the rear truck behind them exploded.

Passing through a defile at that part of the road, the convoy was completely bottled up and the light from the explosions showed a large number of Taliban advancing.

Guns opened up all along the length of the convoy, and Alec started to fire the machine gun as Wally called in on the radio. There was general mayhem now, the tribesmen crying out like banshees, firing as they ran, and several bullets struck the Sultan. Sara crouched to one side in the rear seat and fired her Glock very carefully, taking her time. Frank leaned over, opened the box of RPGs, loaded up and got to work, the first grenade he fired exploding into the advancing ranks. There was a hand grenade hurled in return that fell short, exploding, and Sara was struck by shrapnel just above her left eye.

She fell back, still clutching her Glock, and fired into the face of the bearded man who rushed out of the darkness, the hollow-point cartridges blowing him back, and the man behind him. There was blood in her eye, but she wiped it away with the end of her headcloth and rammed another clip into the butt of the Glock.

Wally, behind the wheel, was firing his AK over the side into the advancing ranks and suddenly cried out as a bullet caught him in the throat. Alec was standing up behind the machine gun, working it furiously from side to side, while Frank fired another grenade and then a third.

The headcloth pressed against the shrapnel wound stemmed the blood, and Sara fired calmly, making every shot count as the Taliban rushed in out of the darkness.

Frank, standing behind her to fire another grenade, cried out, staggered, dropped the launcher, and fell back against the seat, hit in his right side. Above him, Wally was blown backwards from his machine gun, vanishing over the side of the Sultan.

Sara pulled off her headcloth, explored Frank with her fingers until she found the hole in his shirt and the wound itself. She compressed her headcloth and held it firmly in place. As he opened his eyes, she reached for his hand.

His eyes flickered open, and she said, 'Can you hear me?' He nodded dimly. 'Press hard until help comes.'

She scrambled up behind the machine gun, gripped the handles, and started to fire in short bursts at the advancing figures. The gun faltered, the magazine box empty. There weren't as many out there now, but they were still coming. Very slowly, and in great pain, she took off the empty cartridge box and replaced it with the spare. There was blood in her eye, and she was more tired than she had ever been in her life.

She stood there, somehow indomitable in the light of the fires, with her red hair, and the blood on her face, and glanced down at Frank.

'Are you still with me?' He nodded slightly. 'Good man.'

She reached for the machine gun again and was hit somewhere in the right leg so that she had to grab the handles to keep from falling over. There was no particular pain, which was common with gunshot wounds – the pain would come later. She heaved herself up.

A final group of Taliban was moving forward, and she started firing again, methodically sweeping away a whole line of them. Suddenly, they were all gone, fading into the darkness. She stood there, her leg starting to hurt.

There was a sound of helicopters approaching fast, the crackle of flames, the smell of battle, the cries of soldiers calling to one another as they came down the line of trucks. She was still gripping the handles of the machine gun, holding herself upright, but now she let go, wiped her bloody face with the back of her hand, and leaned down.

'It's over, Frank. Are you all right?'

He looked up at her, still clutching her headcloth to his body. 'My God, I wouldn't like to get on the wrong side of you, ma'am,' he croaked.

She reached down, grabbing his other hand, filled with profound relief, and then she became aware of the worst pain she had ever experienced in her life, cried out, and, at that instant, found herself back in her seat on the plane to New York.

NEW YORK

CHAPTER 3

The flight attendant was leaning over her anxiously.

'Are you okay? You called out.'

'Fine, just fine. A bad dream. I've been under a lot of stress lately. I think I'll go to the restroom and freshen up.'

She moved along the aisle, limping slightly, a permanent fixture now, although it didn't bother her unless she got overtired. She stood at the mirror, ran a comb through her hair, touched up what little make-up she wore, and smiled at herself.

'No sad songs, Sara Gideon,' she said. 'We'll go now and have a delicious martini, then think about tonight's reception at the Pierre.'

At Kennedy, her diplomatic status passed her straight through, and she was at the Plaza just after five o'clock. The duty manager escorted her personally to her suite.

'Would you have any news on General Ferguson's time of arrival?' she enquired.

'Eight o'clock, but I believe that's open, ma'am.'

'And his two associates, Mr Dillon and Mr Holley?'

'They booked into the hotel yesterday, but I think they're out. I could check.'

'No, leave it. I think I'll rest. Would you be kind enough to see that no calls are put through, unless it's the general?'

'I'll see to it, ma'am. Your suitcase was delivered this morning. You'll find it in the bedroom. If you need any assistance, the housekeeper will be happy to oblige.'

He withdrew, and she didn't bother to unpack. Instead of lying down, though, she put her laptop on the desk in the sitting room and sat there going over all the material sent to her by Major Giles Roper, whose burned and ravaged face had become as familiar to her as her own, this man who had once been one of the greatest bomb-disposal experts in the British Army, now reduced to life in a wheelchair.

It would be after eleven at night in London, but experience had taught her that if he was sleeping, it would be in his wheelchair anyway, in front of his computer bank, which was where she found him when she called him on Skype.

'Giles, I'm at the Plaza and just in from Arizona. My report on Reaper drones will curl your hair.'

'I look forward to reading it, Sara. You're looking fit.' They'd already become good friends. 'Are you likely to enjoy tonight's little soirée?'

'There will be nothing little about it. No word from the general yet?'

'I've spoken to him. He and Harry Miller have

met with the President and should arrive at Kennedy around eight, if the weather holds. I was going to call you anyway. Your boss, Colonel Hector Grant – boss until midnight anyway – would appreciate you being there before eight.'

'Happy to oblige him. I haven't seen Dillon and Holley. They're apparently out at the moment.'

'Yes, they're seeing to something for Ferguson.'

'In New York? Is that legal?'

'You wouldn't want to know.'

She shook her head. 'This whole business is the weirdest thing that's ever happened to me. That General Charles Ferguson could take over my military career by Prime Minister's warrant, which I never even knew existed, and make me a member of his private hit squad, which I'd always heard rumours about but never believed in.'

'Well, it does.'

'And I find myself in your hands, face-to-face on screen with a man who sits in a wheelchair, hair down to his shoulders, smokes cigarettes, constantly drinks whiskey, and seems to eat only bacon sandwiches at all hours, day and night.'

'I can't deny any of it.'

Tony Doyle, a black London Cockney and sergeant in the military police, appeared beside Roper with a mug of tea. He handed it to him and smiled at Sara. 'Good to see you, ma'am.'

'Tony, just go away.' He laughed and went out.

'It's like a movie, Giles. I only see what *you* want me to. I have to take *your* word for everything.'

'My dearest girl, all that I've told you about Holland Park is true, and you've got photos of everyone who works here, the details of their lives, their doings.'

'So Dillon trying to blow up John Major and his Cabinet in London all those years ago, that's true?'

'And he got well paid for it.'

'And Daniel Holley really was IRA and now he's a millionaire and some sort of a diplomat for the Algerian foreign minister?'

'Absolutely. He's not just a pretty face in a Brioni suit, our Daniel.'

'I didn't say he was.' She shrugged. 'Obviously, he's killed a few people.'

'A lot of people, Sara, don't kid yourself. And he's too old for you. By the way, I went to hear your grandfather give a sermon.'

'You what?'

'I looked him up online. Rabbi Nathan Gideon, Emeritus Professor at London University, and famous for his sermons, so I went to hear one. I saw him at a synagogue in West Hampstead. Tony took me in the van. People were most kind, loaned me a yarmulke for my head and provided one for Tony, also. He thoroughly enjoyed the sermon. Human rights and what to do about its failures. I introduced myself and told him I worked for the Ministry of Defence and that we were going to be colleagues. He asked us back for tea. Whether this broke the Sabbath ruling, I'm not sure, but he did also provide some rather delicious biscuits.'

'And this was at the Highfield Court house in Mayfair?'

'That's right. Tony was fascinated. Your grandfather gave him a book on Judaism, and he talks of nothing else.'

'Are you completely mad?'

'I sometimes think I am, but one thing is certain – Nathan Gideon is a wonderful man, and I'd be privileged to have his friendship.'

'Is there anything else I should know?'

'Yes, since you appear to be interested in Holley. His father was a hardline Protestant who didn't like Catholics, but happened to fall in love with one who came from an equally hardline IRA family.'

'So that explains his foot in both camps?'

'Yes. And it led him as a young man to take refuge with the IRA, who sent him to a terrorist training camp in the Algerian desert, from which he emerged a thoroughly dangerous individual. So be warned. Anything else?'

'Holland Park. What's its purpose?'

'To keep watch over terrorism. London is the dream destination for any jihadist. He can speak openly about intending to destroy our way of life and even involve himself in a plot or two.'

'But the security services and the police are there to do something about that.'

'Like arrest him and then discover that because of human rights laws, he can't even be deported when he entered the country illegally?'

'It's hard to believe that.'

'You'll take worse things than that in your stride when you work for us. A couple of years ago, an Al Qaeda-based unit caused a terrible accident to happen to Harry Miller's limousine on Park Lane. Unfortunately, Harry's wife was using the car that morning. She and the chauffeur were killed.'

'That's terrible. What happened then?'

'The bombmaker was traced. It was an IRA sleeper living in London. He was dying of cancer and fingered his Al Qaeda paymaster. After he died, Dillon called in a disposal team.'

'Disposal team?'

'A quick bullet solves most problems, but you need our personal undertaker, Mr Teague, and his associates to clean up and take the body away. A couple of hours later and it's six pounds of grey ash.'

'What happened to the paymaster?' Sara asked.

'Harry made that personal. Went round to the Al Qaeda guy's house, shot him dead, and left Al Qaeda to clear up. I mean, they wouldn't be likely to call in the police, would they?'

'I wonder if I'm going to be able to cope with Holland Park.'

'You'll do fine. I've seen your file. There were at least twenty Taliban corpses around that Sultan.'

'That was war.'

'And so is this, sweetheart. By the way, I'm told you've been awarded a Military Cross for Abusan.'

She was reeling now. 'But that can't be true.'

'The Intelligence Corps couldn't resist putting their golden girl up for a medal for bravery. Of

54

course, people like us don't get medals, it's too public, so Ferguson isn't pleased. But don't worry, you'll get it. Just don't expect a fuss.'

'Giles, why don't you go to hell and take Ferguson with you?'

'I've been there, Sara, and it wasn't good. Enjoy the Pierre, give my best to Sean, and watch it with Daniel.'

'Just go, Giles.' And he did.

She checked on the screen again, thoroughly annoyed, and brought up Daniel Holley. Medium height, brown hair that was rather long, the slight smile of a man who didn't take his world too seriously and who looked ten years younger than he was.

In spite of the tattoos on his arms, common to convicts who'd spent time in the Lubyanka Prison, there was no sign of the killer on that handsome and rather attractive face, and yet that was exactly what he was. It was all there, his record in the field, meticulously put together by Giles Roper.

She went and unpacked, just the essentials since she was accompanying Ferguson to London, but she'd made sure to bring her dress uniform for tonight's reception. The Yanks would be there, but they were friends. The Russians were another matter, and she had heard that Colonel Josef Lermov of Russian Military Intelligence, the GRU, head of station at the London Embassy, would be present. His book on international terrorism had become essential reading in military circles.

She hung up her uniform tunic with the medal ribbons, the neat skirt, shirt and tie, high-polished shoes, the dress cap. Good old khaki splendour. Just like graduating at Sandhurst, except for the medals. *Ten years of her life.*

'Stop feeling sorry for yourself, Sara,' she murmured, then went into the splendid bathroom and started to fill the tub.

At seven-thirty that evening, Dillon was sitting at a corner seat in the bar at the Pierre, dressed in a black velvet corduroy suit and enjoying a Bushmills whiskey, when Holley entered, wearing a beautifully tailored single-breasted suit of midnight blue, a snow-white shirt, and a blue striped tie.

'Daniel, you look like a whiskey advert. You've excelled yourself. What about our new associate?'

Holley waved to the waiter and called for a vodka on crushed ice. 'I tried to get through to her room, but the duty manager said she was resting. Roper's put everything online, though.'

'Is there much there?'

'The usual identity card photos that make anyone, male or female, look like a prison officer. She has red hair.'

'I look forward to that,' Dillon said. 'I love red hair.'

'There was one unusual thing. Some video footage of her undergoing therapy for her wounded leg at Hadleigh Court.'

'The army rehab centre?' Dillon said.

'I found it a bit disturbing.'

'What's her birth date?'

'Fourth of September.'

'Virgo.' Dillon shook his head. 'The only zodiac sign represented by a female. Still waters run deep with one of those, and you being the wrong sort of Leo, with Mars in opposition to Venus, you've got nothing but trouble on your plate where the ladies are concerned.'

'Thanks very much, Sean, most helpful, particularly as I'm not in the market for a relationship.'

'What did Roper have to say about Sara Gideon?'

'She's a bit bothered about being dragooned into Holland Park. And apparently she's up for a Military Cross for Abusan. He read me the details.'

'Impressive?'

'You could say that. I had a call from Harry. They're about to land, and they'll see us here.'

'And Sara Gideon?'

'I've just checked at the Plaza desk. She left in a military vehicle.'

'Seems a bit excessive, since we're only a few blocks away.'

'It seems her boss, this Colonel Hector Grant, was in the car.'

'Well, there you are,' Dillon told him. 'Privileges of rank. Probably fancies her. Let's drink up, go upstairs, and see if we can ruin his evening.'

The UN reception was all that you might expect: politicians from many countries, plus their military, the great and the good, and many familiar television faces. Waiters passed to and fro, the champagne flowed, and a four-piece band played music, helped out by an attractive vocalist.

A few couples were already taking a turn on the floor, among them Sara Gideon with a grey-haired colonel in British uniform who, at a couple or three inches over six feet, towered above her – at a guess, Colonel Hector Grant.

Holley said, 'That red hair is fantastic.'

'A lovely creature she is, to be sure.' Dillon nodded. 'I'd seize the day if I were you, while I go and embarrass Ferguson and Harry. I can see them over there queuing up with Josef Lermov, waiting their turn to shake hands with the ambassador.'

He walked away, and Holley stayed there, watching. Colonel Grant was smiling fondly, and she was smiling up at him with such charm that it touched the heart. They were dancing slowly, and the limp in her right leg was apparent, but only a little, and she laughed at something the colonel said.

At that moment, they turned and she was facing Holley. She stopped smiling, frowning a little as if she knew him and was surprised to see him there. The music finished. She reached up to speak to the colonel, then turned, glanced briefly at Holley, and moved towards the exit leading to the ladies'.

A voice said, 'Heh, I bet that colonel's more than just her boss. I love a girl in uniform, and that limp is kind of sexy. Maybe I could do myself some good here.'

There were two of them, middle-aged, well-dressed and arrogant, and already drunk. They made for the exit, drinking from their glasses as the music started up again, and Holley went after them.

At that moment, the corridor happened to be empty, just Sara Gideon approaching the restroom door, and the one who was doing all the talking put his glass down on a stand in front of a mirror, moved up fast behind her, and put a hand on her shoulder.

'Hang on there, young lady. I know you soldier girls like a little action. We know just the place to take you.'

'I don't think so,' she said as Holley approached behind them. 'I think my friend wouldn't like that.'

'And which friend would that be?' the second man asked.

Holley punched him very hard in the kidneys and, as he cried in pain and doubled over, kicked his feet from under him and stamped in the small of his back. The other man reached into his inside breast pocket and tried to withdraw what turned out to be a small pistol. Sara put her elbow in the man's mouth, then twisted his wrist in entirely the wrong direction until he moaned with pain and dropped the weapon. Holley picked it up. 'Two-shot derringer with hollow points. I didn't know there were still any of these around. Very lethal.' He smacked the man's face. 'What's your name?'

'Leo,' the man gasped. 'Don't hurt me.'

'The NYPD would just love to catch you with

one of these. You'd be in a cell in Rikers tonight and, what's worse, the showers in the morning. So I suggest you pick your friend up by the scruff of the neck and get out of here while I'm in a good mood.'

'Anything you say, anything.' Leo was terrified and reached down to his friend, hauling him up.

Holley said to Sara, 'I get the impression you know who I am.'

'Let's say I've seen you on screen.'

'Do you still need the loo?'

'No, I think that can wait. I could do with a drink, but I'd prefer to go to the hotel bar for it and catch my breath.'

'The bar it is, then.' He offered her his arm, and, behind them, Leo managed to get his friend on his feet, and they lurched away.

They sat at a corner table and waited until a waiter brought a martini cocktail for her and a large vodka for him. She picked up her glass.

'You don't take prisoners, do you?' she asked.

'I could never see the point. The way you handled that guy with the derringer, though, suggests you could have managed quite well on your own.'

'I have a black belt in aikido. Giles Roper warned me about you, you know.'

'So you're familiar with my wicked past?'

'And Holland Park,' she said. 'And what goes on there. I've been given full access. I must say he's very thorough.'

'He's that, all right.'

'That horrible man.' She sipped her martini. 'He was afraid for his life. You frightened the hell out of him.'

'I meant to, he deserved it.' He took his vodka down in a quick swallow, Russian-style, and she watched him gravely, waiting for more. 'Look, I was involved in a terrible incident years ago that makes it impossible for me to stand by and do nothing when I see a woman in trouble.'

'Being familiar with your file, I understand why.'

'Well, there you are, then,' Holley said. 'Anything else you'd like to know?'

'I saw you watching me dancing with Colonel Grant, but you looked startled for some reason.'

He shrugged. 'Just astonished at finding the best-looking woman I'd seen in a uniform for years.'

She smiled. 'Why, Daniel, you certainly know how to please a lady.'

'No, I don't. I've never had much time for relationships, not in my line of work. Here today and possibly gone forever tomorrow, if you follow me. What about you?'

'If you've immersed yourself in my career, you'll know that the past ten years have been one bloody war after another. There was a chap I got close to in Bosnia who was killed by a Serb sniper. Then there was a major in Iraq who went the same way, courtesy of the Taliban.'

'What about Afghanistan?'

61

'With my Pashtu and Iranian, I travelled the country a lot.' She smiled bleakly. 'Death seemed to follow me around.'

'Well, he must have thought he'd got you in his clutches at last on the road to Abusan.' He smiled. 'If somebody did decide to make a movie, they couldn't do better than let you play yourself.'

'You should be my agent, Daniel.'

'That's the second time you've called me by my first name. That's got to mean something.' He looked beyond her and saw Ferguson, Miller, and Dillon entering the bar, Colonel Josef Lermov with them. 'Look who's here.'

The Russian, instead of his uniform, was wearing an old tweed country suit, blue shirt, and brown woollen tie. He advanced on Holley and hugged him.

'I must say you're looking wonderful, Daniel.' He looked down at Sara. 'And this can only be the remarkable Captain Sara Gideon.' He reached for her hand and kissed it. 'A great honour and privilege, one soldier to another.'

'Coming from the author of *Total War*, Colonel Lermov, I must say the privilege is all mine,' she replied in perfect Russian.

He smiled. 'So your reputation as an exceptional linguist speaks for itself. I'm impressed.'

Miller called for coffee and they all sat down, Ferguson beside Sara. 'Been in the wars, my dear, so Security tells me? You were on camera.'

'I've just seen it, Daniel,' Dillon told Holley. 'You

62

were your normal totally brutal self, and served those bastards right.'

'I agree,' Lermov said. 'Frankly, I'd like to sentence them to a year in Station Gorky in Siberia and see what they made of that. Unfortunately, this is not my parish.'

'So what's going to happen?' Sara asked.

'We've discussed it with management, and the gentlemen involved, having been suitably threatened and banned from ever visiting the hotel again, have departed with their tails between their legs.'

'They can count themselves lucky,' Holley said. 'NYPD could have caused them real trouble over that derringer.'

'Anyway, there it is,' Ferguson said. 'Welcome to the club, Sara, glad to have you on board. Congratulations to you, Dillon and Holley, for your handling of the *Amity* business. Though Murphy wasn't shot to death in Brooklyn, as we thought. He must have been wearing some sort of body armour. He's turned up close to his apartment, stabbed in the heart. Whoever he was dealing with obviously wanted his mouth shut.'

'It must have been a hell of a good vest he was wearing when I shot him into the East River,' Dillon said.

'Yes, but the important thing was the Irish connection you turned up and our old friend Jack Kelly.' Coffee was being passed around and he carried on, 'You may be surprised that we're talking about our highly illegal conduct in Brooklyn in front of

Colonel Lermov here.' He turned to Lermov. 'Perhaps you'd like to make a point, Josef?'

'Of course, Charles.' He removed his spectacles and polished them with a handkerchief. 'In the old Cold War days, we were sworn enemies, but in a world of international terrorism, we'd be fools not to help each other out. Putin agrees with me.' He turned to Holley. 'The Al Qaeda plot to assassinate Putin in Chechnya last year was foiled by information supplied by you, Daniel. He will never forget that.'

'I wish he would,' Holley said.

Ferguson ignored him. 'So we have common interests, but never mind that now. I'll be in touch with you sooner than you think, Josef, but for the moment, we'll say good-bye. We're all heading back to London tonight.'

He shook hands with Lermov, walked to the door, and they all followed, Holley taking Sara's hand. 'Is it always like this?' she demanded.

'Only most of the time,' Dillon said, and turned to glance at them, smiling. 'I see you two seem to have met somewhere.'

And they walked into the night.

LONDON

CHAPTER 4

It was an hour before midnight, New York time, when Ferguson's Gulfstream rose up through heavy rain to 40,000 feet and headed out into the Atlantic. Lacey and Parry, his usual RAF pilots, were at the controls – Sara had met them in the departure lounge and they'd indicated their approval. She was lying back in a red seat, and Parry passed her and spoke to Ferguson.

'Definitely heavy winds in mid-Atlantic, General. Could take us seven hours at least. Will that be all right?'

'It will have to be, Flight Lieutenant,' Ferguson told him. 'Carry on.'

Parry paused as he passed Sara and grinned. 'He can be grumpy on occasion. Sorry we didn't have a steward, but you'll find anything you could want in the kitchen area. We're very free and easy.'

He returned to the cockpit and she stretched out comfortably and listened to what was going on, for they had the screen on and were having a face-to-face with Roper.

'I can see you in the back there, Sara,' Roper called. 'I warned you about Daniel.'

'Enough of this erotic by-play,' Ferguson growled, 'and let's get down to business. These different kinds of IRA dissidents, Giles, is it really possible for them to work together?'

'I don't see why not, but Dillon and Holley are the ones to ask. They've been there and done that, Dillon since he was 19. What's your opinion, Sara? After all, the peace process was supposed to solve things, giving Sinn Fein seats at Stormont.'

'But the ideal to strive for has always been a united Ireland,' Dillon said. 'So as long as Ulster remains with the Crown, dissident factions will have a reason to continue the struggle.'

'A bleak prospect,' Ferguson said. 'Which simply means they – whoever *they* are – have an excuse for continuing general mayhem.'

'I'm afraid so.' Dillon shrugged. 'There are supposed to be sleepers all over London, just awaiting the call to action.'

'Which brings us to Jack Kelly,' Roper said. 'A well-known Provo who's served time in the Maze Prison he may be, but he was automatically pardoned as part of the peace process. So what's to be done?'

'A bullet in the head as he walks home some wet night?' Holley suggested.

Sara said, 'I wonder how many times he did that himself during his years with the IRA.'

'So what *do* we do?' Holley asked. 'Lift him?'

'Impossible,' Roper said. 'His lawyers would run rings around the prosecution.'

'You're all right,' Ferguson told them. 'Even you, Sara, though I would point out that assassination is the business we're in. No, we'll apparently do nothing, leaving you, Roper, genius that you are, to come up with some way of monitoring his comings and goings.'

'That's asking a lot,' Miller said. 'He'll be using only encrypted mobiles.'

Roper shrugged. 'We'll see. Something might turn up.'

'I'd sleep on it if I were you,' Miller told him.

'You clown, Harry, it's breakfast time here.'

The screen went dark and Ferguson promptly fell asleep. Sara was in the rear of the cabin and Holley took the next seat.

'Are you tired?'

'I certainly should be.'

'Because it's all so exciting.' He said it as a statement.

'Disturbing, Daniel, that's what I'd say, and rather frightening.'

Holley smiled through the half-light. 'We'll have to do something about that.'

In front of them, Dillon muttered, 'For God's sake, kiss the girl goodnight, and let's get some sleep.'

Sara smiled and murmured to Holley, 'See you in the morning.'

She pulled a blanket over her knees, closed her eyes, and lay back. Holley watched her for a while, wondering what was happening to him, then he also closed his eyes.

The drone of the engines in flight was the only sound now. Parry peered in from the cockpit and dimmed the lights even further.

Dillon wasn't sleeping, just lying back considering what the day had brought. A lovely young woman, Sara Gideon, and she'd obviously had a profound effect on Holley, but they were in entirely the wrong profession for that kind of thing. A pity, but there it was.

He moved on to analysing the new situation in Ulster. *Always* the same. Reactionary dissidents who would never be satisfied till the sound of gunfire echoed in the streets and the killing began once more. What the hell was Jack Kelly playing at? He'd lost his only son to the conflict, spent years in jail.

'Christ,' Dillon murmured, 'you'd think he'd have learned some sense by now.'

But there was no forgiveness in this world, and he remembered Jean Talbot in the Zion Gallery. She'd appreciated why he'd had to shoot her son, but couldn't possibly forgive, and had put out a contract on him – one of the advantages of being rich, she'd said.

Nothing to be done about that. People had been trying to kill him for years. He remembered the old days, going to the horns in the bullring in Ibiza, waiting for the bull to rush out of the gate of fear. *It comes as God wills,* the toreros used to say, which just about summed it up.

★　　★　　★

One-thirty over the Atlantic, but 7.30 in London, where Jean Talbot was already enjoying the first cup of coffee of the day. She'd lived in the Regency House in Marley Court in Mayfair for years. It was just off Curzon Street, convenient for Hyde Park, and only ten minutes' walk away from Owen Rashid's flat, a decided plus in view of the way their relationship was developing.

Her mobile sounded and there he was. 'Are you up for lunch today? There's something I wanted to run by you.'

'Sorry, Owen, I've got a meeting with the vice-chancellor.' Though she was head of Talbot International, she mostly let her nephew, Gregory, handle things as CEO while she pursued an academic career. 'Are you going for a run in the park?'

'Just about to leave.'

'I'll join you if you like. I'll be at the Hilton end of the subway.'

Which she was, and they walked through, entered Hyde Park, and had a brisk 30-minute jog which ended with coffee by the café at the Serpentine. As always, she thoroughly enjoyed his company. No silly ideas of romance at her age. In a sense, he was filling her son's place, and he was well aware of the fact.

'How did your flight to Rubat go the other day?' she asked, for another link between them was that Rashid Oil kept its private aircraft at Frensham Aero Club, as did Talbot International. Owen had been a private pilot for three years, Jean for considerably longer.

'Now that I've got my rating for jets, it was great fun. I was able to fly the Lear.'

'What was it you wanted to run by me?'

'I wondered if you'd thought any more about my suggestion that Talbot International might consider extending the Bacu Railway line into Rubat.'

She said, 'I've raised the matter with Gregory, and he seems to think that the instability with Yemen next door might raise difficulties.'

Owen said, 'All we're asking for is an extension of the track and the pipelines. It would give us access to Southport and its tankers, and that would be more efficient for us. Remember that one-third of the world's oil from southern Arabia passes through the system. To interfere with that, Yemen would have to invade Rubat, a sovereign state. Any interference with oil supplies would cause chaos on an international scale. If the UN didn't put a stop to it, the Americans would, backed by powerful Arab interests. Yemen would be ground into the dust.'

'I like it when you're this way, Owen, full of enthusiasm.' She smiled. 'You certainly make a good case. I'll speak to Gregory again.'

As they started the return run, he realized with some surprise that she was absolutely right. The idea as put forward by his Al Qaeda masters was totally misconceived.

They crossed Park Lane and he said, 'Tell Gregory there will be a Saudi delegation arriving on

Thursday to be here for the President's visit on Friday. Powerful sheikhs involved in the oil business, but also a general or two, possibly looking for interesting arms deals. I'd be happy to help with introductions.' He frowned. 'But what am I thinking of? There's the reception on the terrace at Parliament.'

'I heard,' she said. 'It's the social event of the year.'

'Well, I've been invited and partners are allowed. Why not come with me?'

She was actually quite thrilled at the idea, but said, 'Good heavens, Owen, are you sure?'

'Talbot International supplies military hardware to half the countries on earth and has an excellent reputation for integrity in the Arab world. Who better to represent it at such an affair than the chairman?'

'I admit I'm tempted.'

'Dinner tonight at San Lorenzo. We'll discuss it then. I'll pick you up at 7.30.'

He half-ran along the pavement. She watched him enter his apartment block, then turned and walked away, suddenly absurdly happy.

As Owen crossed the sitting room, making for the bedroom suite, pulling his sweater over his head, a phone sounded. He hurried into his office and took a mobile from the top drawer. It was his sole link with Al Qaeda through an individual he'd come to know only as Abu. The man spoke the perfect dry and precise English of an academic, with no clue as to age or nationality.

'Good morning, Owen,' Abu said. 'Did you enjoy your run in Hyde Park with Jean?'

Owen had got past being surprised at how up-to-date Abu's information was, particularly about Rubat. He had got used to the idea that he was under some sort of surveillance.

'She's excellent company!'

'What's the feedback regarding the extension to the Bacu?'

Owen gave him chapter and verse. 'Frankly, it's exactly what I expected the company to say. Yemen makes everyone nervous these days, including my own people in Rubat.'

'Our orders demand that we persist.'

'I'm doing the best I can. As you know, I'm a guest at the terrace reception for the President. I've invited her to join me, with a promise to introduce her to various Saudi dignitaries.'

'I like that,' Abu said. 'It's good for business from a Talbot International point of view. It could possibly have an effect on their attitude to the Bacu extension. You've done well.'

'We aim to please.'

'Kelly has filled me in on the Murphy business in New York.'

'Yes, I suggested he speak to you personally,' Owen said.

'You were quite right. We need to do something about Ferguson and his Holland Park set-up. The wretched people he employs have been a thorn in our sides for years. Now we have Ferguson's latest recruit, this Sara Gideon. Jewish, I understand. She probably has ties to Mossad.'

'I wouldn't blame her. That bus bombing that killed her parents in Jerusalem saw off fourteen Palestinians as well. It was rather careless of Hamas.'

'Take care,' Abu said. 'Or we may start to wonder whose side you're on.'

'That's easy. I'm on Owen Rashid's side. What's our next move?'

'I'll order Kelly to activate some of his sleepers here in London. He's boasted of them enough, so let's see if we can give Ferguson and his people a few problems.'

Owen said, 'Let's be practical. Ferguson and Miller spent years fighting a war in Ireland. Dillon and Holley were on the other side and have now crossed over. Their friend Harry Salter may be a wealthy developer now, but he was a notorious gangster in his day, and his nephew has taken after him. And the Gideon girl's record speaks for itself. What do you think you'll be able to accomplish?'

'I've been doing some research. Are you familiar with the Irish National Liberation Army? Their members were recruited from the professional classes. Years ago, they killed an MP with a car bomb as he drove out of Parliament. No one was ever caught.'

'All right, but that was a long time ago,' Owen said. 'What are you saying?'

'I'm saying some things never go out of style. I'm going to speak to Kelly. I want this Charles Ferguson business taken care of once and for all.'

Owen Rashid, with plenty to think about, went into the bathroom and stood under a hot shower, cursing the day he'd got involved with Al Qaeda, but he was, and would have to make the best of it.

As he finished dressing and moved into his office area, the phone sounded. It was Kelly, and he wasn't pleased.

'I don't like being ordered around by that creep Abu. He sounds like an undertaker.'

'I suppose that's what he is in a way,' Owen told him. 'You could always resurrect one of your sleeper cells and give instructions to bump him off.'

'If only it were that simple,' Kelly said. 'Just like I have visions of getting Charles Ferguson and his entire outfit all together in a van, so it would only take one bomb planted underneath to get rid of them all.'

'And pigs might fly,' Owen said. 'Anyway, Abu thinks we need something special. He's discovered that INLA once killed a Member of Parliament with a car bomb.'

'But that was years ago.'

'Well, he's impressed – not only that they got away with it but that the cell consisted of middle-class professionals.'

'Yeah, that was a newspaper story that got out of hand.' Kelly laughed harshly. 'Each time it reprinted, a bit more was added, until in the end, it was better than the midnight movie.'

Owen Rashid found himself genuinely interested. 'How do you know?'

'Because I've always suspected a friend of mine was involved. He wasn't Irish, and his only connection with the IRA was a girl named Mary Barry, whom he loved beyond rubies.'

'Tell me about him.'

'In 1976, like a lot of IRA volunteers, I was sent to a training camp in the middle of the Algerian desert, courtesy of Colonel Gaddafi. We were trained in all kinds of weaponry and shown how to make what they now call improvised explosive devices, car bombs and such.'

'So what's this got to do with anything?' Owen Rashid demanded.

'Our instructor was named Henri Legrande. He spent three years in the Foreign Legion in the Algerian War. Joined at eighteen, got wounded and decorated, and discharged on his twenty-first birthday. Then he was recruited by Algerians and got well paid to give people like me the benefit of his experience for six months.'

'What happened to him when you left the camp?'

'We were his last group. He had an English aunt in London who'd left him well provided for, and her estate included an antiques shop with a flat above it in Shepherd Market.'

'That's not far from here,' Owen said. 'Lots of shops like that there.'

'He decided to go to London University to study literature and fine arts, of all things. It was still a popular destination with Irish students like Mary Barry, the daughter of a friend of mine. I told her to look him up.'

'And they fell in love.'

'She moved in with him, and had two years of bliss before she went home to Belfast one day, got involved in a street protest, was manhandled by soldiers, handed over to the police, and was found dead in a cell the following morning. Choked on her own vomit. There was a suggestion of abuse, but nothing was ever proved.'

'Well, there wouldn't be, would there?' Owen said.

'We all know that, but there was nothing to be done. I was on the run at the time, took a chance and went to the funeral. St Mary's, Bombay Street in Belfast, the church packed. Just before the service, the door banged and there was Henri over from London. The look on his face would have frightened the devil. He had a single red rose in his hand, walked straight up the aisle, ignoring the priest, placed the rose between her folded hands, leaned over, kissed her, and walked out.'

'What did you do?'

'Went after him, took him for a drink. I asked him if he intended to return to France. He told me he would never leave London, because as long as he stayed, her presence would always be with him.'

'True love.' Owen reached for a cigarette and lit it. 'So you suppose that he was responsible for the death of that MP all those years ago as an act of revenge?'

'It was more complicated than that. I told you that Henri had given us a thorough training on the construction of explosive devices.'

'What about it?'

'One of the car bombs he demonstrated was of Russian origin and was unusual in that it used mercury as part of the trigger mechanism. Three months after Mary's death, the army colonel whose men had been involved in that riot was killed with the same sort of car bomb right here in London.'

'Which could hardly be a coincidence,' Owen said.

'Not when you consider that two months later, the Royal Ulster Constabulary chief superintendent who'd been commanding the police station where Mary had died met a similar fate.'

'I'd say that's pretty convincing proof, but why would Legrande target the Member of Parliament? He didn't have anything to do with what happened to Mary Barry, did he?'

'No, but there was an election going on at the time, the government was taking a very anti-IRA line, and the MP was a spokesman. Who knows what was going on in Henri's head? The important thing was that there were no more mercury tilt bombs after that.'

'What happened when you put all this to Legrande?' Owen asked.

'But I never did,' Kelly told him. 'I was serving five life sentences for murder in the Maze Prison until the peace process pardoned me.'

'So what is Legrande doing now?'

'I haven't a clue. I wasn't certain whether people like me were still under police surveillance, so I decided to leave well enough alone where certain old friends were concerned.'

Owen, who'd been examining the phone book on his desk, said, 'Here we are. Henri Legrande. Rare books, fine art, antiques. It's called Mary's Bower.'

Kelly said, 'Well, we know where the shop's name comes from. Where are you going with this?'

'Abu is just a messenger boy passing on orders, but orders they are. You've boasted of your sleepers in London. Now you're supposed to activate them to sort out Ferguson and his people.'

Kelly said, 'It isn't as easy as that. When the Troubles were in full swing, we had a network of them, but . . .'

'Are you telling me it would be impossible?'

Kelly had an edge of desperation in his voice. 'It would be difficult.'

'Then you're a dead man walking, because you've been lying to Abu and Al Qaeda. I don't intend for you to pull me down with you. Stay on the phone for five minutes. I'll be back.'

He went out to the kitchen and dialled a number on the wall phone. A man's voice answered. Owen listened, then said, 'Sorry, wrong number.' He spoke into his mobile: 'Are you still there, Jack?'

'Yes, what the hell are we going to do?'

'Revisit your glory days. You used to be the pride of the IRA – now you're going to take on Ferguson yourself. I'll provide you with money if you need to hire three or four foot soldiers. All you need is a plan.'

'And where would that come from?'

'Henri Legrande, of course. He survived the Legion, the Casbah, the Battle of Algiers. If he can't sort your problem, nobody can.'

'But I don't know if he's still around,' Kelly said. 'We haven't spoken in years.'

'I just phoned him three minutes ago. When he answered, I said sorry, wrong number. What I suggest is you phone him, tell him you'll be in London later today and thought you'd look him up.'

'But what do I say to him?'

'Stick with the truth. After all, your IRA past is no surprise to him. Stress that all you're seeking is his expertise on the best way to handle Ferguson, and that you're not expecting him to carry a gun for you or anything like that. Don't offer him money – the kind of man he is would be offended, and I suspect he's got more than he knows what to do with.'

Kelly said, 'Owen, you're a genius.'

'I'm not going to argue with that. Now, get moving.'

'Right,' Kelly said. 'I'll phone Henri, then I'll get the Beech Baron to pick me up from Drumgoole. I'll cover my back by phoning the finance director at Talbot International and telling him I need to discuss the estate's books. What are you up to?'

'I'm taking Jean out to dinner tonight.'

'You seem to be seeing a lot of her these days.'

'Don't get ideas. I'm just a substitute for her son. You once told me he apologized to her in front of you for not having told her he'd served in the SAS and that he'd killed many members of the Provisional IRA.'

'That's true.'

'And you really think she wasn't aware of his involvement with Al Qaeda?'

'I'm sure of it, Owen,' Kelly said. 'I was as close to him as anyone, and he didn't tell me about it until the last couple of months of his life. Why do you ask?'

'I like Jean very much, but I also feel a certain amount of guilt where she is concerned.'

'Why is that?' Kelly asked.

'She adored her son, she makes that very obvious, and yet the blunt truth is that he lied to her about his life and what he'd been doing.'

'So what are you saying?'

'I'm doing the same to her, and I don't like it.'

'Explain that,' Kelly told him.

'It concerns Rubat and an old railway that Talbot

International owns. Al Qaeda would like to see it extended for their own reasons.' He gave Kelly chapter and verse and ended by saying, 'But just as her son did, I'm feeding her Al Qaeda lies. What the hell can I do?'

'Nothing,' Kelly told him. 'And don't go beating yourself up. Poor wild Justin suffered at the hands of Al Qaeda, and you and I are caught in the same web – there isn't a thing we can do about it. I wouldn't worry too much if I were you. The Saudis, backed by America and the UN, will never allow the Bacu extension. It would be madness.'

'Let's hope you're right.'

'Well, sometimes I am.' Kelly laughed. 'You know something, Owen? I'm feeling better already, so let's just play the hand the Good Lord's given us for the moment and see where it leads. You take Jean out tonight and give her a good time, but drop the idea of being the son substitute. It doesn't suit you.'

He rang off, and Owen crossed to the window and opened it to the terrace. The morning traffic was nose-to-tail and he stood there, smoking a cigarette and thinking about what Kelly had said. One thing was certain. The advent of Henri Legrande was going to make life very interesting.

He flicked his cigarette out into the traffic and went back inside.

CHAPTER 5

Later that day, Jack Kelly was on the corner of Park Lane and Curzon Street, walking down towards Shepherd Market, carrying a modest overnight bag. He had never visited this area before, and it fascinated him, the narrow streets, the wide variety of restaurants and shops.

He found Mary's Bower, two narrow windows, each featuring a painting, flanking a Georgian door with a brass knocker, a lovely hand-painted sign above with the name above a drooping mulberry over an empty sofa. He felt sad about that, realizing what the imagery meant, and stepped back into a doorway as it started to rain.

The truth was that he hadn't phoned Legrande, perhaps because of a fear of rejection, and yet he *had* come, which had to mean something. At that moment, the red velvet curtain behind the painting in the window to the left was pulled back and the Frenchman appeared.

Despite the years, it was undeniably the Henri Legrande who had meant so much in the life of Jack Kelly all those years ago. A little heavier, grey-haired, wearing steel-rimmed spectacles and a green apron. He made an adjustment to the painting on its easel, glanced up, and saw Kelly. He stood there, very still, then disappeared behind the curtain. A moment later, the door opened.

Kelly crossed over, and Legrande said, 'Jack, is it really you?'

'As ever was, Henri.'

Legrande removed his spectacles, stuffed them into his apron pocket, hugged him, and kissed him on both cheeks. 'After all these years. Come in at once.'

In the Victorian sitting room in the flat above the shop, Kelly was amazed at the number of photos, not only of Mary but of Mary and Henri. Legrande found him examining them when he came in with champagne.

'So she's still with you,' Kelly said.

'Always has been.'

'No room for another woman in your life.'

Henri thumbed off the champagne cork and paused. 'Now and then. After all, a man needs a woman, but nothing serious.' He raised his glass. 'To me and to you and all those other young bastards at Camp Fuad, most of whom are probably dead by now.'

'I can certainly think of a few Provos who are,' Kelly told him.

Henri poured him another and they sat down. 'You were in the news when this peace process went through,' Henri said. 'There were lists of the prisoners pardoned. So you were serving five life sentences in the Maze Prison? A formidable record.'

'I never shot anyone who wasn't shooting at me first,' Kelly said. 'We were fighting a war.'

'So what do you do now, how do you make a living?' Henri reached for a second bottle and opened it. 'Get on with it – I want to know it all.'

So Kelly did, talking through the drink and, while Henri Legrande sat there impassively, smoking one Gauloise after another, taking in everything, including the Talbot saga, which somehow merged seamlessly into the Al Qaeda connection.

There was a long silence when Kelly finished talking, and then Henri Legrande sighed and shook his head. 'You would appear to be in deep shite here, my friend – isn't that what you say in Ulster? The situation seems plain. Either you sort out this General Ferguson and his people or Al Qaeda's merry men will hold you to account, and whatever they decide is bound to be unpleasant.'

'So what the hell do I do?' Kelly asked.

'You go and have a long hot shower and sober up.' Henri checked his watch. 'I've got to close the shop and make some calls, so you sort yourself out and we'll go and have a great dinner somewhere and decide on our next move later tonight. I'm going to help you to get you out of this stupid mess you've got yourself into. Who better than your old teacher?'

'For God's sake, Henri, I turn up out of the blue

after all these years.' Kelly shook his head. 'It's not right.'

'As it happens, it's exactly what I need.'

Kelly frowned. 'What do you mean?'

'I've got cancer, my friend, a bad one. I've got six months at the most.' He smiled. 'So you see, this will be as much for me as it is for you.'

He turned and walked through the shop. Kelly stood there for a moment, then picked up his over-night bag and went in search of the spare bedroom.

The Gulfstream had landed, and its passengers were going their separate ways. Ferguson in his Daimler was dropping Harry Miller at his house in Dover Street. Dillon had his Mini Cooper, and Holley an Alfa Romeo Spider.

'I'm staying at the Dorchester,' he said to Sara. 'Highfield Court is only just up the road, isn't it? I'll drop you off if you'd like.'

'Why not?' she said, and got in the Alfa.

Ferguson called: 'Take a break. We'll meet at noon on Thursday to take one last look at the security plans. That includes the RAF,' he added as Parry and Lacey emerged from the Gulfstream.

'No peace for the wicked,' Squadron Leader Lacey said.

'Stop moaning. You could be in Afghanistan,' Holley told him.

'All right for some people, getting to chauffeur good-looking women,' Parry called.

Holley slid behind the wheel. 'Bloody flyboys.'

He drove away, and Sara said, 'What have you got against pilots?'

'Not a thing. As it happens, I'm one myself.'

'Is there no end to your talents?'

'Well, that remains to be seen, doesn't it?'

Which for the moment shut her up, and he turned out onto the main road and headed for London.

She fiddled with his CD player and immediately found Sinatra belting out 'Night and Day'. She joined in for a while, word perfect.

As it finished, Holley said, 'You like Cole Porter, then?'

'Love him. It's not just the music – the lyrics stand up as poetry in their own right.'

She tilted her seat a little and lay back, listening.

Holley said, 'Are you feeling reasonably happy about things now? I mean, Ferguson forcing you to join the team?'

She glanced at him sharply. 'Are you worried about me?'

'Of course not.'

She smiled. 'Oh yes, you are.'

'Worried about the hero of Abusan? Why would I be?'

Instead of annoying her, the remark made her smile, but with a certain complacency. 'Poor Daniel,' she said, turned up the volume, and started to hum along with Sinatra.

He left Park Lane at the Dorchester Hotel and drove along South Audley Street, turning right before Grosvenor Square into Highfield Court. It was a fine mid-Victorian property of four storeys, standing back from the road so that there was no parking problem. He drove into the drive, got out of the Alfa, and retrieved her luggage.

'Why don't you come in? I'd like you to meet my grandfather.'

She turned, walked to the door, and he followed, suddenly awkward. As she got her key out, he said, 'Look, you've been away for some time. He'll be thrilled to see you. I'll just be intruding.'

She turned to look at him, quite calm. 'Daniel, do you have a problem with me?'

For a moment he was speechless, then he said, 'Look, Sara, what is this?'

She prodded a finger into his chest. 'I'd like you to meet my grandfather because I think you should.'

'And what's that supposed to mean?'

'You'll have to work that out for yourself.'

As she turned, the door was opened by a comfortable-looking dark-haired woman who wore horn-rimmed spectacles and a green smock. 'So you're back?' she said. 'We wondered when to expect you. You've never heard of the telephone? A great invention.'

'Sadie, I love you desperately.' She gave the woman a quick hug and a kiss on the cheek. 'I was in Arizona, the other end of the world. Is Granddad at home?'

'In the study. But he's going out this evening.'

She was examining Holley as she spoke, and Sara said, 'Mrs Cohen is our housekeeper, Daniel.'

That the woman was running an eye over him made Holley feel foolish, standing there with a bag in each hand. He put them down.

'A pleasure, Mrs Cohen.' He held out his hand.

She took it briefly, then turned to Sara. 'I'll bring you tea.'

She moved down a wide corridor, obviously making for the kitchen area. They followed her for a moment, then Sara opened a large mahogany door to the left and led the way in.

The room was a relic from the past, a wonderful Victorian library, walls lined with mahogany panelling or bookshelves, a period fireplace, Turkish carpeting on the floor. Rabbi Nathan Gideon was seated at his desk in a swivel chair and turned around as they entered. He had the look of a scholar and wise man, but with the kind of face that seemed ready to break into a smile at any time. The fringe of grey beard suited him, and his unruly hair topped by a black velvet yarmulke somehow made him look quite dashing. So did the old black velvet smoking jacket he wore.

He flung his arms wide and stood to greet her, removing his reading glasses. 'My dearest girl, how wonderful to see you.'

They hugged for a few moments. 'I love you so damn much, Granddad,' she said fiercely.

'Such language,' he told her. 'You're bringing

tears to my eyes.' He took out a hanky to dab at them. 'What will your friend think?'

'That you're a lucky man to have such a beautiful grand-daughter, Rabbi.' Holley held out his hand. 'Daniel Holley. Sara and I are colleagues.'

'Is that so?' Nathan Gideon led the way across to the fireplace, where two sofas faced each other across a glass coffee table. He sat down with Sara in one, Daniel facing them. The door opened and Sadie Cohen pushed in a trolley.

'Do you also work at the Ministry of Defence, like that nice Major Roper who came to hear my sermon?' the rabbi enquired.

'Now and then, if I'm needed,' Holley said. 'I'm also in the shipping business.'

'But somehow a colleague of my granddaughter who's a captain in the Intelligence Corps. This I don't understand.'

He accepted the cup of tea Sadie handed him, and Sara said, 'The thing is, I won't be wearing the uniform much any more.'

'Except if you have to go to the Palace to get your Military Cross,' Holley said.

The news was received with astonishment, Sadie missing a cup entirely while pouring more tea.

'The Military Cross?' Nathan Gideon was amazed. 'Sara, you never said a word.'

'I only just heard,' she said. 'And it was totally unexpected. Frank, my sergeant, deserved it more.'

'I don't think he'd agree,' Holley told her. 'It was his account of your actions that night that led to you being put up for the award in the first place.' He stood up. 'Look, sir, you're a sensible man and I get the impression that Mrs Cohen is pretty smart, too, so please listen. Major Roper, Sara, myself, and a few other people work for a top secret intelligence unit, responsible only to the Prime Minister.'

He turned to Sara inquiringly and she nodded in agreement. 'What Daniel says is true, Granddad. But you know you can't say anything about this, right? Neither of you. It's under the Official Secrets Act.'

Her grandfather gaped at her in astonishment as Sadie said, 'So no more wars, no more Afghanistan?'

Sara smiled and then said, 'Sadie, I'd be perfectly happy if I never have to clap eyes on the place again.'

'So you will be living at home? That's good. Now, you get that tea down you, and I'll see to the trolley when you're finished.'

She went out, and Nathan said, 'I'd like to thank you for clearing the air about all this, Daniel. We all know where we stand now, and you can rely on me and Sadie to play our parts.' He smiled mischievously. 'Such as they are.'

Holley said, 'I'll get out of your way, because I know you must have a lot to talk about, and I know you're going out later.'

'That's true. A big fundraiser with a speech, unfortunately. But I suspect we'll be seeing each other again.'

They shook hands, and Holley followed Sara

out to the hall. 'He's a rather wonderful man, isn't he?'

'You could say that. And very special to me after what happened to my parents.' His tie had loosened, and she reached up and adjusted it. 'Thanks for what you told him. It needed doing, and I didn't know how.'

The rush of tenderness he felt at that moment was a totally new experience. He said to her, 'Doing things for you comes easy.'

She went back along the corridor to the study. The door of the cloakroom opened and Sadie came out with towels. 'Still here?'

'Just leaving.'

She nodded and moved closer. 'She's a lovely girl. Do anything to hurt her—'

Holley cut her off. 'I know, you'll kill me,' he said cheerfully.

'Just remember that.'

Seeing Sara returning, she retreated into the cloakroom. Sara opened the front door, turned, and smiled at him. 'Seven-thirty okay with you?'

'Do you mean it?'

'Not too dressy. Somewhere interesting. Don't be late – I'm hungry.'

She pushed him outside, shut the door and leaned against it, smiling as Sadie emerged from the cloakroom. 'So you're going out on a date with him?'

'I know what you're going to say. He isn't Jewish.'

'Why would I say that, and what does it matter

as long as it's you having the kids?' Sadie told her. 'As it happens, I like him, so there.' She turned and went back to her kitchen.

The moment he was out of the shower, and sober, Jack Kelly lost no time in contacting Owen Rashid, who was delighted with the turn of events.

'Legrande is obviously the right man for this, no question. Don't tell him you've told me about his cancer. I don't think he'd like that.'

'I'll keep that from him, then,' Kelly said. 'But it will make that bastard Abu sit up and take notice. It should keep him off our backs for a while.'

'Let's make sure of that by getting things moving right away. I'll expect you at my flat in half an hour. I'd like to meet him.'

He was immediately impressed with the Frenchman, who was everything he could have wished for. Rashid had been putting on his tie when they arrived, told them to help themselves to a drink, and found them enjoying a whiskey at the table by the open terrace window.

'I've been looking at your record, Henri, and I think you're the man for this job. Do you?'

'But certainly, Monsieur Rashid, or I wouldn't be here.'

Owen reached for the red file and put it on the table. 'Every scrap of information Al Qaeda has on Ferguson and his people is in there.'

'The facts in here are all guaranteed, then?' Legrande asked.

'Yes. Unfortunately, we don't have an internal source in his organization, so we can't *tell* you what his intentions are.'

'It would be a miracle if you could with an old fox like Ferguson,' Henri said.

'Money is no problem,' Owen said. 'Anything you need, you get. My people want him finished once and for all.'

'It will be my pleasure.' Henri shook hands and led the way out.

Jean rang a couple of minutes later. 'I don't really feel like anything exotic tonight. Would you mind if we just go to that little Italian place at the end of Curzon Street?'

'Not at all,' he said. 'We might as well walk. Not worth taking the car.'

Fifteen minutes later, he was pressing the bell at her front door. She was out in a moment, wearing a French beret and a short navy blue bridge coat. He kissed her on the cheek, and she took his arm.

'You look very Parisian tonight,' he told her. 'Most becoming. How are you?'

'I had students to see, end-of-term papers to discuss with other staff. Dammit, Owen, I'm a painter, an artist, that's what it's all about.'

'I know that,' he said.

'This title I have, visiting professor in fine arts, sounds very prestigious, and I suppose it is for some people, but I couldn't care less. The only difference between me and my colleagues is that I'm filthy rich. I feel guilty about that.'

'Don't be silly. I'm in the same position when it comes to money. I haven't the slightest intention of feeling guilty about it. What else is new?'

'Just that Kelly's in town,' she said.

'You didn't mention he was coming.'

'I didn't know. It's happening in a hurry. He's needed to see my finance director at the firm about the estate accounts for some time, then he discovered that a man he was involved with in his wild youth, and thought was dead, is running an antiques shop in Shepherd Market.'

'By his wild youth do we mean his IRA days?' Owen asked. 'You did tell me all about that, remember.'

'Yes, the friend is French, as I understand it. Anyway, I've told Jack that under the circumstances he might as well make a bit of a holiday out of it. He's staying at this chap's place for a few days.'

'Well, there you are, then,' Owen said, and a moment later, they reached the restaurant.

They sat in a corner booth, had a bottle of cheap red wine, and shared some lasagna and crunchy bread that was warm from the oven.

Over cognac he said, 'Kelly's IRA activity must have been a problem for you, with your son being an officer in the British Army. But when you had me over, it was heartwarming to discover the great affection the people in Kilmartin have for you.'

'You mean with their being IRA to the core and me a Protestant?' All at once, she felt like

96

unburdening herself. 'I knew my son served in the SAS and I kept quiet about it. Kelly found out and lied for me, so that the villagers have never known of my guilt. They never knew that my wild son's madness resulted in his Al Qaeda connection, nor that he took his own life.' She put a hand on his. 'So there you are – lies, deceit, and enough wickedness to choke on.'

None of this was new to him, but hearing it from her own mouth moved him deeply. He had been so sure that he had served merely as a substitute for the son she had lost so tragically, but realized now that the truth was rather different.

He paid the bill, and they walked up Curzon Street in silence, arm in arm. When they reached the house, she rummaged in her purse to find her key and he took it from her.

'Let me,' he said, and opened the door.

She turned to face him, trying to smile but in obvious distress. 'So sorry, Owen, to unload all that garbage and guilt on you like that. I get so damn lonely.' She was close to tears. 'Just look at me, chairman of Talbot International, the woman who's got everything and nothing.'

'What nonsense. You've got me, haven't you?' He kissed her lightly on the mouth. 'That's better, isn't it?'

As if not quite believing what he had done, she glanced up at him in astonishment and then smiled. 'Yes, it is, actually. Would you by any chance fancy a coffee before you go?'

'I thought you'd never ask,' he said, then stepped inside and closed the door.

On leaving Owen Rashid's flat, Henri Legrande and Jack Kelly had returned to the antiques shop, where the Frenchman started to work his way through the file Rashid had given him. Leafing through it, he was immediately aware of the most recent addition, and he read it quickly.

'Look what we have here,' he said to Kelly. 'Captain Sara Gideon just joined Ferguson's staff from the Intelligence Corps.'

'A nice-looking woman,' Kelly said, examining Sara's photograph.

'There's a damn sight more to her than good looks,' Henri told him. 'Her military record is remarkable, and I know her grandfather by reputation, Rabbi Nathan Gideon. Very popular with the interfaith movement. Preaches all over the place, even in Christian churches. He's good – I've heard him.'

'So where would he fit in?'

'When she's not serving abroad, she lives with him. Since she was a passenger on that Gulfstream of Ferguson's that just got in from New York, I think we can assume she's with him now.'

'Do you want to take a look?'

'Why not? I'll need to check where all Ferguson's people live, but she'll do for a start. We'll take my car.'

*   *   *

98

Twenty minutes later, he was behind the wheel of his small and battered Citroën van, Kelly beside him, observing Highfield Court, when the Alfa Romeo Spider turned into the drive.

'Now, there's a nice car,' Kelly said, and then Holley got out and approached the front door. 'It's Daniel Holley. I know the bastard well. Sean Dillon's friend. Top Provos in their day, but damn traitors now.'

The door opened and Sara Gideon appeared, Sadie behind her. She looked very striking, the red hair contrasting vividly with a bomber jacket, shirt, and loose leggings in black raw silk.

Sadie said, 'Don't let it go to your head, but you look fantastic.'

'Well, he's not looking too bad himself, is he?' Sara nodded to Daniel, standing by the Alfa in a leather flying jacket and jeans.

'For an older guy,' Sadie told her.

'Don't be boring.' Sara kissed her on the cheek. 'Go and check us out on your tarot cards or something.' She went down the steps and said to Holley, 'You're looking very sharp. Love the jacket.'

'I told you I was a pilot.' He handed her into the Alfa and slid behind the wheel. 'For someone who said not too dressy, you look amazing.'

'Thank you, Daniel, but the other thing I stipulated was somewhere interesting, so what's it to be?'

'You've got to meet Harry and Billy Salter sometime, so I thought we'd combine business with pleasure and visit the Dark Man down on Cable Wharf at Wapping. That's Harry's pub.'

'Well, that sounds fun,' she said as they drove away. The Citroën went after them, and Kelly said, 'What are we going to do?'

'Who knows?' Henri told him. 'We'll just hang in there and see where they go.'

CHAPTER 6

It was dark below by the Thames as the Alfa moved down the hill and pulled up in front of the pub, which was ablaze with lights.

'Well, here we are, the Dark Man, the first piece of property Harry Salter ever owned, the beginnings of his empire.'

Sara smiled. 'Oh, he has one of those, does he?'

'Ever since he discovered there was more money to be made from business than crime. He was known in the London underworld as a right villain. He only did prison time once in his youth, and that was enough. These days he's behind some of the biggest developments on the river.'

'And his connection with Ferguson? What's all that about?'

'A bit like the rest of us, pulling together in these uncertain times to keep the ship afloat. London gangsters have their uses.'

'Just like reformed IRA gunmen.' She got out and limped quite heavily to the edge of the jetty, looking across at a passing riverboat, music echoing over the water. 'I love all this, even the smell of it.'

He moved to her side. 'Are you okay?'

She glanced at him. 'You're worried about my leg, aren't you? I'm fine, really I am. So I get a bit cramped in a car and I need to loosen up a touch when I'm on my feet.'

He felt suddenly awkward. 'I was just concerned.'

'I know, but it is what I am now. It won't go away.'

'So I won't mention it again.' He took a pack of cigarettes from his pocket, put one in his mouth. 'Do you use these?'

'Good heavens, no, and neither should you.'

He'd taken out his lighter and paused. She took it from him, tossed it into the water, and held out her hand, palm up, without a word. He hesitated, then passed the cigarette pack across. It followed the lighter into the Thames.

'Do you always get your own way?' he asked.

'When I'm in the right, I do. I insist on it.' She took his arm and walked him a little way along the jetty. 'What's the boat tied up there at the end?'

'An old riverboat, the *Linda Jones*, Harry's pride and joy. He owns bigger boats that do the tourist runs and so on. He knows the Thames better than anyone – a river rat since childhood.'

'Well, let's go and meet him, then,' she said, and they turned and walked towards the entrance of the pub.

Henri Legrande had kept the Citroën well back and he and Kelly sat there, waiting for Holley and Sara to go inside. When they had gone, he turned on the Citroën's interior light and leafed through the file, paying particular attention to the photos.

'So here we are, Harry and Billy Salter, but perhaps there could be others in there with them,' he said, and he checked through all the photos again.

'So what do you want to do?' Kelly asked. 'If Holley sees me, we're done for. He knows me well.'

'But not me.' Henri smiled and closed the file. 'A drink at the bar is called for. You keep your head down. I won't be long.' He turned off the interior light and walked to the entrance.

The bar was at least half full, certainly enough for him not to feel out of place. He recognized the Salters sitting in the corner booth and also their minders, standing behind them, Joe Baxter and Sam Hall. Sara was receiving considerable attention from the men, Holley watching.

The blonde barmaid approached Henri and said, 'And what can I do for you, dear?'

He'd been looking up at the bar shelves and said, 'I see you have a bottle of Pernod there. I'll have a large one.'

She reached up and took the bottle down. 'It's been up here for ever such a long time. Not even open. A funny-looking screw cap.' She tried it and made a face. 'I can't do a thing with this.'

'If you would allow me, mam'selle.' He eased the top open effortlessly.

She pushed a glass over. 'You must have a strong

hand. Have a large one on the house. I'll find a stopper for it.'

'Why, thank you.' He poured and toasted her.

Harry Salter called, 'Over here, Dora, you've got to meet this lady.' He was back with Sara again now. 'You'll have something to eat, I hope? Dora's hotpot is out of this world.'

'Well, I certainly wouldn't want to miss that,' Sara told him, and shook hands with Dora as she came round the bar to meet her.

'I've heard all about you, love,' said Dora, 'getting a medal for bravery and everything. Marvellous what a real woman can do when she puts her mind to it. Shows the bleeding men the way for a change.'

'Well, I don't know about that,' Sara said.

'Well, I do. Here, come and have a look at my kitchen.'

Sara smiled helplessly at Holley and went off with her, and Harry said, 'Sit down, my old son. What an amazing girl she is, and how many Taliban did she knock out with that machine gun?'

'A lot,' Holley said.

'The newspapers will really go to town with it. A great story.'

'I don't think they'll be allowed to tell it,' Holley said. 'A question of security.'

'Have you told her that?'

'That's Ferguson's job, not mine.'

'What's this meeting about on Thursday? Roper left a message saying we had to report in.'

'Something to do with the President flying in on Friday morning.'

'Is it right he's only here for 24 hours?'

'A whistle-stop tour. Paris, Berlin, Brussels. Harry Miller's coordinated all the security. Maybe he's got jobs for us.'

'We'll see,' Harry Salter said, and at that moment the two women returned, Dora pushing a trolley.

'Right, sit round the tables, the lot of you, and let's get started.'

Henri, apparently absorbed in an *Evening Standard* he'd found at the end of the bar, put it down, finished his Pernod, and went out and rejoined Kelly in the Citroën.

'So what's the story?'

Henri told him everything. 'It would be interesting to know what's being said at the meeting on Thursday.'

'Well, there's not much you can do about that,' Kelly said.

'Perhaps not, but it might be amusing to cause a little mischief right now.'

'Like what?'

'Watch and learn.' He reached across, opened the glove compartment, and took out a torch and a pair of vicious-looking steel wire cutters. 'That should do the trick. You stay here.'

He walked down to the Alfa, ducked until he was out of sight. Kelly couldn't even get a hint of what he was doing, afraid that someone might emerge from the pub entrance at any moment.

Luck was certainly on Henri's side, for as he reappeared and started to walk back, the door opened to a burst of laughter, and three men emerged. They got into a car and drove away.

As Henri joined him, Kelly said, 'By God, that was close. What were you up to?'

Henri replaced the torch and the wire cutters where he had found them, took out a duster, and wiped his hands.

'What's that smell?' Kelly asked.

'Hydraulic braking fluid. I sliced the main tube. I'm afraid the next time friend Holley drives his car and tries to brake, he'll get a nasty surprise.'

'You bastard,' Kelly said. 'Are we going to stay to watch?'

'We don't need to be here. The accident will occur whether we are or not. But it might be amusing. Let's give it half an hour.'

Which they did, and quite a few people left during that period. In fact, forty-five minutes had elapsed when Henri said, 'To hell with it, we'll go.'

At that moment, Sara and Holley appeared, followed by the Salters, with Baxter and Hall standing in the entrance. There was a short exchange, laughter, then Sara and Holley got in the Alfa. The engine fired, and the Alfa moved forward, turning in a wide circle to point towards the exit road. Suddenly, the engine note deepened, and the Alfa swerved violently towards the edge of the wharf, bouncing sideways into a bollard, which was the only thing that saved it from going over into the Thames.

Holley scrambled out, turned, and reached for Sara, whose door was jammed. He pulled her towards him and she said, 'I'm fine, really I am.'

The Salters arrived with Baxter and Hall, and Holley said, 'I braked on the turn and nothing happened. I can't understand it.'

Baxter was already on his knees, peering under the car. 'Brake fluid dripping all over the bloody place, Harry.' He reached inside and pushed on the pedal. 'Nothing doing.'

'You were bloody lucky, my old son,' Harry said. 'If it hadn't been for that bollard, you'd have been down on the bottom and fighting to get out. It's ten feet deep down there.'

Billy said, 'Sure you're okay, Sara?'

'I'm good,' she said. 'No problem. What happens now?'

Harry said to Baxter, 'You handle this, Joe, get the garage on it. Meanwhile, give Daniel the keys to one of the Mercedes.' He turned to Holley. 'We've got three here, so you might as well take one. You'll need it to get to Holland Park in the morning.'

'That's brilliant,' Holley said.

A number of people had emerged from the pub, paused to see what was going on, and then had moved on to their parked cars. Henri and Kelly joined in the general exodus.

'My God, we nearly had them,' Kelly said.

'Yes, we did, but never mind,' Henri told him. 'There will be other times.'

As they passed the Tower of London on the way back, Holley said, 'Are you sure that you're all right, Sara?'

'Of course I am. It could have turned nasty, it didn't. I wouldn't say no to a drink.' She looked at her watch. 'It's only ten o'clock. Can we drop in at the Dorchester Bar?'

'Of course we can.'

'What an evening,' she said. 'It was fun. I liked the Salters.'

'And Dora's hotpot.'

'Was bloody marvellous. She should patent it.'

He pulled in at the front of the Dorchester, handed his keys over, and they went in. It was busy, but there was nothing surprising in that. The problem was, the bar was packed, and so was the concourse, with the late-supper trade.

'It would appear to be just one of those nights,' he said. 'I can only apologize.'

'What for? I'm sure you have an absolutely wonderful suite waiting upstairs. Can we take a look?'

The maids had dimmed the lights and left the French windows in the sitting room open to the night air, because that was the way Holley liked it. The white gossamer curtains stirred constantly, like living things, giving the whole room an eerie feeling.

'This is extraordinary,' Sara told him.

'What would you like to drink?'

'Champagne, please.'

The curtains were like cobwebs to be brushed aside as she went through, but the view from the terrace high up above Mayfair and Hyde Park, the splendour of the city at night, lights stretching into the distance, was incredible.

Holley came out with a bottle of Dom Perignon in an ice bucket with two glasses. He filled them and offered her one. She ran the ice-cold glass against her forehead.

'That's lovely,' she said.

'What do we drink to?'

'Oh, to love in spite of war, and to this incredibly wonderful place we're in now, which is not the real world and never could be. Out there, one way or the other, it's all Afghanistan, where the beast rules.'

'I think I see where you're coming from,' Holley told her. 'But what exactly are you saying?'

'You pointed out that you never had much time for relationships in your line of work, because although you were here today, you were very possibly gone tomorrow, and you meant permanently.'

'Which is true.'

'What would you say if I said I'd like you to take me to bed?'

'I'd say no.'

'But why?' She looked genuinely bewildered. 'I know how you feel about me. It's been obvious from the moment we met. In case you hadn't noticed, I'm a woman. We know about these things.'

He took her empty glass from her hand and refilled it. 'Would you just listen to me? In the old days, I ran guns out of Algiers to the Mafia, so I was familiar with the part of Sicilian folklore that speaks of the thunderbolt that strikes a man when he meets the special woman, the *only* woman.'

She stopped drinking, just stared at him. 'What are you trying to say?'

'That I always thought it was nonsense until I saw the most desirable and endearing woman I'd ever set eyes on limping around that dance floor at the Pierre.'

'So why won't you take me to bed?'

'Well, God help anyone who tries to do you harm, but regarding anything else . . . Sara, I fear I'm carrying too much baggage. And as you may have noticed, I'm too old for you.'

Her expression was unreadable, though there was a touch of triumph there. 'Oh, you poor old boy.' She emptied her glass and dropped it into the champagne bucket. 'You can take me home now.'

She was smiling as they went down in the lift, smiled at the doorman when he got the Mercedes for them, was still smiling when they turned into Highfield Court, and Holley, leaving his engine running, went round and opened the door for her.

'What a gentleman,' she said.

'It's an older-guy thing,' he told her. 'I'll leave

you till tomorrow. You'll want to spend some quality time with your granddad. I'll pick you up for Thursday around noon.'

As he moved away, she said, 'Aren't you forgetting something?' He turned, and she stepped in close, reached up and kissed him on the mouth, held the moment, then smiled. 'Not bad. Not bad at all for a poor old boy.' She turned and went in.

Sadie was hovering in the hall. 'Did you have a good evening?'

'It was very interesting.'

'I saw you kissing him. You haven't been doing anything silly, have you?'

'Well, I offered, but he turned me down.' Sara laughed. 'Would you like to know why? Because he loves me too much.' She shook her head and spoke as if to herself. 'I'm really going to have to do something about you, Daniel.'

'You don't think it would be more sensible to let him go?' Sadie asked.

'What a waste of a good man that would be. They're in short supply, or hadn't you noticed?'

Sadie was annoyed. 'Why has everything got to be such a joke to you?'

'Because sometimes life is a joke, like Afghanistan was a joke. If I hadn't been able to see that, two tours in that hellhole would have driven me insane.' The wildness, the pain that erupted on Sara's face was frightening.

Sadie was immediately contrite. 'I'm sorry, darling.'

'Aren't we all. When's Granddad due?'

'Sometime after midnight. They'll send him home with a chauffeur, they always do. I'm going to wait up for him. What about you?'

'I'd better go to bed. New York was a long time ago, and Tucson is just a distant memory.'

'You must be exhausted. A holiday is what you need.'

'No chance. After all, I've only just started with this new outfit. I've got to find my way. I've got tomorrow off anyway.' Sara was yawning now. 'Night bless, Sadie, I'm going to get my head down.'

Holley was enjoying a glass of the Dom Perignon as a nightcap when Roper called him on his Codex. 'Harry's been in touch. I understand you took Sara down to the Dark Man tonight and there was an incident.'

'An accident of sorts. I was driving the Alfa, and when we were leaving I suddenly lost all braking power. We could have gone in the river, but fortunately a bollard got in the way.'

'Sara's all right, is she?'

'We both are. Harry's sorting it. Loaned me a Merc.'

'Well, he's had the night crew down from that garage he owns, and it wasn't any accident. A main tube feeding the hydraulic system was deliberately severed. As it's steel mesh-covered, it would have needed a special cutter to do it, used by someone who knew his business.'

'That doesn't fit the profile of some ordinary vandal,' Holley said.

'Daniel, Harry Salter is still revered in certain circles, because he was once one of the most powerful guvnors in the London underworld. Vandals and hoodlums and the like would never try to pull something at his own pub. It would be like committing suicide.'

'You're saying we were targeted?'

'That's about the size of it.'

'Sara and I were there for about an hour and a half. It wasn't particularly busy, well-behaved people having a night out, enjoying themselves. Did any of Harry's folk have anything to report?'

'Come to think of it, Dora did mention something unusual.'

'Such as?'

'Some French guy asked for a Pernod.'

'And did she give him one?'

'Apparently, she had a bottle on the bar shelf that had been standing there forever and never opened, and he did it for her. She said he was very charming, grey-haired, with those steel-rimmed round spectacles, and he wore a black trench coat.'

'And she'd never seen him before?'

'Never. Do you think it's important?'

'It's certainly unusual, especially considering the coincidence that Sara and I were visiting.'

'True,' Roper said. 'And the third unusual fact, Watson, as Sherlock would have said, concerns the Alfa Romeo that almost went into the Thames.'

'So it could be we were followed with evil intent by an unknown Frenchman seeking an opportunity to do us harm. No hint of Islam there?'

'Dora said he spoke English like Maurice Chevalier and looked like Jean Gabin in one of those old gangster movies – you know, the ones where he's just out of jail to do one last job, looks permanently tired, and you know it's all going to end badly.'

'Well, that's something,' Holley said. 'A starting point. We've known for some time now that the French Secret Service operates undercover in London. Get on to your friends at DGSE headquarters in Paris and see if they can help.'

'They'll deny being here.'

'Then phone one of the guys who isn't supposed to be here, such as Claude Duval, and see what he has to say. I'll go to bed now. I'm bushed.'

It was quiet in the computer room at Holland Park, the multiplicity of screens from around the world somehow enclosing Roper as he sat there thinking about the conversation he'd just had.

Sergeant Doyle came in with a mug of tea and a bacon sandwich. 'There you go, Major. I'll be having a lie-down in the duty room. I won't say take it easy, because you never do.'

'I love you, too, Tony.'

He lit a cigarette and made a phone call. A voice echoed round the room in French. 'Duval here. Who in the hell is that? It's one o'clock in the morning.'

114

Roper answered in English. 'Roper. Just turn your back on whichever delectable lady is sharing your bed, Claude, and listen to me.'

'So what is it now, Giles?' Duval said in English.

'I'm sure it's no news to you that we've taken on new blood at Holland Park.'

'You mean, of course, the magnificent Captain Sara Gideon?' Duval was much more alert now. 'Is there a problem?'

Roper recounted the episode at the Dark Man in detail. 'What do you think?'

'That Sherlock Holmes would be proud of you, and I agree: The Pernod-drinking Frenchman is too much of a coincidence. The good Dora's description is remarkable. She should have been a film critic. I used to love those black-and-white gangster movies with people like Jean Gabin. I'll bear what she said in mind.'

'I'd be grateful.'

'Needless to say, he was not one of ours.'

'Perish the thought,' Roper told him, and switched off.

Holley didn't raise his head until 10.30, the travel catching up with him. The telephone brought him back to life.

It was Sara. 'Did you sleep well?'

'Like a log. What about you?'

'Drifted in and out. I do that a lot. I often leave my radio on.'

'What have you got planned?'

115

'That should be what has Rabbi Nathan Gideon got planned. He's doing one of his big fundraising tours, all for charity. Four days, maybe five. Leeds, Manchester, Edinburgh, they can't get enough of him. He left half an hour ago. What are you up to?'

'I sometimes go for a run.'

'Which is beyond me these days.'

'Well, I may be an older guy, but I'm still up for a stroll in the park.'

'That sounds good to me. I'll be waiting.'

He showered and dressed, and just before he left, two things happened. The concierge phoned to say the Alfa had just been delivered, and they'd exchanged it for the Mercedes. Next came Roper to inform him of his conversation with Claude Duval.

'So you see,' he said when he had finished, 'He believes our Pernod-drinking Frenchman to be too much of a coincidence. Duval's a good man to have on our side.'

'I'm sure he is.'

'I'm just leaving to go and meet up with him in Hyde Park. Tony's taking me in the van.'

'What's that all about? I'm picking up Sara in a few minutes to go for a walk in the park.'

'Claude and I have a mutual interest in someone who's agitating at Speakers' Corner this morning, Ali Selim.'

'What's he rabble-rousing about now?'

'The President's visit on Friday. What he's already calling the Great Satan's descent on London.'

'That could lead to a riot, Giles. Not exactly the right scene for a man in a wheelchair.'

'Oh, the police will be out in force, but if you are going anywhere near, make sure you've both got your warrant cards with you.'

When Holley drove the Alfa into Highfield Court, Sara came out to meet him wearing a khaki linen suit, a brown leather bag over one shoulder. He was wearing Ray-Bans, his flying jacket, and blue cords.

'You're still looking very sharp,' she told him. 'We don't need the car, it's only a short walk to Park Lane, and the subway will take us straight into Hyde Park.'

'And right next to Speakers' Corner,' he said. 'I was going to talk to you about that. Have you got your warrant card?'

'Oh yes, it was a present from Roper in a package he had delivered to the house along with this.' She opened her bag and took out a snub-nosed .22 Colt. 'With the new silencer.'

'Plus hollow points?'

'Naturally.'

'Well, you must carry them at all times. There's been a development. Put your fine Intelligence Corps mind on this.'

He told her what had been discovered about the Alfa, the Frenchman at the Dark Man, Claude Duval, everything.

As they turned into Park Lane, she said, 'Whoever

117

it is, it must be you they're targeting, Daniel. I've only just joined.'

'That's a fair point,' Holley said.

'Let's talk as we walk.' She slipped her hand into his arm.

Henri Legrande and Kelly had followed the Alfa from the Dorchester and were sitting in the Citroën in South Audley Street waiting for the Alfa to emerge.

When Holley and Sara appeared, Henri said, 'I'm going to follow on foot. I can walk around with impunity, but not you. Holley would recognize you instantly. Wait for me in Grosvenor Square somewhere by the American Embassy. I'll find you.'

Kelly said, 'You're right,' scrambled behind the wheel of the Citroën as the Frenchman got out, and drove away.

When Holley and Sara went up the steps from the subway and entered Hyde Park, they could hear the noise from Speakers' Corner at once. They paused to listen.

'Who is this Ali Selim?' Sara asked.

'British-born, three months ago he came back home from several years in Pakistan and started to agitate as the mullah at the Pond Street Mosque in Hackney. You were in Arizona for that period, so you wouldn't have heard of him. Would you like to go see what's happening?'

118

'Actually, I'd like to meet Giles Roper for real. So far I've only seen him on screen.'

'Well, let's see if we can find him.'

He took her hand and they followed the path, the noise getting louder, until they reached Speakers' Corner. The crowd was already large. Individual speakers worked from their stands to offer a wide range of topics, some from people who took their politics seriously, but there were also cranks of every persuasion. There were a number of police vehicles parked on the fringe, the officers a mixed bag of men and women in normal uniform, riot police in full gear in the background.

'There's the van parked to the right of that police line.' Holley pointed. 'That's Roper in his wheelchair talking to Claude Duval in the navy blue trench coat, and the black guy standing at the front of the vehicle is Sergeant Tony Doyle.'

Roper saw them and waved, and they approached. 'We meet properly at last, Sara. Tony, you've only met on screen, like me.'

Doyle held out his hand. 'My pleasure, ma'am.'

Roper turned to the man in the trench coat. 'This is Claude Duval of the DGSE, who is not supposed to be here at all.'

Duval took her hand and kissed it gallantly. 'Your behaviour at Abusan was truly remarkable. It is an honour to meet you.'

She said, 'I appreciate the compliment coming from a man like you, Colonel, but when you think

119

about it, I didn't have much choice at Abusan. It was fight or die.'

He turned to the others. 'Only a woman could be so practical.'

'This Ali Selim that Daniel has mentioned – he's not here yet, I presume?'

'No, but he's what most people are waiting for, and he explains the police presence,' Roper said. 'There are many young Muslims in the crowd, the sort of people he's been urging to fight the good fight for a new Muslim empire, and pointing out that it's their duty to break as many wicked Western laws as possible.'

Holley said, 'To the Arab world, the British government is the villain of the piece here, for harassing a devout holy man.'

'What if that's exactly what he is?' Sara said.

Claude Duval said, 'What he is, Sara, is Al Qaeda's most important mover and shaker in London. He's been responsible for recruiting scores of young British Muslims for training camps in Waziristan.'

Roper said, 'The Prime Minister and the government have handled him with kid gloves so far, but yesterday he made a very unhelpful speech regarding the President's visit here on Friday. That can't be allowed.'

'If you examine the crowd carefully,' Holley said to Sara, 'you'll notice a decidedly rough element.'

Tony Doyle put in, 'So as soon as Selim starts preaching fire and brimstone, they'll begin throwing things, the Muslims will respond, and we'll have a riot situation because the police will have to contain it.'

'Looking like Fascist bullyboys to the Arab world,' Roper said. 'Which is exactly what Ali Selim wants.' There was an outcry just beyond the crowd. 'Unless I'm very much mistaken, here he comes.'

Henri Legrande had been standing as close as he dared to the van, hoping to hear something useful, and found himself among those who were not interested in getting involved in this unfolding drama but wanted to see what was going on. At the sound of Ali Selim's approach, pressure from behind caused a surge forward and scuffling broke out.

Henri, involved in the pushing and shoving, voiced his displeasure in bad language, French-style. Claude Duval, close by in the mêlée, hearing him, called in French, 'What do you expect, they're English!'

They were swept apart, and Henri lost himself in the crowd fast. He had not been close enough to hear the exchanges between Roper and the others, so he did not realize who Duval was, but there had been something about him, a face from the past perhaps.

The group of Muslims who forced their way through the crowd covered a wide age range. Some wore Western clothes, others wholly traditional, and there were those who wore a mixture of both.

Ali Selim sat in a palanquin carried on the shoulders of six men. He wore a large white skullcap, his long black hair flecked with silver, as was his beard, and his face was fiercely intelligent. A young woman ran alongside, a hand on the palanquin. She was all in black, as if mourning, and wore a silk chador, a loose shirt, and leggings. She had big eyes and high cheekbones in an olive face.

As the group passed, Selim's eyes swept over Roper and his party, showing no interest, no emotion, as if they didn't exist, and two people plunged on into the crowd, joined up with others waiting beside a stand. The palanquin was lowered, disappearing from view, and a moment later Ali Selim was standing high above the crowd to a roar of acclaim and an equally loud chorus of jeers and shouts. His voice boomed through a loudspeaker.

'I have a right to be here, to speak the truth. As a British citizen, I am affronted that the President of the United States can be welcomed here in the city of my birth without any consultation with those citizens who think as I do. He is a war criminal who deserves only execution as retribution for the thousands of innocents who have died in an unjust war. Praise be to he who becomes his executioner!'

An egg hit him on the side of the face, and as he turned he was caught by another, and then some sort of ball struck him in the mouth, which immediately started to bleed. He disappeared quickly, and the crowd roared as fighting began.

The riot police surged past the van, their shields up, batons ready, and Roper said, 'That's it, folks. Heave me inside, Tony, and let's get out of here.'

Holley helped, wheeling him onto the hydraulic lift, which had the chair inside in seconds. 'If anyone wants a lift, jump in,' Roper said.

'I'll walk,' Duval said. 'I've other things to do, but I'll be in touch.'

'You don't want to hang about here,' Roper said to Holley and Sara. 'Maggie Hall does a lovely lunch at Holland Park.'

'You could try your new weapon on the firing range,' Holley suggested.

'Good idea,' Sara said. 'We'll do that.'

CHAPTER 7

They climbed in, and Tony turned from the rioting mob and drove off. Henri Legrande, some little distance away, saw them go, and Duval make his way towards the subway, as many people did, fleeing from the violence. He joined in, keeping an eye on Duval, who was some distance ahead.

On the other side, some people made for bus stops and others hailed taxis or walked down Park Lane. Duval was on the heels of a group of seven or eight who turned into Upper Brook Street. As Henri rounded the corner, Duval, concealed in a doorway on the other side of the street, took a photo with his mobile phone.

Henri hurried after the group, realizing that he had lost his quarry when they reached Grosvenor Square, not that it really mattered. He'd just been interested in who the fellow Frenchman might be. Kelly was parked across from the American Embassy, and Henri joined him.

'What was it like?' Kelly asked.

'Terrible. A real bloody riot,' Henri told him, and

Kelly drove away, passing Duval, who had been watching.

Duval called Roper on his mobile and told him what had happened. Roper said, 'I must say, Claude, it would be a remarkable coincidence.'

'My dear Giles, I understand life to be full of them, but admit I could be wrong. If he hadn't cursed someone he was wrestling with in that mob in rather rude French, I would not have paid him the slightest attention, but why was he following me?'

'You're quite right, so first things first. I'll have Dora look at the photo. If she says it's the Pernod drinker from the Dark Man, then we'll obviously seek assistance from your Paris files.'

'Excellent. Give me your number and I'll patch the photo through now.'

Roper did as he was asked. 'We're still in the van on the way to Holland Park, but it will be waiting when we get there.'

Duval lit a cigarette, thinking of the sign he had noticed on the side of the Citroën van as it passed. *Mary's Bower.* Quite intriguing, that. Something to do with religion perhaps. And he walked away.

When they arrived at Holland Park, the four of them went into the computer room, and Henri Legrande was on one of the many screens. Roper had explained the situation to them on the way.

He said to Doyle, 'You're the copper. What do

you think?' Doyle said, 'Mid-sixties, could be older. Very self-contained. Don't let the glasses fool you – that's just age. He's been a soldier.'

Sara said, 'How can you be sure of that?'

'Because I've been a military policeman for seventeen years. We guard the wall, we take care of the bad things that ordinary folk can't face. We can kill when we have to. Not many people can do that.'

'Now then, Tony, you're waxing lyrical again.'

'Yes, I'll put myself on report, Major. There was some talk of Captain Gideon trying out her new weapon on the firing range. Shall I go down and prepare?'

'An excellent idea,' Roper said. 'You carry on, Tony, and we'll catch up with you in fifteen minutes.'

The firing range was at the rear of the main building, a long concrete bunker under the garden and dating from the Second World War. It was reached by a lengthy sloping tunnel, Roper leading the way into a cold and gloomy room, harsh white light at one end, illuminating a line of twelve targets representing charging soldiers in uniform, nationality unspecified. Tony Doyle was standing at a long table with a range of handguns laid out and sound mufflers for everyone.

'Here we are, then,' Roper said. 'What have you got for us, Tony?'

'There's a Glock here, a Browning Hi-Power,

126

a .44 Magnum, and a Beretta.' Tony picked up the Browning. 'My personal favourite, Major.'

'Give it to me.' Roper held out his hand, took the weapon, and lifted it. 'It's been a long time.'

Tony slipped some mufflers on him. Roper gripped the left arm of his chair and fired from left to right three times, hitting each target in the chest.

'You're still up for it, sir,' Tony said, and Roper handed him the weapon. 'You finish.'

Which Tony did, all heart shots. 'Will that do, sir?'

'Try not to sound so satisfied, Tony,' Roper said. 'And see to Captain Gideon.'

Sara had covered her ears, taken the Colt from her shoulder bag, and loaded it. She weighed it, then fired, double-handed, very fast at the fourth target, riddling the heart and chest area.

Tony took the Colt from her. 'Not much left with those hollow points, ma'am.'

She picked up the Glock, remembering, face serious, extended her arm, and shot the fifth target in the heart. No one said a word, and she laid it down carefully. 'A good gun to have in a bad place.'

She picked up her Colt and returned it to her shoulder bag, and Holley said, 'Lunch, anyone?'

Roper sat there, a slight smile on his face, as if waiting for something, and Tony picked up the Browning, held it out without saying a word, and Holley took it. 'Do I have to?'

'Josef Lermov called it a gift from God,' said Roper. 'We must show Sara.'

'More like a curse.' Holley turned sideways, left hand on hip, right arm extended like some old Western gunfighter and double-tapped the last three soldiers, shooting out their eyes.

'Oh, my God,' Sara said softly.

'Satisfied, Giles?' Holley asked.

'Absolutely,' Roper said calmly. 'Let's go and have Maggie Hall's idea of a simple lunch. French onion soup, tossed salad, poached salmon with Lyonnais potatoes. Join us, Tony, when you're finished here.'

He coasted out in his electric chair. Sara took Holley's hand without a word, and they walked after him.

After the meal, they went to the computer room and discovered the news screen alive with footage of the riot in Hyde Park. It had all been caught: Ali Selim's dramatic arrival, his appearance and subversive speech high above the crowd, including the rain of missiles, the riot police surging past the van. There was some further footage of Ali Selim, with what appeared to be blood on his face, emerging from the crowd, surrounded by minders, who bundled him into the back of a van waiting beside the Marble Arch entrance to the park and which had last been seen driving towards Bayswater.

A Scotland Yard commissioner made excuses for the police failure to arrest and detain Ali Selim, who could not be found at his home or the Pond Street Mosque. The Prime Minister emerged from 10 Downing Street to inform journalists that the speech could only be construed as advocating the assassination of the President of the United States and every effort would be made to find and arrest Selim.

Roper cleared the screen for a while. 'You noticed Ferguson, of course, standing at the back with a few other functionaries?'

'We certainly did,' Holley said.

'For future information, Sara, the rather jolly-looking chap with the permanent smile and the blond hair is a good friend of ours. Henry Frankel, the Cabinet Secretary.'

'He looked nice,' she said. 'But what do you think Ali Selim was up to making such a speech? Was it really incitement to murder?'

'Others have made similar speeches with the hope that they will be imprisoned. They need martyrs to attract more followers to their cause. Al Qaeda knows damn well that the majority of Muslims don't want this kind of trouble.'

'So what do you think he's done?'

'Who knows?' Roper said. 'Gone into hiding, done a runner. Maybe Al Qaeda has a plan for him. Anyway, I was thinking, Sara, maybe it would be a good idea if you spent the afternoon with me. I'll show you everything we get up to here, who our contacts are with outfits like GCHQ, the CIA, and the GRU, all the tricks of our rather nefarious trade.'

'I'd like that very much,' she said. 'What do you think, Daniel?'

'I think it's an excellent idea. They coined the word *Machiavellian* for the great Giles Roper. Cunning and underhanded, but in the nicest possible way.'

'I would suggest you leave now,' Roper said.

'Well, make sure Tony takes the lady home.' He smiled at Sara. 'Noon tomorrow, I'll pick you up.'

Tony followed him out, and Sara found a swivel chair and sat beside Roper, looking up at the screens. 'It must make you feel like sort of lord of the universe.'

'That's true, particularly when I'm watching people, their comings and goings. And the really spooky thing is they have no idea that it's happening.'

Tony came in at that moment. 'Sorry to break this up, but it's shower time, Major, the full works. Can't have you sitting there smelling like an ashtray all day.'

'I hear and obey.' Roper turned to Sara. 'Here's an exercise for you. Look up Professor Jean Talbot and a man named Jack Kelly.'

At that precise moment, Mullah Ali Selim was enjoying a cup of coffee in the library of a country house called Stukely Towers. There was a knock at the door, it opened, and the young woman Sara Gideon had noticed running beside the palanquin entered, followed by a darkly handsome young man in jeans and a black bomber jacket. He was her fiancé, Jemal Fateh, and she

130

was Asan Selim, the mullah's niece. They were both dedicated jihadists.

'So there you are,' he said. 'Do you approve of the house, Asan?'

'Quite wonderful, Uncle.'

'Owned by a wealthy sheikh from the Gulf, one of many dedicated friends that we can always rely on. He also keeps a jet just ten miles from here.'

'I am glad to hear it. Now that Osama has been so brutally torn from our lives, your safety from our enemies is of crucial importance. You must leave England as soon as possible,' she said.

'Not yet. For the moment, I am safe here. Eventually, I shall leave for Pakistan, for Peshawar, and from there cross the border to a village called Amira, west of the Khyber Pass. I'll be safe among friends there, and I can plan our future campaign in peace. America, the Great Satan, shall pay for what they did to Osama. This I promise you.'

'In what way can we serve, master?' Jemal asked.

'Come with me and I'll show you,' Ali Selim said, and led the way out.

It took a sizeable staff to take care of such a house, and yet there was no sign of anyone, as if they were keeping out of sight. Selim led the way to a rear conservatory, through a tunnel, and they emerged in a vast garage containing many vehicles, the most interesting of which was an imposing yellow Central Accident & Emergency ambulance.

'This is exactly the same as the old and battered

one you both spent two days being taught at the proving ground last week,' Ali Selim said. 'The only difference is that this one is brand new and provided by the Brotherhood. Inside you will find uniforms and identity cards, plus a worksheet authorizing you to deliver emergency oxygen cylinders to level three of the underground garage at the House of Commons.'

'May we try driving it, master?' Jemal asked.

'Of course, but only in the courtyard. I'll see you in an hour – and wear your uniforms.'

He was going over papers at the library desk when the knock came, and they entered and stood together in the yellow uniforms, waiting for his approval.

'Excellent.' He nodded. 'It should work, particularly because there'll be so many vehicles that day. An obvious workhorse has a better chance than anything else of being accepted. Now, sit down and let me explain what we're attempting here.'

'Yes, Uncle,' Asan said, and she and Jemal pulled chairs forward and sat.

'Both of you can pass as Europeans – particularly you, Asan, with your hair cut and dyed. You proved that by going on that guided tour of Parliament last week, when they showed you and the other tourists the terrace.'

'Which was interesting,' Jemal said. 'But I don't see how we could possibly get that far on Friday.'

'Of course not,' Ali Selim said. 'Certainly not in uniform, and not with this.'

He picked up a large and very yellow paramedic's bag and dumped it on the desk.

'You're not going to the terrace. There's no way you could get close enough to blow up the Prime Minister and the President, as wonderful as that would be. But there is something we can do. We can remind them that Al Qaeda is still a force to be reckoned with. We're going to blow up the underground garage in the House of Commons. It will reverberate around the entire world. There's enough Semtex in the bag to cause huge damage. All you have to do is leave the ambulance there and switch on the timer. You'll have thirty minutes to walk away.'

'And what then?' Jemal asked.

'Cross from Parliament to Northend Street, where a Mr Aziz will be waiting in a white Ford van. You will change in the back of the van while he drives you back here, then we'll leave at once for the jet. Naturally, I'll be taking you to Pakistan with me.'

There was a heavy silence as they glanced at each other, Asan with rather more enthusiasm than Jemal. Her eyes were shining as she said to Ali Selim, 'It is an honour to do this, Uncle.'

'You make me proud, child.' He nodded to Jemal. 'I'd appreciate a word with my niece alone.'

'Of course, master,' Jemal told him, got up with some reluctance, and went out.

Ali Selim took a small pillbox from a drawer, got up, came round the desk, and placed a hand

133

on her head. 'Bless you, my child. Your parents would have been so proud. If anything untoward happens, if you were to fall into the hands of our enemies, I fear what they might do. These evil ones use torture of the worst kind.'

She looked up in adoration. 'Nothing could ever make me speak, Uncle.'

'I'm sure you would do your best, but I'd hate to think of you suffering.' He slipped the small pillbox into her hand. 'The capsule in there will take you to eternity in an instant, where you will wait for me until my time comes. Hold it in your mouth until all is lost and then bite on it.'

She took the box without hesitation. 'You are so good to me.'

'This is our secret, of course – Jemal would not understand. You, child, have become a woman, and he is still a boy.' He patted her on the head. 'Go to him now.'

Jemal was waiting in the hall anxiously and took her hand. 'What did he say to you?'

'My uncle only wished to hear that I was strong enough for this, and I was able to assure him I am. We are privileged to be tasked with such a thing, Jemal, so let us be as one.'

He nodded, still a touch reluctant. 'If that is how you see it, so be it.'

'It is, loved one.' She took his hand. 'Now we are no longer two, but one, and it is a time for acting, not talking,' and she led him towards the kitchen.

★   ★   ★

134

At Holland Park, when Roper returned, he found Sara watching the news. 'Anything of interest?'

'Still no sign of Selim.'

'And how have you been getting on with the Talbot saga?'

'It's an incredible story. I can see where Jack Kelly would give you a problem. The peace process totally wiped the slate clean for men like him.' She shook her head. 'And now he's at it again. Do you think Jean Talbot knows?'

'The received wisdom would be that she doesn't, but I was never totally certain about her.'

'So what can you do about Kelly?'

'The IRA threat at the moment is from a ragbag army composed of various factions,' Roper said. 'Kelly, with all those years in the Provisional IRA under his belt, has a membership in the Army Council and is a force to be reckoned with, but coming to grips legally with men like him is very difficult. After all, some of them are serving in Parliament at Stormont.'

'So how do you keep an eye on him?'

'I allow my computer to do that. Apparently, he flew in on a private Talbot plane yesterday. If he turns up at Jean Talbot's house, we'll know.'

'How?'

'We have an asset in the area. Talbot goes for a run in Hyde Park most mornings, and often has dinner with Owen Rashid of Rashid Oil. Good-looking chap, unmarried, younger than her. Welsh mother, Bedu father. Lives in Park Lane.'

'You mean she's under surveillance?' She frowned. 'I don't like the sound of that.'

'Her son was a traitor to the Crown, and she is chairman of one of the biggest arms groups in the world. It's the name of the game. Do you want to go on?'

She took a deep breath. 'Of course I do. So what next?'

Holley had spent his day on Malik Shipping business, dealing with agents worldwide, mainly on screen. A final hour had been with Hamid Malik, his partner in Algiers, who treated him like a recalcitrant son.

'Why can't the firm be enough for you, Daniel? Business has never been better. We're making millions.'

'I've got millions,' Holley told him.

'Since they gave you Algerian nationality, the foreign minister is delighted with how well you speak for us abroad, even the President.'

'I'm glad to do it, and not only for the diplomatic immunity it gives me. Algeria means a lot to me.'

'But still you crave for this violent world of action that Ferguson offers you. You're soon to be fifty, and still no woman in your life.'

Holley answered instinctively, 'Oh, I wouldn't say that.'

Malik was on it like a tiger. 'Ah, so there is someone? Tell me at once, Daniel. After all these years, am I not a father to you? Who is she?'

'It doesn't matter. She's twenty years too young for me.'

'Are you mad?' Malik demanded. 'What is twenty years to a man and a woman in love? In any case, the way you live your life, you could take the fatal bullet at any time – and probably will if you don't change your ways.'

'She also happens to be a Sephardic Jew.'

Malik was suddenly angry. 'Daniel, I've managed to survive with a Christian for my partner for almost thirty years. I'm that kind of Muslim. Seize the day. Now go in peace. And by the way, there were Sephardic Jews living in Algiers a thousand years ago.'

He was so tired that he undressed and went to bed in the early evening and drifted into sleep. It was the sound of his mobile that pulled him awake at ten-thirty. He was surprised at how late it was, but then, it had been a long day.

It was Sara. 'It's me, Daniel – what a day I've had. Roper is a hard taskmaster. Come and pick me up. I'd love to sit on the terrace and have a drink with you.'

He wanted to say yes, but forced himself to say no. It couldn't go on, it wasn't right, and to his surprise he realized that for once in a reasonably self-centred life, he was thinking of the welfare of another human being as more important than his own.

'I don't think so, Sara. We've got a big day

tomorrow, the noon meeting. Try and get a good night's sleep.'

'Damn you, Daniel Holley.' She sounded close to tears. 'I'm going to walk all the way down South Audley Street to the Dorchester, look up and imagine you in your solitary splendour on the terrace, wish you a thoroughly rotten night, and then walk back.'

She clicked off. Holley lay there thinking about it. Was it a tantrum or had she really meant it? But then, he didn't have a choice, because if they *were* being targeted, the last thing she should be doing was walking down any street at night, even in Mayfair. So he got out of bed and dressed quickly, cords and boots, a khaki shirt and his flying jacket, the holster on his right ankle. He was out the door fast, and behind him the curtains ballooned, stirred, then settled again.

Events had made it clear to Henri Legrande that Holley and Sara were more than just good friends. Their behaviour on the walk to Hyde Park and during the riot had convinced him that they were a couple. The chance that Holley would deliver Sara home late from dinner or a show one night seemed obvious, as did the planning of an ambush. It might take two or three nights of waiting, but the moment would surely come.

He sat behind the wheel of the Citroën now, Kelly beside him, and behind were two hard-headed London Irish boys named Fahy and Regan,

138

who had salivated over the prospect of a thousand pounds cash between them for crippling Daniel Holley. They were already drunk, a half-bottle of whiskey shared between them, and were rowdy with it.

'Where the fuck is this red Alfa you're going on about?' Fahy demanded. 'We've been here for an hour, man.'

'Just shut up and wait,' Henri said grimly. 'That's if you want to see the other half of your money.'

From the dark end of Highfield Court where they were parked, they could see the house, and suddenly the door opened and security lights came on and Sara appeared. She was wearing a black leather belted coat, a scarf around her neck, carried a walking stick in her right hand, and her shoulder bag was slung across her front. She started to walk briskly, using the stick, already limping.

'Would you look at that?' Fahy cried. 'A fella could have a great time giving that one a seeing-to.'

'I saw her first.' Regan reached for the door handle.

'Leave it,' Henri said. 'She's not the target.' He triggered the internal locking device, securing all four doors.

Fahy said, 'She's getting away, for Christ's sake. This is stupid.'

He reached over and punched Henri in the side of the head, leaned down, and unlocked the doors. The next moment he was standing on the pavement, pulling up his friend, who'd fallen out. They were both swaying a little with the drink taken.

'Get back in, you bloody fools,' Henri said, tried to open his door, but Regan kicked it closed.

They both broke into a shambling run. Along the pavement and for the full length ahead, the only sign of life was Sara.

'Will you wait for us, darling?' Fahy called. 'We'll give you the time of your life.'

She glanced over her shoulder, then turned and hurried on, her hand reaching for the Colt, which she was carrying in the right pocket of her leather coat for easy access.

'We must do something,' Kelly said.

'Yes, like getting the hell out of here,' Henri told him as the Alfa appeared down the road, and he swerved the Citroën into the nearest side street, parked, then jumped out and moved back to the corner to see what was going on. As he watched, Kelly joined him, peering over his shoulder.

Sara had just reached the corner of a dark cobbled lane. Regan was a few yards behind and Fahy reached her first, grabbing her scarf, forcing her round and swinging her into the entrance of the lane. She went down, and as she drew the Colt, he leaned over and tried to kiss her. She shot off the lobe of his left ear, and he cried out, blood staining his fingers.

Holley swung the Alfa into the curb, was out in a flash and, as Fahy tried to get up, booted him

140

in the face, sending him backwards into the gutter. Regan took one look, swerved into the lane, and kept on running. Fahy heaved himself up, a hand to his ear, and backed away in horror from the Colt in Sara's right hand, shaking his head dumbly, then turned and stumbled into the darkness.

Sara offered her hand. 'A drunken mugger, Daniel. It's the times we live in.'

He pulled her up. 'Are you okay?'

'Of course I am.' She held up the Colt. 'I was ready to blow that bastard's brains out.'

'I'll take you home.'

'Oh no you won't. There's only one place you're going to take me, and that's the Dorchester.' Henri Legrande watched the Alfa drive away, having heard and seen everything that had taken place. Kelly said, 'What a mess that turned out to be.'

'It could have been worse. He might have beaten the truth out of those two, but his only concern was the woman, which enabled them to get away.'

Henri said, 'This lady is quite exceptional. We'll have to take care with these two.'

They turned and went back to the Citroën.

Rain drummed against the canopy, which Holley had sent out over the terrace at the touch of a button. He sat in the half-light, an open bottle of Dom Perignon on the table. There was only one glass, Sara having taken a refill with her when she had decided to soak in a hot bath in marble splendour.

He poured another and drank it slowly, considering what had happened. The two men involved in the assault had been luckier than they knew, but he felt curiously calm. That she was safe and unharmed was all that mattered.

He called Roper on his Codex and told him what had happened. 'What do you think?' he asked.

'That you're losing your edge. The important question here is: Were these guys just drunken muggers, as Sara said, or were they a couple of thugs hired by somebody to do their worst? What you should have done was kick hell out of one of them until he talked.'

'All right, so I didn't.'

'And we both know why. While you were making sure Sara was okay, they were able to leg it. She *is* all right, isn't she?'

'So you care, do you?'

'Of course I do.'

'I'll tell her that. I'm sure she'll be thrilled.'

'She's not still there, is she?'

'She felt like having a hot bath after what happened. I'll be taking her home shortly.' Roper burst into laughter, and Holley said, 'What's so funny?'

'You are, Daniel, I'll see you at noon tomorrow. Say goodnight to Sara for me.'

A moment later, she walked in wearing a terry-cloth robe. 'The bath was lovely.'

Holley said, 'You're not dressed. Don't you want to go home?'

142

'On a night like this? It's pouring out there and I'd be alone. Sadie's gone to Manchester to see her niece, who's just had a baby girl, and she'll be staying for a few days. I thought you wouldn't mind me sleeping over in the second bedroom, the smaller one you never told me about. I see the maid has only turned down the covers on yours. I'd better go and sort the other one out.'

Suddenly, she looked very tired indeed, the stress finally catching up with her, and although she would never admit it to him, her leg was really hurting.

'Just take the master bedroom,' Holley told her. 'I'll be fine.'

'Thanks, Daniel, I believe I will. I've got such a headache. You wouldn't have something for that, would you?'

'As it happens, I do. I'll get it for you.' He went to his study, got two pills from his field service kit, went into the bedroom with a glass of water, and found her already under the covers, her head raised on a pillow.

'These act incredibly quickly, and they'll help you sleep.'

She got them down and put the glass on a side table. 'Sometimes I hate men, Daniel. What absolute bastards those guys were. A woman on her own on a dark street, and a cripple into the bargain. That just about sums them up.'

He sat beside her on the bed and held her hand. 'With a pistol in her hand and ready to use it. That creep doesn't realize he's lucky to be alive.'

She managed a smile and touched his face. 'Poor Daniel. I'm a problem for you, aren't I?'

'A nice problem. Just go to sleep.'

She closed her eyes, and he sat there until her hand slipped away. Only then did he quietly leave the room.

They arrived at Holland Park in good time for the noon meeting, to find that it had been cancelled. They found only Roper and Dillon enjoying a cup of tea together in the computer room.

'What's going on?' Holley asked.

'Ferguson and Miller have been called for a Cabinet Office discussion about Ali Selim.'

'Is there anything to suggest he's left the country?' Dillon asked.

'No, but I'd say it's a strong possibility,' Roper told him. 'Think of the times you've been involved with beating the air traffic control system, dropping in and out again from some decaying airfield deep in the countryside.'

'True enough,' Dillon said. 'He could be over the English Channel in a small plane inside two hours, and once in France, transfer to a jet, and the world's his oyster.'

'There was a chance that the President's Secret Service people would persuade him to cancel and carry straight on to Paris, though that would have left the Prime Minister with egg on his face.'

'But he's still coming?' Sara asked.

'Insisted on it, but the Prime Minister is as

incandescent on the whole matter as Ferguson is with you two,' Roper carried on.

'You told him about last night?' Holley said.

'Come off it, Daniel,' Dillon put in. 'Club rules, old son. Even if the threat is only a possibility, it's the kind of thing that touches us all. An attempted mugging is one thing, assault as a result of being targeted is something else again. Roper's right – you should have squeezed the truth out of one of them.'

'Just shut up, the both of you.' Sara was angry. 'It wasn't Daniel's fault. So those two guys were pretty foul, but I shouldn't have been there in the first place. I was being childish and stupid. The truth is this is a whole different world I've been plunged into.'

Dillon put an arm about her shoulders. 'You'll be fine, girl dear, just give it time.'

'It's all right saying that, Sean.' She smiled bitterly. 'But perhaps I *was* being targeted. Who knows?'

'Well, it won't happen again, because I'll see it doesn't.' Holley turned to Roper. 'So what now?'

'I've had orders to go down to the House of Commons and check out the terrace, and I'm to take you three with me. Tony is going to take us in the van.'

'Well, that will certainly be a new experience,' Sara said.

'Not for Dillon,' Roper said. 'He's something of an expert where the terrace is concerned, but I'll tell you about that when we get there. Let's get moving.'

At the House of Commons, Tony stayed with the van while Roper and his friends joined the queue to get in. It was mainly constituents hoping to see their MP or people on official business. Tourists were being turned away by the security staff, obviously because of the pending arrival of the President. Some were complaining bitterly as they were firmly moved on.

A uniformed police inspector, obviously in charge, standing back surveying the scene, wore the campaign medal for Ireland, among others. He stared at Roper, then walked forward.

'Major Roper, isn't it? What a pleasure to see you, sir. My name's Halloran. I was the military police sergeant-major in charge of the entrance to the Portland Hotel in Belfast when you spent nine hours defusing that bomb in the foyer.'

'I remember you well.' Roper shook hands. 'You were on that door when I went in, and you were still there when I came out.'

'A privilege to be there, Major. I'll never forget it.'

'We're here on behalf of the Cabinet Office to have a look at the security situation on the terrace.'

'I was notified about it, Major. I just didn't realize it was going to be you. Allow me to lead the way.'

★　　★　　★

He left them on the terrace beside the Thames, which was surprisingly busy – MPs enjoying a drink, waiters passing to and fro from what was called the Terrace Bar. It was very pleasant there, slightly chilly but the sun shining enough to bring the awnings out, and the famous tall Victorian lamps ranged along the parapet added to the scene.

'I've never been here before,' Sara said. 'Why is the carpet green here and red up there?'

'That's the House of Lords end,' Dillon said, and ordered champagne for all of them from a passing waiter. 'A grand place, this, restaurants and bars all over the show.'

With remarkable speed, the waiter was back with four glasses of champagne on a tray, and they each took one. 'So what makes you such an expert on the terrace?' Sara demanded.

'An old story, my love, no big deal. I've no wish to bore you.'

'What a humbug you are.' Roper touched glasses with Sara. 'Some years ago, President Clinton graced the terrace with a visit, and the security services will never forgive Dillon for turning up as a waiter and serving canapés to President Clinton and the Prime Minister.'

Sara turned in appeal to Holley, who shrugged. 'Before my time.'

Which left only Dillon. 'But how did you do that?' she asked.

'It was very simple. The Salters dropped me in the river from a passing boat in the middle of the night. I hauled myself up to the terrace, hid in a storage room, and stayed there until the action started, when I came out dressed as a waiter.'

Before she could say a word, Henry Frankel appeared, a file under his arm, and he was smiling hugely.

'Captain Gideon, what a pleasure.' He shook Sara's hand warmly. 'You exceed my expectations, and that doesn't happen very often.' He turned to Dillon. 'So, what have you got to say, Sean? Is our security acceptable?'

'Well, there's still twenty-six restaurants and bars, entrances and exits galore, MPs, workmen, cleaning staff – in other words, far too many people, and you notice I haven't even mentioned the river?'

'Well, we'd rather you didn't,' Henry Frankel told him. 'We don't want to be alarmist.'

'I'm just being realistic, Henry. In Belfast in the bad days of the Troubles, Catholic women of all ages queued up to get jobs as cleaning ladies in schools and factories that housed British troops. There were sympathizers to the Cause in the Royal Ulster Constabulary itself, and the civil service.'

'What are you trying to say?' Frankel asked.

'We live in a cosmopolitan society, Henry, and London is a splendid example. We've left a vehicle in the underground garage, where people in over-alls, obviously from many cultures, work as mechanics and sweepers. It was the same coming through the House of Commons to get here – lots of cleaning women in the corridors, for example. The champagne I ordered? The waiter was obviously Muslim. People were talking and didn't notice that I ordered in Arabic, which pleased him, by the way. Did you notice, Daniel?'

Holley shook his head. 'No. I didn't notice.'

'The place is a sieve, Henry, but so is the whole country, just like Belfast was. People can't help hearing conversations, good people who don't want to be involved with terrorism, but when you've got a family, you'll respond to pressure for obvious reasons.'

'Everything you say is true,' Henry Frankel said. 'We can only travel hopefully. You are team leader, Giles,' he said to Roper. 'Everybody loves a hero, and the George Cross certainly makes you that. We are keeping quiet about your exploits at Abusan, Sara. There are good reasons why, so no offence.'

'None taken,' she said.

'Blake Johnson tells me the President asked for you, Dillon, to be included in the luncheon, and you, Daniel. I believe he knows both of you.'

'True enough,' Dillon acknowledged.

'So the four of you return tomorrow morning. Harry Miller and Charles Ferguson have been ordered to stay at the Prime Minister's beck and call all day.' Frankel chuckled. 'I've never seen Ferguson so fussed. He said to tell you, Giles, to make sure there's no more nonsense with Daniel and Sara, whatever that means. I'd love to know,

149

but I haven't got time to listen. Ciao, everyone, I'll see you in the morning,' and he was gone.

Roper smiled at Sara. 'Well, there you are. You've been warned to avoid bad company at all times.'

'Thanks very much,' Holley told him. 'Can we go to lunch now?'

Roper laughed and led the way out.

CHAPTER 8

With only failure to report, Henri Legrande and Kelly had kept quiet about the two attempts to cause mischief with Holley and Sara. It left Owen Rashid, seated at his laptop by the terrace in his flat, with little to say when Abu came on the line.

'I've heard nothing from you. What's happening with Legrande and Kelly?'

'I understand they're familiarizing themselves with the background of Ferguson's people.'

'Then I trust they were at the riot in Hyde Park yesterday morning. They were all there.'

'What do you want from me?' Owen asked him.

'I thought I'd made that clear. Ferguson and his people have not only caused constant trouble for Ali Selim, they have murdered some of our most important people over the last few years. Death for death, Owen, that's what they deserve and it's a result I intend to have.'

'And this includes the woman?'

'I'm surprised you need to ask. Her service record speaks for itself, and not only in Afghanistan. Owen, these people call us terrorists and speak of being at war with us. Well, we are at war with them, and to the knife. So what about some action from the Frenchman? He was supposed to be serious business, but I've seen little evidence of it. A bullet in the back when your target walks home in the rain is serious business; so is a bomb under someone's car. What I'm getting here is nothing.'

'He's only been on the case for a couple of days,' Owen protested.

'I'm not interested in excuses. If he lets me down, my retribution will be not only swift but final. I want results and I want them now. Fire from heaven, Owen. That would be appropriate while the President is in town, don't you think?'

Owen sat there thinking about it, thoroughly angry at the position he was in, but there was no way out, so he phoned Kelly.

'Where are you?'

'The shop.'

'And Legrande is with you?'

'Yes. Is there a problem?'

'Not for me, for you. I've had Abu on my back, and he isn't pleased at the lack of action from you two. I'll be round in fifteen minutes.'

Henri Legrande was in the workshop repairing an antique chair when Kelly hurried in to warn him of Owen Rashid's imminent arrival. He was worried, and it showed.

'What the hell are we going to do?'

'Well, for one thing, we still keep quiet about the Dark Man affair and the business with the woman last night,' Henri told him. 'Failure is the last thing Abu wants to hear about, so not a hint to Rashid. So we tell him we've been making a general reconnaissance, checked out the Salters' pub, followed Holley from the Dorchester to Highfield Court, where the woman lives, sussed out the situation at her house.'

'And you followed them to Hyde Park,' Kelly said.

'Exactly. Not bad for two days.'

There was no time for more, because the bell sounded as the shop door opened and Owen Rashid called, 'I'm here. Where are you?'

Henri produced a bottle of Beaujolais and three glasses. They sat around the workbench, and Owen told them exactly what Abu had said. Henri offered the defence he and Kelly had prepared, pointing out that he had followed Sara and Holley to Hyde Park and witnessed Ali Selim's speech and the riot that had followed.

'We've been on the case – surely you can see that?'

'I can, but that isn't the point. I've told you what Abu said. The bullet in the back, the car bomb.'

'I heard you,' Henri told him. 'Fire from heaven.'

'And can you handle that?'

Henri got up and went to a door in one corner. He reached up to a lintel, found a key and opened it, and switched on a light. 'Have a look, why don't you?'

Owen was amazed. There were three shotguns, two Lee Enfield rifles and an AK-47, ranged neatly against one wall on racks. A shelf on the other side displayed a number of handguns. There were boxes of assorted ammunition and several large tin boxes painted khaki green.

'What's that?' Owen asked.

'Semtex in one, pencil timers in the other. I've had this stuff for years. The guns came from house sales. It's astonishing what turns up in the antiques business.'

Kelly was examining a Beretta. 'This is in lovely condition.' He replaced it on the shelf and took another. 'Walther PPK with a Carswell silencer. Real stopping power.'

Owen said, 'When did you last use any of these?'

'This particular weaponry? Never. It just came into my possession through the house sales, as I told you. The Semtex is a different matter, but I've kept it carefully preserved. I'm sure Jack has told you my story. It was last used many years ago when I sought retribution for a great wrong.'

They went out, and he locked the door, then poured them each another glass of wine. Owen said, 'Fire from heaven, a spectacular to ruin the President's visit and demonstrate the power of Al Qaeda. Would you be up for that – a car bomb?'

'I don't see why not.'

'It would be like old times to Jack here, he was involved in so many similar affairs during his IRA past. But why are you sure of yourself?'

So Legrande told him. 'As Jack knows, I have a cancer. Six months is all I've got.'

Owen pretended shock. 'My God, that's terrible.'

'No it isn't, it's a fact, so I don't give a damn about anything any more. That's why I took on the job.'

'And if the woman were involved?'

'To me, my friend, she is no longer a woman as you mean it. She is a soldier, and a damn good one, so she is just another member of Ferguson's team.'

Owen nodded. 'So what do you intend to do?'

'I haven't the slightest idea what Holley plans for this evening. With a man like him as my quarry, I'll certainly wear a bullet-proof vest. I may be on borrowed time, but there's no need to hurry things. All I can say is that if a suitable opportunity presents itself, I'll take advantage of it, but Abu must understand that I can't promise anything.'

'Which is perfectly reasonable,' Owen said. 'The only problem there is that he's the most unreasonable sod I know.' He stood up. 'I'd better go and leave you to get on with it. I'll be in touch,' and he went out.

Lunch at a Lebanese restaurant in Shepherd Market had been so convivial that it lasted until three.

'Nine-thirty tomorrow morning at Holland Park,' Roper said as Tony Doyle loaded him into the van, Dillon already on board.

'Well, that was nice.' Sara slipped her hand inside Holley's arm as they started the short walk to the Dorchester. 'What shall we do tonight?'

'I haven't the slightest idea.'

They arrived at the small art-house cinema on the corner, the Curzon. She paused to look at the posters and said, 'Hey, they're showing *Manhattan*.'

'Woody Allen. A great movie,' Holley said.

She was checking the performance times and turned, delight on her face. 'It's starting in fifteen minutes. I truly adore this film, Daniel, all that glorious Gershwin music.'

'Then let's go and see it.' He put an arm around her, pushed open the door, and they went in.

It was a quarter to six when they came out, happy, into the early-evening darkness and walked back towards the Dorchester.

'What are you going to do?' Holley asked. 'Come up to my suite?'

'Love to, but it might be a good idea to check the house out, since Sadie is away – get the mail and so on.'

'Fine by me,' he said. 'I'll tell them to bring the Alfa round.'

Standing on the steps a few moments later, handing his car keys to the doorman, Sara at his side, he was immediately spotted by Jack Kelly, who had taken turns with Henri to stand on the corner of the side street where they'd parked the Citroën. He watched them for a moment, then hurried back to the Frenchman, who sat behind

156

the wheel with a magazine, the silenced Walther in his pocket.

'They're here,' he said, and got in the Citroën.

'About time. What are they doing?' Henri asked.

'It looks like they're waiting for the Alfa to be brought round.'

'Then let's be ready,' Henri said. 'You drive. Take me round to South Audley Street to wait for them. My bet is they're going to her home. I'll get ready in the rear.'

There was a magnet on the lid of the cake tin box that he held on his knees. He removed the lid, revealing the block of Semtex, three scarlet-rimmed pencil timers in a small box beside it. He sat back.

A few moments later, the Alfa passed him, and Kelly went after it. 'Don't follow them into Highfield Court,' Henri said. 'Drop me at the entrance of the street, then continue into Grosvenor Square and wait for me. It will all happen very fast, so be ready for a quick departure.'

The Alfa swung into the drive of the house and the security lights came on. Holley switched off the engine. Sara got out, taking the key from her shoulder bag, and as she went up the steps, a lean brown Burmese cat meowed and brushed her feet.

'On your way, Samson,' she said, and glanced at Holley as she turned the key. 'From next door. An absolute rascal.'

She went into the hall, switched on the light,

and Holley followed her, closing the door behind him. The security lights died as she started to take off her coat.

Henri had been waiting for the dark. He gave each pencil timer a half-turn, inserted them into the Semtex, replaced the lid, and left the Citroën quickly, crouching as low as possible to avoid activating the lights, dropped on his knees, and reached under the Alfa with the cake box, the magnet clicking firmly into place. At the same moment, Samson, who had been crouching underneath, let out a loud wailing cry and fled, bounding up the steps and leaping onto the balustrade of the side terrace, the security lights turning the darkness into day.

Holley had just helped Sara off with her coat. 'Samson again. What's wrong with him?' She glanced out through the window beside the door and saw Henri as he rose up. 'Daniel, there's a man outside,' she said, and reached for her Colt, which she was carrying in a spring holster against the small of her back.

Holley moved on the instant, reaching to open the door with one hand, drawing his Colt with the other. Henri, dazzled by the sudden lights, pulled out the Walther, fired blindly in the general direction of the door, and ran for it, Holley's shot chasing him into the street, missing by inches and striking the gate post.

He got there in time to see Henri vanish round the corner, hesitated, then turned. Seeing no sign of Sara, he ran in panic up the steps and through the open door. He found her on one knee, pulling herself up with the aid of a large chair, the cheval mirror on the wall starred with a bullet hole.

'I'm all right,' she said as he reached her. 'A dull thud was all I heard. I dropped down instinctively.'

'He was probably using a Carswell.' He pulled her close, for a moment holding her tight, and she smiled. 'At least we now know for certain that we *are* being targeted.'

'What was he doing when you saw him?'

'He just rose up as if he'd been crouching beside the car. Could he have been messing about with the brakes again?'

'I'll take a look. Do you have a light?'

'There's a spotlight in the cloakroom.'

She gave it to him, and followed as he went down the steps to the Alfa, got on his knees, and found the cake tin.

'Oh, dear,' he said, and straightened. 'I've got a strong feeling that if I ask you to go away, you'll refuse.'

'Yes, I damn well will, if it's what I think it is. What are you going to do?'

'Well, I'm trying to be logical. If whatever is in the cake tin that's attached to this car was remote-controlled, we'd have been blown to bits by now. He'd have already activated it while he was running away.'

She said calmly, 'Which would leave pencil timers. Fifteen-minute, thirty, one-hour?'

'I'd say thirty to give him ample time to be elsewhere.'

'That would seem reasonable.'

'Let's hope so. I'd just like to say I love you.'

'I know you do.' She smiled gravely. 'You'd better get on with it, then.'

He handed her the spotlight, got on his back, reached up, gripped the box in both hands, and pulled so hard that it came away from the lid. He eased back, got up, staring down at the red-ringed pencil timers, pulled them out quickly, and tossed them into the birdbath beside the steps.

'You must live right, Sara Gideon. They were fifteens – fifteen bloody minutes. We should have been dead by now, and, somewhere, the bastard who concocted this very special cake is kicking himself because he's been waiting for the sound of an explosion that hasn't come.'

'I suppose you'll have to report in? Ferguson will go ballistic.'

'I'll call Roper now,' he said as they went up the steps.

There was a meow, and Samson slipped out of the darkness, wound himself around her right ankle. She reached for him, and he faded into the night again.

'He saved our lives,' Sara said. 'It's as simple as that.' She turned and smiled at him as they went into the hall. 'Thank you for your dying declaration. Naturally, I'll hold you to it.'

'Somehow I thought you would.'

★　★　★

Henri had found Kelly in Grosvenor Square with no problem, then scrambled into the Citroën, breathless from his running.

'Is it done?' Kelly demanded as he switched on and drove round the square past the Eisenhower statue.

'If you mean did I plant the bomb, yes. We should hear the explosion any moment, so pull over.'

They sat waiting, Henri checking his watch until, with a certain despair in his voice, he said, 'I put in three pencils, the extras just to make sure in case of a malfunction. Fifteen minutes. They should have heard the explosion all over Mayfair by now. Let's get going – I'm beginning to feel cursed.'

'But what went wrong?' Kelly asked as he drove away.

'I'd just placed the bomb under the Alfa when Holley appeared. There was an exchange of fire, silenced shots, I ran for it. I can only conclude he suspected a device and found it just in time to remove the pencils.' He didn't mention the cat – it would have been too embarrassing.

'Well, Rashid won't be pleased.'

'We don't tell Rashid we tried again and failed. It's beginning to smack of burlesque.'

'If you think so,' Kelly said. 'What do you want to do now?'

'Well, at this particular moment, getting drunk sounds like a very attractive idea.'

★   ★   ★

161

Dillon happened to be at Holland Park when Roper received the news, so they all came together to Sara Gideon's house. Tony Doyle recovered the box's lid from the Alfa's chassis, and they were now sitting in the Victorian library by the fireplace while Roper examined the Semtex with a professional eye.

'This has been around for years,' he said. 'Highly volatile. It's absolutely incredible that you got away with handling it, Daniel. These pencil timers remind me of my Irish time as a bomb-disposal officer – wouldn't you agree, Tony?'

Doyle was checking one of them now, and he nodded. 'Takes me back to Ulster in the bad days, but on the other hand, I can remember stuff like this turning up years ago right here in London when IRA sympathizers were run to earth. Maybe it's just been sitting around in somebody's cellar.'

'I agree,' Roper said. 'But it's dangerous stuff. It's a miracle you two are with us.'

'Which raises the obvious question,' Dillon said. 'What's going on? Who's behind this?'

'I haven't the slightest idea,' Roper said. 'All I would say is that it makes it highly unlikely that the attack on Sara last night was a mugging. There's a pattern to all this. If only we'd caught them.'

'I admit I should have done better,' Holley said. 'But if I'd given chase to tonight's villain, Sara would have come out of the front door in search of me and walked straight into the Alfa blowing up.'

'We can all see that,' Roper said, and his Codex signaled. 'Yes, General?' He made a gesture to them and went out into the hall, returning ten minutes later.

'So tell us the worst,' Dillon said.

'Well, no surprises here. With the President's visit, talk of car bombs is the last thing the government wants. In other words, this little incident never happened. No police involvement. It is entirely our baby.'

'And we can do that?' Sara asked.

'Charles Ferguson can do anything, Sara,' Dillon said. 'Get used to that now. What happens here, Giles?'

'Best not to stay in the house right now. I doubt they'll return here now that we're onto them, but it's safer if you stay somewhere else for the next few days.'

'She can stay with me,' Holley said. 'What about Parliament tomorrow?'

'I'll join Roper at Holland Park,' Dillon told him. 'We'll pick you up at 10.30 tomorrow morning.'

'Excellent,' Holley said. 'Let's all get some sleep. To put it mildly, it's been a memorable evening.'

To Owen Rashid, who was dressing the following morning before picking up Jean Talbot for the reception, Abu's phone call came as no surprise.

'I've been waiting to hear from you about the Saudi delegation that was due to arrive yesterday.

You said you would introduce them to Talbot's nephew.'

'Which I did. They arrived yesterday, two sheikhs and a couple of generals. I took them to the Le Caprice for lunch and persuaded Jean to join the party. They were impressed with her, and the fact that she owns most of the stock in Talbot International impressed them even more.'

'Hmm. You know, it occurs to me that it might suit our plans if you could persuade her to make a trip to Rubat with you. She could see the Bacu Railway for herself, meet Sultan Ibrahim Rashid, your uncle.'

The prospect did not particularly appeal to Owen, but, as usual, it was diplomatic to agree. 'It's certainly an idea worth pursuing.'

'See what she thinks about it. I'll let you go now. I look forward to a full report on the reception. It should be memorable.'

A slight chuckle, and he was gone. Owen puzzled over it for a moment, then reached for his blazer, pulled it on, walked out into the sitting room, and as he approached the balcony window, a flurry of rain tapped against it. Good old British weather. You could always rely on it to be bad when it was particularly essential that it should be good. There were awnings there, however, so the show could go on. He found himself a light raincoat in the cloakroom, slipped it on, and went to pick up Jean. It was far too early, but it didn't matter. It would take her ages to dress, but what else was new?

164

After all, she was meeting the President of the United States of America for drinks.

An hour and a half earlier, Ali Selim had said goodbye at Stukely Towers to Asan and Jemal, holding his niece close to him for a moment.

'Allah protect you, child, and aid you in this great enterprise.'

'It is a privilege to have been chosen, Uncle.'

He shook Jemal's hand. 'My blessings go with you both, and I await your return anxiously. I shall spend the day in prayer for you.'

They got into the ambulance, Asan at the wheel, for she was a better driver, and as she drove round the circular lawn, she reached out and waved to her uncle. He waved back, and then they were out of the main gate and on their way.

Ali Selim turned to the steps leading up to the front door, which was opened by an Arab in a chauffeur's uniform. 'Are you ready to leave, master?'

'Certainly, Mahmud. Have you brought down my luggage?'

'It's already in the Mercedes in the rear court-yard. I'll go and get it.'

'You've notified the airfield that I'm ready to leave?'

'I called them the moment I saw the ambulance start down the drive, master. The Hawker will depart as soon as we get there.'

He put up an umbrella, since it had started to

rain, and hurried away, and Ali Selim stepped back into the porch. The sooner he was out of England, the better. There was nothing to stay for, certainly not his niece and Jemal. They were the walking dead now. He had no doubt the ambulance would be admitted, and, once inside, when the real plan came into play, the one they knew nothing about, the results would be shattering. Ali Selim's bomb maker had packed every possible cavity in the ambulance with Semtex, and the electronic timer in the paramedic's bag, which Jemal had been told was timed to give them thirty minutes to walk away, was actually set for the instant it was turned on. The explosion was bound to be catastrophic, although unfortunate for Asan and Jemal. On the other hand, that was no bad thing. He had, after all, been too open with them concerning the flight to Peshawar and his stay in Amira. There was no advantage in making that public at the moment.

The Mercedes came round the side of the house. Mahmud got out and raised an umbrella and mounted the steps. Ali Selim flicked the stub of the cigarette into a flower bed.

'Fast as you like, Mahmud,' he said as he joined him. 'I can't wait to get out of here.'

Doyle, Dillon, and Roper pulled up at the Dorchester, where Sara and Holley waited at the top of the steps, sheltering under the canopy from the rain. A doorman held an umbrella for them as they piled in, and Doyle pulled out into the Park Lane traffic.

'Well, the President won't be impressed with the weather, that's for sure,' Sara said.

'So they'll have the canopies out,' Dillon said. 'And everybody crowding in a bit, but on the good side, there's Captain Sara Gideon, with red hair to thank God for, and nicely set off by a scarlet blazer from Valentino, and I adore those navy blue raw-silk jeans. That's got to be Gucci. You'll be a sensation, girl dear.'

'Why, Sean, is it your feminine side you're revealing?'

'Well, I *was* once an actor,' he told her.

'Yes, we all know that, but you'll have to spend more time on your lines. The silk jeans are Valentino and the blazer's by Gucci. Not bad for an alpha male, though.'

Sara turned round to Roper in his wheelchair behind her. 'Are you looking forward to meeting the great man?'

'You could say that. He's certainly a remarkable human being, but with anything as important as this, all I want is for it to be over. All those years with the bombs in Belfast taught me one thing with complete certainty. No matter how well you organize and plan, something unlooked for comes round the next corner and screws everything up. It's a kind of chaos theory.'

They were into the press of traffic heading to Westminster, vehicles three abreast. As Sara glanced out, looking to the left across Holley, she saw the yellow ambulance ease past, noticed particularly the young girl at the wheel for no better reason than that she was extremely pretty. Asan glanced over briefly, then eased the ambulance forward in the column of vehicles aiming for the entrance to the underground garage at the House of Commons.

Sara frowned, leaning across Holley as the van moved close to the ambulance again. He said, 'What is it?'

The ambulance had moved again, for they had joined the double queue of vehicles entering the garage.

'The driver of that ambulance,' Sara told him.

Dillon said, 'I noticed her, too. Pretty girl. What about her?'

The ambulance was being passed through. 'It's just that I seem to know her from somewhere.'

With the documents Doyle showed the security men, they were passed through themselves, and as they moved forward, it struck Sara like a thunderbolt.

'Oh, my God, I know where I've seen her before.'

Roper said, 'What are you talking about, Sara?'

'That girl was at Speakers' Corner with the men carrying Ali Selim. She was running alongside with a hand clutching his palanquin. She was all in black and wore a silk chador.'

Doyle braked to a halt involuntarily, and Dillon said, 'God in heaven, girl, are you sure about this?'

168

'Of course she is,' Roper said. 'Get after them, Tony. There's no place for them to hide, not in that ambulance. If it's a bomb job, there's no time to lose, so be ready to go in hard.'

Asan and Jemal had no idea they were in trouble. The trip into London had been without incident, and their identities and the work documents relating to the delivery of oxygen cylinders to level 3 had been accepted without question. Level 3 itself seemed pretty parked up, so Asan cruised, glancing from side to side, and it was Jemal who was stressed and cursing softly.

'Calm yourself, Jemal, all will be well,' she said serenely, for she was on a complete high, never so certain. A moment later, at the far end, they came to a section of what obviously were work vehicles of one kind or another, and she pulled in on the end at a row and switched off. There was a wide gap to the next vehicle, a red Ford van.

'So it begins,' she said. 'Just as my uncle said it would. We are here.'

Jemal was so nervous that he was close to coming apart at the seams. 'And here we'll stay one way or another unless we get out of here fast. I'll go and set the timer.'

Which was in the paramedic's bag in the back of the ambulance. He got out, went to open the rear door, and Dillon's van arrived in a sudden rush as Doyle took it past in a burst of speed. Jemal pulled out the silenced Walther he had been provided with and fired twice, and the van turned in to the other side of the red Ford for protection.

Jemal opened the door on the passenger side of the ambulance, reached in, and pulled Asan across. There was a look of total astonishment on her face as she tumbled out, then struggled to her feet.

Roper's voice boomed out. 'It's over. Throw any weapons into the open and then lie down.'

'I don't know who they are, but he's right,' Jemal said. 'It's finished.'

'Only if I say so.' Her left hand found the pillbox, and she pulled out the capsule it contained, put it in her mouth, then took out her own Walther. She stood, leaned across to the driver's window, which she had left open, and fired several times across at the red Ford. It was a strange and eerie sensation, only the dull thuds of the silenced weapons as Dillon and Holley returned fire.

Jemal grabbed at her, turning her and slapping her face. 'No more. It's over.'

She pushed him away, turned, and fired wildly again at the van, her teeth crunching down on the capsule, the sickly sweet smell of cyanide apparent at once. He had no idea what it was, only that it was bad, and he pushed a fresh clip into his Walther.

'Damn you to hell,' he called, and emptied the gun into the van. It was Sara, crouched on the other side with Dillon and Holley, who took the practical approach.

She dropped down flat and saw Asan's body at

once, and the lower half of Jemal's legs beside it. He was at that moment reloading. She took careful aim and shot him through the right kneecap. He cried out, lurched backwards into a Mercedes limousine, and went down.

'That's the man taken care of,' Sara said. 'But I get a bad feeling about the girl.'

'Then we'd better go and see,' Holley told her.

Doyle had found a large police sign saying 'Entry Prohibited,' and placed it at the entrance to give them peace. Jemal was lying beside Asan, an arm around her, blood oozing from his shattered kneecap. He looked up in agony at Sara. 'It wasn't supposed to be like this. What's the smell on her mouth?'

'Cyanide, I'm afraid,' Sara said. 'A quick exit to the next world. The Nazis made it popular after they lost their war. Hitler handed them out like candy to his nearest and dearest.'

Jemal came apart then. 'Oh, dear God, it's her uncle who's responsible for this. He must have given it to her.'

Tony Doyle had pushed Roper close in his wheelchair, and with Dillon and Holley they stood waiting for Sara to put the obvious question.

'And who is her uncle?'

'Mullah Ali Selim. I can see now he was using us. I only got involved because I adored her beyond reason.'

'I see.' She frowned at the others, motioning

them to be still. 'I think we're going to have to do something about your knee.' She turned to Doyle. 'See if you can find a first-aid kit in the rear, Tony.'

Jemal said dully, 'Better take care. There's a couple of blocks of Semtex in a bag, and a thirty-minute timer I was supposed to switch on.'

There was a stillness for a moment, then Giles Roper said, 'Well, as you haven't done that, it leaves the Semtex about as deadly as a large block of plasticine. Bring the bag to me, Tony, and find a first-aid kit for Sara.'

As Roper questioned Jemal further, Sara worked deftly, bandaging Jemal's knee, giving him morphine, aided by Holley and Dillon, a double dose to help with the pain. 'Battlefield style,' she said. 'He could be crippled. How do you feel, Jemal?'

'Lousy, but the pain is not as much. Who are you?'

'I'm the person who shot you.'

'Allah will forgive you for that.'

'I don't think so, but Jehovah might. I'm Jewish.'

'Well, that's not your fault.' He was fading fast.

Roper, who'd got on his Codex, said, 'Don't fall asleep yet, Jemal. You did say he intended to leave Frensham in a Hawker jet and would be waiting for you and Asan to join him?'

'That's true.' The boy sounded very tired, his words slurring.

'Such a plane did leave Frensham about four hours ago, and I do know one thing for certain.'

'What's that?' Jemal really was almost out of it now.

'He wasn't waiting around for you, because he knew you wouldn't be coming back. That timer I took to pieces wasn't thirty minutes, it was instant. You and Asan would have been vaporized the moment you switched it on.'

'But she was his niece.' Jemal shook his head. 'What kind of man would do such a thing? May he rot in hell.'

His head rolled, and Dillon and Holley picked him up and passed him to Doyle in the ambulance, who laid him out on one of the stretchers. Asan lay on the other in a body bag. Some of the panelling of the ambulance had been pulled away to disclose a considerable quantity of Semtex.

'The major's suspicions were right,' Doyle said. 'It would have been a total disaster, one of the worst bombs to hit London since the Second World War.' He looked up. 'No telling what it could have done to this garage – and the building above it.'

'Well, it didn't,' Roper said. 'I noticed a couple of paramedic jackets in one of the lockers. Put one on, you'll be driving.'

'Rosedene?'

'No, the disposal unit. I've warned Mr Teague. He's familiar with Muslim customs, so he'll ensure she's properly treated, God rest her.'

'And the boy?'

'Bellamy knows what to expect. The general will see we do right by him. To be frank, now the iron's entered his soul, he might prove useful. Is that okay with you, Sara?'

She surprised herself by saying, 'If you mean does it worry me that he'll walk with a limp for the rest of his life because I shot him in the kneecap, no it doesn't. That's what you get.' She gave a crooked smile. 'And there's a bonus – you can always tell it's going to rain, because your leg hurts even before you get out of bed, just like mine did this morning.'

'Point taken,' Roper said. 'Wave goodbye to Tony, everybody.'

They watched him go, stop to move the No Entry sign, then get back in and drive away. Sara said, 'I can't say I'm impressed with the security here. Where are the police, for God's sake? We must have been on every camera in the place.'

'No, we haven't, thanks to this.' Roper held up what looked like a TV remote. 'This is a Howler. The moment we started to chase them, I punched a button that killed the entire camera system on this floor. There's no record of any of this happening. It's also highly illegal, needless to say.'

'Too bad we can't market it,' said Dillon. 'We'd make a fortune.'

'I'm sure we would. Now let me call Ferguson.'

He pressed a priority button on his Codex.

Ferguson answered at once and said in a half-whisper, 'Not now, Major, I'm with the Prime Minister and the President. What on earth can be so urgent?'

'We've just experienced a serious incident involving Empire, General.'

Ferguson's voice changed completely. During the Second World War, there had been several attempts on Winston Churchill's life, and the term had come to refer only to matters of the highest seriousness concerning the leadership of the country at either the royal or political level.

'Just a moment,' Ferguson said, and there was a brief pause before he returned. 'Meet me at once at the Cabinet Office.'

'Of course, General. What about the others? Dillon, Holley, Gideon?'

'Too many people might cause curiosity. We don't want people talking. You fill me in, Roper. The others can go to the reception, act normal.'

Roper put his Codex away. 'Rage in heaven over this one. How could it happen?'

'But we stopped it,' Sara said. 'That's all that counts.'

Dillon said, 'Jesus, girl, but you really do have a lot to learn. They're very unreasonable, politicians. The way they look at it, we should have known it was going to happen before it did happen.'

'That's politicians for you,' she said.

'Exactly,' Holley told her. 'But let's get Roper upstairs to the Cabinet Office before they set the dogs on him, and we'll all go on our merry way and try to pretend it didn't happen.'

★　　★　　★

175

On the terrace at lunchtime, all the awnings were out, as the rain showed no sign of stopping. Members of Parliament were starting to appear, guests crowding in behind them, some in traditional dress. In spite of the rain, there was a good atmosphere, a sense of expectancy. And then Jean Talbot appeared, and stopped as she saw Dillon.

She looked remarkably attractive, astonishingly so for her age. Granted, the streaked blonde hair owed a great deal to an expert hairdresser, but the black velvet jacket over a white blouse contrasted well with the vivid blue skirt. Owen Rashid paused behind her.

'Why, Mr Dillon, still alive and kicking?' said Talbot.

'As ever was, ma'am,' Dillon told her.

'We'll have to see if we can do something about that.'

'Well, as I've told you before: People have been trying to kill me for years. I'm still here. You're welcome to try.' He offered her a visiting card, and she accepted.

'You may regret that invitation.' She smiled at Sara. 'I don't know who you are, my dear, but it's a pity to see a charming young woman like you in such bad company.'

She turned away, and Owen, who couldn't think of a thing to say, went after her. She took a glass of champagne from the tray of a passing waiter and leaned against the balustrade, sipping it as Owen reached her.

'The young woman looked interesting,' she said. 'I wonder who she is.'

Owen answered without thinking. 'She's an army captain, wounded and decorated in Afghanistan. A gifted linguist, I understand. Her name's Sara Gideon.'

'Any connection with the Gideon Bank?'

'She inherited it some years ago when her parents were killed in a bomb attack in Israel. Her grandfather sits in for her as chairman.'

'So what is she doing with Dillon and Holley?'

There was no way round it except to tell the truth. 'I believe Charles Ferguson has recruited her for his team.'

'You seem very well informed.'

'Well, you know how it is these days. It pays to keep up, and there's not much that can't be found on a computer.'

There was more to it, she knew that, but she shied away from perhaps learning an uncomfortable truth about him. In any case, an announcement sounded over the loudspeakers.

'Ladies and gentlemen, the Prime Minister and the President of the United States.'

They came through the entrance, Ferguson, Miller, Roper, and Blake Johnson behind them, and the applause was deafening.

The glad-handing went on for thirty or forty minutes, Blake Johnson at the President's side the whole time, as was Harry Miller with the Prime

Minister. Ferguson, who had been standing back, crossed the terrace to speak to them.

'It's not over yet.'

'No problem,' Dillon said.

Ferguson turned to Sara. 'Your performance since you've joined us has been remarkable. I'm beginning to wonder how on earth we managed without you.'

'It was a daily occurrence in Afghanistan, General, this sort of thing.'

'But not in Mayfair,' he said. 'At least not since the high tide of the IRA's London campaign. We've still got the rest of the day to get through. Then there's the early-evening cocktail party at Downing Street, but you won't be required for that. The President flies out to Berlin at ten o'clock, and then it will all be over.'

'Watch out behind you, General,' Dillon said, and Ferguson turned to find both the Prime Minister and the President aiming for the doorway.

The President said, 'Mr Dillon, Mr Holley, good to see you.' But it was the man in the wheelchair to whom he extended his hand. 'Major Roper, it's an honour to see you. The official accounts I've read of your bravery are outstanding – especially that time in the Portland Hotel foyer nine hours on your own.'

'Not quite true, Mr President. I had the bomb as company, which I found myself occasionally talking to.'

The President roared with laughter. 'It's been a joy meeting you, and if I could, I'd give you the Congressional Medal of Honour to go with your George Cross.'

The words were for public consumption, but at a private meeting he had said as much to Roper already, along with a commendation to all of them for the way they'd handled the incident in the garage, which the powers that be had decided had *not* taken place at all. No point giving Al Qaeda the oxygen of publicity.

He shook Roper's hand warmly and went out, followed by the Prime Minister and his entourage. Ferguson said quietly to Roper as he passed, 'I'll speak to you soon.'

Suddenly it was all over, people drifting out in twos and threes, no sign of Jean Talbot and Owen Rashid.

'Now what?' Sara asked.

'Back to Holland Park. Let's see if any interesting business has come our way.' He took his wheelchair out through the entrance, and they followed.

Early evening, Owen Rashid gave Jean Talbot a call and invited her to join him in an Irish bar in Shepherd Market. They sat in a corner booth and had Irish coffees.

'What did the President say to you?' Owen asked. 'I got caught up with the crowd the Secret Service were holding back.'

'Oh, he said what a tragic accident it was, the

plane crashing into the Irish Sea like that with my son inside.'

'Do you think he believed that?'

'No, he was just being civilized. Dillon, Holley, Kelly, and myself were all there when Justin slammed the door on all of us and flew off to his death. The President would have been told the facts.' She smiled a little bleakly. 'Don't worry about me, Owen. I've survived, and I'll go on surviving.'

He took her hand. 'You're a remarkable woman.'

'Not really, just practical. Now that the President's come and gone, what's next on your agenda?'

'I need to go to Rubat for a few days. I haven't been for a while, as you know.'

'Because you don't want to go.' She laughed. 'Without Mayfair, you're like a fish out of water.'

'On the other hand, the Sultan does like to see me every so often. I mean, it's protocol even if he is my uncle. Just a few days, a week at the most.' He took her hand again. 'Is there any chance you'd consider coming with me? You've often talked about it. I could show you the Bacu Railway.'

'When would this be?' she asked.

'I'm pretty flexible where that's concerned.'

'Well, as it happens, we have a half-term vacation coming up at the university on Friday.'

'How long for?'

'Two weeks.'

'So you'll come?'

'Only if you take me to dinner tonight. Do you think we could go to that little Italian place again?'

He smiled. 'Only if you ask me in for coffee afterwards.'

'Oh, I think that could be arranged. Let's go, shall we?'

At the antiques shop, Kelly was in the kitchen, checking on an Irish stew he was preparing for the evening meal. Henri was dozing in a wingback chair beside the fire when he came awake with a start, because he'd suddenly realized why that Frenchman's face at Hyde Park had been familiar to him.

Kelly appeared in the kitchen doorway. 'Are you okay?'

'I've just realized that I can put a name to the face of that Frenchman I was following. Colonel Claude Duval. He's with the DGSE, the Secret Service. His face was in newspapers a lot six months ago, having to do with a Muslim terrorism trial.'

'What would he be doing over here?' Kelly asked.

'How do I know? It explains why he was in Roper's company, though.' Kelly returned to the kitchen, and Henri followed him, found a bottle of red wine, and poured two glasses. 'I've been thinking. If Rashid phones, which he probably will, I'll tell him our impression is that the Gideon woman is staying at the hotel with Holley, so we're looking at a new target.'

'And what would that be?'

'The Salters' place, the Dark Man, down by the river.'

'It's a thought,' Kelly said. 'Okay, that's what we'll say. Mind you, I think Rashid's occupied with other things at the moment.'

'Like your boss?'

'I think so. She doesn't answer her mobile, and I walked round again today and knocked on her door in Marley Court, but no answer.'

'Wasn't I with you twice yesterday and no response? Perhaps they were in bed. She's no spring chicken, but she's a fine-looking woman for all that.'

'Maybe so,' Kelly said. 'Anyway, go and sit down, and I'll serve the meal.'

So Henri took the two glasses and the bottle of wine and went off to the dining room.

At Holland Park, Dillon had decided to keep Roper company by staying over in staff quarters, something he often did. Holley and Sara, having long since departed for the Dorchester, had dined in The Grill and ended up, as before, enjoying a nightcap on the terrace of his suite.

Holley checked his watch. 'Eleven o'clock, so the President is well on his way by now, and things can get back to normal.'

'Whatever normal means to you people,' Sara said.

His Codex sounded, Roper on the line, and

Holley switched to speaker. Roper's voice boomed. 'All hell's broken out at Downing Street.'

'Why?'

'The Prime Minister feels humiliated about what happened while he was entertaining the world's most important head of state—'

'But we prevented it from happening,' Sara cut in.

'That's not good enough, it seems. Young Jemal – the boy you shot, Sara – has told us exactly what Ali Selim's plans are, and where he's going. The Prime Minister has ordered Ferguson to take us in hot pursuit. Ferguson will bring you up to speed on everything. He's on his way now. You'd better get here fast.'

He switched off, and Holley said, 'So much for the quiet life. You heard the man, Sara. Get dressed, and I'll call the doorman to have the Alfa ready.'

CHAPTER 9

When they got to Holland Park, Ferguson was sitting with Dillon and Roper, Doyle serving tea and coffee.

'There you are.' Ferguson was remarkably cheerful. 'Let's get started. It could be a long night, thanks to Ali Selim. The Prime Minister is furious, thinks the whole business makes us look very bad in Washington, so Ali Selim must be dealt with once and for all.'

'Which is where hot pursuit comes in,' Sara said. 'But what does that mean, sir?'

'Exactly what I was going to ask,' Dillon said. 'Do we try and capture the man or just put a bullet between his eyes?'

'That would obviously depend on the situation,' Ferguson told him.

'But the bullet would make more sense,' Holley said. 'In any case, do we know if he's actually reached Peshawar?'

'Not to our knowledge,' Roper said. 'His plane had a flight plan to Bahrain. Since then it's dropped out of view. It's an Arab plane owned by a wealthy sheikh, flying in Gulf airspace.' He shrugged. 'It might as well be invisible. On the other hand, if it has landed at Peshawar, it hasn't done anything wrong. We all know how corrupt the situation is in Pakistan. It's easy for Ali Selim to be passed through, and after all, he isn't going to stay there. According to Jemal, he intends to cross the border into Afghanistan to this village called Amira.'

'One thing in our favour,' Ferguson said. 'Our old friend Seleman Hamza has been promoted to colonel in charge of the military police headquarters in Peshawar. He's not only on our side, he hates Al Qaeda.'

'So you are completely in charge, General, not the Cabinet Office,' Roper said.

A statement, not a query, and Ferguson smiled. 'Just the way I like it. Tell me about this Amira place.'

'About forty miles inside Afghanistan, west of the Khyber Pass.'

'So an illegal crossing is necessary.' Ferguson nodded, thinking about it.

'Definitely,' Roper said. 'A dangerous trip by road in the back-country, which I believe they call the Wilderness. A helicopter would be better.'

'Which would mean the Pakistani Army having to look the other way. That's where Colonel Hamza would be useful. I believe there are private firms flying cargo in old Soviet Raptor helicopters and vehicles like that. Money talks, so something could be arranged. He's bound to have the right contacts.'

185

It was Dillon who said, 'Remember Ben Carver, who we used to use in Hazar? He sold his air taxi firm to a guy named Greg Slay, a captain in the Army Air Corps. Helicopters and fixed-wing. Got a DFC in Iraq. The old military airfield where he's based is used regularly for refuelling by RAF traffic on the way to the war zone in Pakistan.'

'Good thinking,' Ferguson said. 'Get in touch with him, Giles. Make him an offer he can't refuse, and tell him I want him at Peshawar International Airport within twelve hours. He'll arrange a lift, I've no doubt, from some RAF transport plane passing through.'

'I'll get right on it.'

'I suggest we all stay over in staff quarters, but I'll be in my office for a while discussing things with the Cabinet Office. So contact this chap Slay, Giles, then Colonel Hamza in Peshawar, and notify Parry and Lacey to be on standby with the Gulfstream at Farley Field. Have I missed anything?'

'With respect, sir, it's important to know every aspect of the situation, and I don't think we have that,' Sara said.

Ferguson frowned. 'In what way are we lacking?'

'*The Art of War* says: Allowing your enemy to choose the field of battle will only serve *his* purpose, not yours.'

'And what exactly is that pearl of wisdom supposed to tell us?'

'The village of Amira. Why has he chosen it and what goes on there?'

Roper cut in. 'I looked it up, Sara. The population is no more than seventeen or so. It's too barren for poppy cultivation, and the climate isn't right – there's rain and a certain amount of snow at this time of year. It's goats, sheep, subsistence farming. They're mountain people, and Pashtu speaking.'

'A fair description of Poverty Row,' Dillon put in.

'So what's his agenda and what's he doing there? We fought a battle in the garage with silenced weapons, foiled his bomb attack on Parliament, his niece is dead, Jemal is in our hands. There's been nothing in the newspapers or on television, so he can only conclude that it all ended in failure,' Sara said.

'So what are you saying?' Ferguson demanded.

'When you're on the run, having done bad things, you expect to be hounded. It's the law of nature. For every action, there's a reaction.'

Ferguson said patiently, 'And what would that be, my dear?'

She took a deep breath, glanced at the others, then back to Ferguson and smiled sweetly. 'I haven't the slightest idea, General, dear, except that you'll be in a village at the backside of nowhere with a bunch of tough mountain Pashtu-speaking boys who won't even go to the lavatory without an AK-47 dangling from one shoulder, and maybe, just maybe, Ali Selim is *waiting* for you to turn up.'

Ferguson burst into laughter. 'Sara Gideon, I suspected you were a woman of parts, and I've just been proved right. Anything to add?'

'Well, I would point out that you all speak Arabic to some degree or other, but as Pashtu was one of the main reasons you recruited me, I do think I should be included on this one. I'm good, sir, my Pashtu is fluent, and I can pass myself off as an Afghan woman.'

Holley couldn't help himself. 'Not with that scarlet mop of hair, you can't.'

'I've done it before in the right clothing, Daniel – you'll see.'

He wasn't pleased, but he gave up. Ferguson said, 'My decision. You'll go as interpreter, Sara, I'll supervise things in Peshawar. Harry will be representing the Prime Minister, and Dillon and Daniel can handle any rough stuff. Now I really must go to my office.'

Ferguson reappeared almost an hour later to find Sara, Holley, and Dillon deep in conversation while Roper worked at his screens. 'They want me back at Downing Street. Sergeant Doyle can drive me. What's been happening?'

Roper said, 'I contacted Greg Slay in Hazar, and he snapped my hand off before I even got a chance to discuss money. He'll definitely be there when we reach Peshawar. I contacted Colonel Hamza. The Hawker landed three hours ago and is still there. They can't touch it because the owner is too important politically. No sign of Ali Selim, who is obviously on the other side of the border making for Amira. Colonel Hamza will give us all the support he can, but it will have to be unofficial.'

'Fair enough,' Ferguson said.

'He's suggested an air taxi firm run by a man named Wali Hussein as our best bet if we want to hire a helicopter. Hussein apparently operates three old Russian Raptors and has the right dodgy reputation – smuggling, illegal pickups over the border, that kind of thing. Colonel Hamza is going to suggest to him that it would be in his best interests to help us. It will be a comfort to have an exceptional pilot like Slay along.'

'You seem to have covered just about everything,' Ferguson said.

'We aim to please,' Roper told him. 'We're going to be in and out on this one, so no point in staying at one of the downtown hotels. Colonel Hamza suggests a place called the Rangoon close to the airport. He's having a word with them.'

'Excellent,' Ferguson said. 'I've got a good feeling about this, but I'd better get moving and see what they want at Downing Street.'

He went out, followed by Doyle, and Sara said to Holley, 'Is he always so cheerful?'

'A rare occurrence. Enjoy it while you can.'

Dillon said, 'The smell of power, the possibility of action, is what brings an old soldier to life again, Sara, so you've got something to look forward to. I'd grab a little shut-eye while you can, if I were you. You've got a long flight ahead of you tomorrow morning.'

'A sensible thought. I'll see you here later.' She gave Holley that special smile and walked out.

At the same moment, Ferguson had arrived outside the Prime Minister's study at Downing Street to find Henry Frankel, sitting alone and working his way through a file.

He glanced up. 'You look agitated, Charles.'

'I am, Henry. We've got a lot on, and that's putting it mildly.'

'Miller's already here, Charles. The PM wanted a private word.'

Ferguson frowned. 'Without me? Why is that?'

'To be frank, I think the PM believes this enterprise to be rather more hazardous than he at first thought.'

Ferguson was immensely irritated. 'I'm damned if I can see why.'

Frankel smiled pleasantly. 'Well, you can go and find out, Charles, they're ready for you now.' He went and opened the study door and ushered Ferguson in.

Harry Miller got up from his seat opposite the PM, who said, 'There you are, Charles, do come in. I wanted to have a word with Harry to make sure that he fully appreciates the personal risk he is taking in this matter.'

'But, Prime Minister, the whole thing will be quite simple, I can assure you. I shall be at our

Peshawar base to handle matters, the Pakistan authorities will look the other way, and I have arranged for a clandestine helicopter flight with a trusted pilot to take in Major Miller and my two best operatives to assess the situation.'

'Of course, he may not be there at all.'

'We'll only know that by taking a look at the place. I doubt young Jemal is lying. He's too distressed,' Ferguson said.

'I accept that,' the Prime Minister said. 'But on the other hand, Amira may be a nest of Taliban, who would like nothing better than laying hands on my personal representative here. Harry has years of experience in British intelligence that would make him liquid gold to Al Qaeda.'

Ferguson was badly thrown as he tried to think of the right thing to say, and it was Harry Miller who intervened. 'On the other hand, nothing is ever wholly certain in this business. I'm willing to take a risk as long as my friends appreciate the danger.'

The PM said to Ferguson, 'Do you, Charles?'

'Of course I do, Prime Minister.'

The Prime Minister sighed. 'All right. Then I can only wish you Godspeed,' and he shook hands with both of them.

Sitting in the rear of the Daimler as it turned into Whitehall, Ferguson said, 'What on earth was all that about? Stirring it up a bit, weren't you?'

'Nothing to do with me,' Miller told him. 'I got a call from Henry Frankel changing the time of the meeting. When I arrived, I was surprised to find you weren't there.'

'Bloody Henry, sticking his nose in again.' Ferguson was annoyed.

'He was only doing his job as Cabinet Secretary,' Miller said. 'He saw an element of danger in the plan.'

'And that's your opinion, too?' Ferguson demanded.

'Yes, but I also think it's worth taking the risk. I want to make sure both things are made clear to everyone. Is that agreed?'

'Yes, damn you, I suppose it is,' Ferguson said, and spent the rest of the trip scowling out the window.

When they arrived at Holland Park, Ferguson went straight to his office, and Miller to the computer room, where he found Gideon and Holley talking to Roper and Dillon.

'What's happened to the general?' Roper asked.

'He's in a black mood. We've just been to see the PM at Downing Street, who was having second thoughts about what we intend.'

'And why would that be?' Holley asked.

So Miller obliged. Dillon said cheerfully, 'For once, a politician is acting like a human being. He actually cares what happens to us, folks, it warms my heart.'

'Well, it didn't exactly please the general,' Miller said. 'I've made it clear I'm willing to take my chances, but I don't think anyone should be ordered to do this one, and there's one thing I want you all to remember. Al Qaeda terrorists have taken many people hostage, and they have had a bad track record of not only keeping them for a long time but occasionally beheading them on video.'

'Yes, we had heard,' Dillon said. 'Anything else?'

'Yes, I'd be remiss not to point out what would happen to a good-looking London lady who fell into their hands, particularly when they discovered she was Jewish.' There was a heavy silence. 'I just want you all to consider these facts.'

Sara said to Roper, 'Giles, I believe you have quite a collection of costumes here for people going into the field?'

'Yes, we do,' Roper said. 'I'll lead the way.'

She turned and put a hand on Holley's arm as he stirred, ignoring everyone else. 'No, love, I'd rather do this by myself.'

She followed Roper's wheelchair as he coasted along the corridor, taking a remote control from a pocket in his chair and activating it. A broad door slid back at the far end and revealed a theatrical treasure-house.

There was anything one could ever need. Full make-up facilities at mirrored tables ranged against the rear wall; there were changing- and shower-room facilities; and walk-in wardrobes with sliding doors contained a wide selection of clothes and uniforms, both military and police, as authentic as could be wished for.

'All this is amazing.' She emerged from one wardrobe, holding up a uniform. 'A captain in the GRU. I could wear this in Moscow and be totally accepted.'

'But not in the wilderness of North Afghanistan,' he said. 'What would you wear?'

'I've already seen it, Giles. Wait here.'

She vanished into a wardrobe she'd paused at earlier; he lit a cigarette and sat there waiting. The shock when she appeared was considerable, for she drifted towards him, a strange and ghostly figure, wearing a head-to-toe black burka and a black face veil that left only the eyes exposed.

'What do you think?' she asked.

'Perhaps a little dark eye shadow to reinforce the illusion, but first I would recommend a black cowl over that flaming hair of yours, just to make sure. Let's take another look.'

They went back to the particular wardrobe, where she found what he'd suggested and held it up. 'The very thing.'

'Now to the armoury down here. The end wardrobe.'

When she slid back the door, she found a selection of body armour on display, starting with heavy flak jackets. She took one in particular down.

'I wore this in three different wars.'

'Put it back. You need something a bit more

sophisticated.' He pointed to one that looked rather flimsy. 'That will suit you very well.'

'Why, it's so light,' she said in wonder.

'Nylon and titanium, we all have one. It will stop a Magnum round at point-blank range. I'd wear it at all times now, if I were you.'

'I will.'

'Excellent. Let's return and see what the others make of you.'

Lacey and Parry had appeared, and Ferguson was talking to everybody. He stopped abruptly on seeing Sara, and she drifted into the room to the astonishment of all.

'Will I do?' she demanded.

'Oh yes.' Ferguson smiled. 'I think we can all agree on that. You look absolutely splendid.' He turned to the others. 'So, as we all agree, it's a go. We'll leave at ten o'clock in the morning from Farley Field.'

Sara said, 'I'd better go and change.' She pulled down the veil, made a face at Holley, beckoned, and he followed her. 'I need to disrobe and pack my burka for the plane trip. Warm up the car, and I'll see you in a few minutes.'

She emerged, looking amused, dumped a large bag in the back of the car, and sat next to him. 'Ferguson wanted a word.'

'What about?' Holley asked as he drove away.

'He said he was sorry for plunging me into the deep end so soon after joining the department. If there were problems, I must say so. Hasn't he read my file? I've spent the last ten years fighting wars.'

'So where are we going?'

'My place for clothes and things, and the Dorchester for you, then back here.'

'What about your granddad and Sadie?'

'Well, it's useful that both of them are away. With luck, this could just be an in-and-out job, forty-eight hours at the most.' She shrugged. 'We'll see.'

'Well, let's hope you're right,' Holley told her, and turned the Alfa out into the main road.

PAKISTAN

PESHAWAR

AFGHANISTAN

CHAPTER 10

Four hours earlier, Greg Slay had been sitting at the desk of his small office at the old railway airfield in Hazar, bemoaning the fact to his partner, Hakim Amal, that business was seriously slack, when his mobile had sounded. The names of Major Giles Roper and General Charles Ferguson were more than impressive to any old army man, and the use of phrases like 'highly dangerous' and 'top secret' finished it off nicely.

A call to the control tower produced information that a jet was due to refuel in thirty minutes, then proceed onwards to Peshawar with a cargo of jeeps for the Pakistani Army. It wasn't RAF, but the captain knew Greg Slay and was able to offer a lift.

So he was a happy man, striding purposefully across the cracked concrete of the old runway. He was an inch or so over six feet, wearing jeans and a bush shirt under an old Luftwaffe flying jacket, and Ray-Bans that shrouded a heavily tanned face with tousled hair that had needed a barber for some considerable time.

He said hello to the crew on the flight deck, then went to the rest area, where there was a small kitchen, a shower, and some seats, and belted up for the take-off. Everything had happened so fast. He glanced at his watch. Only an hour and a half had elapsed since Roper's call, and he still didn't know what he'd let himself in for. He tilted back in his seat, lay there thinking about it, and fell asleep.

Two hours later, he awakened with a start and realized how much time had elapsed. He phoned Roper and got him at once. 'It's Slay here. I'm on my way and doing well.'

'Excellent,' Roper said. 'Although you're going to be there a long time before Ferguson and his party, but, then, I think you'll be able to make good use of it. You were Army Air Corps.'

'That's right.'

'Retired in the rank of captain last year. Why did they give you an RAF decoration, the DFC?'

'I was a passenger on a Chinook medevac RAF flight. One pilot was killed, the other wounded, and there were passengers, so I brought her in.'

'Though wounded yourself.'

'I was hardly playing heroes. I was saving my neck. Anyway, what is it you want me to do?'

'Have you ever heard of a Raptor helicopter?'

'Of course I have. Medium-size, general-purpose load of Russian crap. Imagine a flying tractor, or, even worse, a tractor trying to fly.'

'I love your sense of humour,' Roper told him. 'So laugh this off. We want you to make an illegal flight across the border to a village called Amira, approximately forty-five miles into Afghanistan. What do you say to that?'

'What I'd like to say is, you've got to be kidding, but I don't think you are. Tell me the rest or the worst, whichever comes first.'

Which Roper did, covering the plan of campaign, the players, everything. 'How is it now?' he asked. 'Laughing or crying?'

'Well, I've often wondered who was running the lunatic asylum. Now I see it's you. On the other hand, I'm a bit of a lunatic myself, so when do we start?'

'As soon as you get to Peshawar. There's no sense in hanging around waiting for the others to arrive. You've got a room at this Rangoon place, so book in. Sign for anything you want, it's taken care of. I've told you all you need to know about Colonel Hamza. He'll be in touch and sort you out the moment you arrive. Enjoy the rest of the flight.'

Greg sat there, thinking about it, and then called his partner, Hakim, in Hazar, who answered quite quickly. 'It's me,' Greg said. 'How are things with you?'

'That new well they've been drilling at Gila has come in big. They're going to need me on a daily basis with a Scorpion. Things are looking good. What are you up to?'

'Advising an old friend in Peshawar who's having

problems with his Russian Raptors. I should be back maybe in three days.'

'The other Scorpion is standing idle. Do I find another pilot?'

Thinking of the situation he faced with the trip to Amira in the antiquated Raptor over the Afghan wilderness populated by very unfriendly people, it suddenly occurred to Greg Slay that he couldn't answer Hakim's question properly, as there was a distinct possibility he might not get back at all.

'I'll let you know, Hakim,' he said, and switched off.

The jet landed at Peshawar International in the early evening and taxied to its designated unloading point, where a squad of soldiers waited to handle the jeeps. A lieutenant, wearing combat fatigues like the rest of his men, was talking to a full colonel in khaki summer uniform with medal ribbons above the pocket. He was clean-shaven, handsome enough, and looked young for the rank, although the scars on his face indicated combat experience. He touched the side of his forehead with his swagger stick as Greg went to meet him.

'Captain Slay? Hamza's the name. I command the military police here, but Roper will have told you that. You're an old Sandhurst hand, I hear.'

'That's right, and so are you.'

'Something in common. I'll take you to your hotel.' A jeep roared up, a bearded sergeant in a scarlet turban at the wheel. They drove away, and Hamza said, 'It's better to stay out of the down-town area. Lots of refugees from the tribal areas. Al Qaeda's made us one of the most bombed cities in the world.'

'There seems to be no end in sight,' Greg said.

They turned in through an archway with a faded painted sign above it that said 'Rangoon Hotel' and strongly hinted of better days, as did the cracks in the walls of the main building, but there was a fountain, which was actually working, and, inside, the old-fashioned fans stirred the air as they must have done for years.

Colonel Hamza introduced the manager, a digni-fied and bearded old man who wore a frock coat over traditional dress. 'Omar has never forgiven the British for leaving India.'

'You are wrong, Colonel. I have never forgiven myself for not leaving with them,' Omar said, and told a porter, 'Captain Slay's bag to cottage 3.'

'Let him take it, but you come and have tea on the terrace with me,' Hamza said to Greg. 'We need to talk.' He led the way through an extensive bar area, where staff were already turning on lights and making ready for the evening.

'A caravanserai for travellers, just like the old days, only these are pilots, cabin crews, transients between planes. No tourists at all, as you would expect. Terrorism is strangling the world.'

They sat on old wicker chairs opposite each other

at a small table. The waiter who served them was so old, he seemed to move in slow motion.

Hamza sipped his tea. 'I have history with Ferguson and Miller, and I hate everything Al Qaeda stands for, so in this matter I'm totally on your side. Commanding the military police has given me considerable power. People tend to do as I say.'

'I bet they do,' Greg said.

'On the other hand, the Pakistani Army can't be seen to be involved with anything that takes place across the border. That's why the only solution to the present problem is an illegal flight.'

'In an ageing Russian helicopter that wasn't much good in the first place,' Greg told him. 'What does this Wali Hussein get up to anyway?'

'Drug trafficking, mostly, and guns for the Taliban. A very unsavoury crook. His mother is American, and when his father was killed, she took the boy to Florida and raised him there until he was eighteen, so he can't speak Pashtu – not that it matters. Nearly everybody can speak English here. He came back because his grandfather left him property here.'

'He doesn't sound like the most trustworthy guy on the block,' Slay said.

'He isn't. How did you get mixed up in this?'

'I was recruited by Major Giles Roper because of my experience flying helicopters in war zones. I have my own set-up in Hazar now, next to Rubat and Yemen.'

'So I understand. What do you know about General Charles Ferguson?'

'A great soldier who walks on corpses, if needed, to get the job done.'

'And Roper?'

'A George Cross man, Colonel.' Slay nodded. 'A true hero.'

'So tell me what he expects you to do.'

'Fly the Prime Minister's personal representative and his support team in across the border to Amira to snatch Mullah Ali Selim.'

'Oh, is that all?'

'Roper warned that Downing Street is all a-twitter, worried about the possibility that Amira might be swarming with Taliban, putting Miller in danger – putting them all in danger, comes to that.'

'What's your opinion?' Hamza said.

'I don't have one. I'm a pilot. I fly missions, that's what I do. And I do it well.'

'Yes, I'm sure you are adept at looking after yourself. Are you carrying?'

'With the kind of security in airports these days?' Slay smiled. 'Do I look like that kind of guy?'

'Yes, you do.' Slay produced a .25 Belgian Leon from the holster on his right ankle.

'Some people might say it's a woman's gun.' Hamza weighed it in his hands.

'Not with hollow-point cartridges.'

'Yes, that would make a difference.' Hamza checked his watch. 'The Gulfstream won't be in for some time. We'll drop you at the hotel while I show my face at headquarters, then I'll take you to meet Wali Hussein, and you can run your eye over the Raptor.'

Hussein Air, as it was called, was in one of several old aircraft hangars on the outer edge of the complex, and about as far from the control block and concourse as it was possible to be. The doors of the hangar were closed, but there was a small Judas gate through which Slay and the colonel entered, leaving the sergeant and the jeep outside.

The hangar was in half-darkness and there was an all-pervading odour that was a mixture of damp cold, oil, and aviation fuel. There was music playing softly from above, Latin American rhythms, and a flight of steel steps led up to a railed landing and an office with glass walls and a light on.

'Wali Hussein, where are you?' Hamza called in English.

There was an old Cessna 310 to one side of the hangar and a Raptor helicopter parked towards the rear, close to the engineering section, where an engine, suspended by chains and pulleys, hung close to one of the benches.

'Nothing to do with our requirements, I hope,' Hamza said.

The main door of the Raptor had been pushed back so that one could see into the interior, and Slay was already pulling himself inside. Hamza joined him. It was larger than Slay had expected, quite cavernous, with a bench seat and a high superstructure, housing seats for two pilots. He mounted four steel rungs and slid into the right-hand seat.

He had never flown this aircraft before, but it felt completely familiar to him, in spite of the fact that all the instrumentation was in Russian, which he could not read. He knew exactly what everything was for, though, after the vast range of helicopters he'd flown over the years.

'It's a dinosaur, it belongs in a museum, but I like it,' he said.

'She'll fly *you*,' a voice broke in, and they turned to view the man who was leaning in. 'Raptors have a mind of their own.' He was small and aggressive, his skin olive and eyes blue, hinting at his mixed blood. He wore a khaki shirt and jeans, and a baseball cap pulled down over long hair.

'Where are the other two?' Hamza asked.

'Islamabad. They both needed work done on the engines that I can't do here.' He had a distinct American accent.

'Where are your flight mechanics?' Greg asked.

'Islamabad with my two pilots.'

'So what if we want this up and running first thing in the morning?' Greg asked. 'Are you capable of checking it out?'

'Hey, I fly them, but I'm no mechanic, man.' He was obviously on something. 'Anyway, I was flying it yesterday, and it was fine.'

'Not for me, my friend, not when we're faced

with the kind of flight we're going to make on the other side. It's a long night ahead, so you can help me.'

'Can I? Hell, that wasn't in the deal. You wanted to hire a helicopter, and there it is. What makes you so special anyway?'

'Because as a captain in the British Army Air Corps for the last fifteen years, he's flown more helicopters in more wars than you've had hot dinners,' Hamza said.

He lightly tapped his swagger stick against Wali's chest. 'You've been snorting coke again, I can always tell. I imagine you've left your supply on the desk. I'll send Sergeant Hamid to find it. He's a religious man, so he'll be disgusted enough to take you down to the military prison. We're rather full at the moment. It can be very unpleasant in the showers.'

'You lousy bastard,' Wali Hussein said.

'Time you learned that.' Hamza turned to Slay. 'Is there anything else?'

'There's a mounting for a machine gun.'

'Have you got it?' Hamza asked Wali Hussein.

'They didn't have the guns when I bought them.'

Hamza said to Slay, 'I'll see you get one.'

'Pineapple fragmentation grenades would be good, and a couple of AK-47s. A launcher and some RPGs would also be useful.'

'You're going to war, then?'

'A few of those grenades dropped from on high can have a salutary effect.'

'I can imagine. I'll see you later when the others get in. After Sergeant Hamid drops me, I'll send him back. He speaks English, and he's a good man. Maybe he can help you with that engine, and he can certainly kick Wali Hussein up the backside if he needs it.'

He went out through the Judas, and Slay turned to notice that Hussein had mounted the steel steps and was going up to the office. He went after him, found the door open and Hussein leaning across the desk.

There was a line of cocaine lying ready, a bag of the stuff beside it, the white powder round his mouth and nose when he turned to look at Slay. There was also an open bottle of Cossack vodka, a half-filled glass beside it.

Slay picked it up. 'They wouldn't be very pleased about this down at the mosque.' The toilet door was ajar; he walked in and emptied the bottle down the bowl.

'You bastard.' Hussein lunged at him.

Slay slapped him back-handed twice, then picked up the bag of cocaine. 'Let's just flush it away.'

Hussein's face was contorted, and he was close to tears. 'No, don't do that,' he pleaded.

'Then let's play question-and-answer. This place Amira – it's Taliban, isn't it? Don't tell me you don't know. The colonel seems to think you deal in guns with them.'

'You don't go to them unless they send for you, and they've never sent for me from Amira. Most of the people only speak Pashtu, and I can't. Blame my Yank mother. The rest speak very little English. I only know it by reputation. It's a bad place.'

'No word of anyone special being there?'

'No!' Wali Hussein cried. 'And if I start asking round the bazaar, they'd be at my door within the hour, wanting to know what was going on. Get one thing straight, pal.' He was suddenly all-American. 'These Taliban bastards make the Mafia look like a Sunday-school outing. They think they've got God on their side when they cut your throat.'

'And what about Al Qaeda?'

Wali Hussein laughed wearily. 'So what can I say? It's in the police force, it's in government, it's in the schools, and the Taliban are the foot soldiers. They probably know about you now, but if they don't, they soon will. I'd go back to where you came from, I really would.'

There was the sound of the jeep down below. Slay said, 'That will be Sergeant Hamid, arriving to give me a hand.' He tossed the bag of cocaine to Hussein. 'I notice a convenient bunk back there. I'd go to bed, if I were you, and stay out of his way.'

Hussein retreated, and Slay went down the steps, taking off his flying jacket as Hamid got out of the jeep and came to join him with a bag in one hand. He had opened the hangar doors to get in, and it was raining outside.

'Not good flying weather,' Slay said.

'The forecast is bad for the next few days, sahib.'

210

Hamid held up the bag. 'Tea and coffee, various things to eat and keep us going.' He put the bag on the bench. 'So what do we do first?'

'We need the engine cowling off,' Slay told him. 'So let's get started.'

It was seven o'clock in the morning when the Gulfstream landed at Peshawar International, the normally impressive background of the mountains of the north-west frontier shrouded in heavy rain.

Colonel Hamza was standing under a canopy, a Burberry trench coat hanging from his shoulders, a van beside him, and another of his sergeants wearing a yellow oilskin. A couple of porters ran forward with large umbrellas as Ferguson led the way down the steps.

'My goodness, Colonel, the rains seem to have come early this year. It's good to see you.'

'I'll take you along to the Rangoon and help you settle in,' Hamza said. 'You're just in time for breakfast.'

Lacey called from the Gulfstream. 'We've got to sort out a few things with the plane, sir. We'll be in touch later.'

The rest of them piled into the van. As it drove away, Ferguson asked, 'Where's Captain Slay? I thought he'd be here.'

'He and one of my sergeants have been working all night. I called on them a short while ago with weaponry he wanted, including a machine gun for

211

mounting in the Raptor. He told me the engine was now ready.'

'And this Wali Hussein chap?'

'Knows where he stands, as far as I'm concerned. I don't know whether he'll be much good to you.'

'Well, I must say Gregory Slay has come up trumps in my book,' Ferguson said. 'I look forward to meeting him.'

Slay and Hamid showered in the staff quarters at the back of the hangar. It had been a hard night, but it had been worth it, Slay told himself as he got dressed. There had been plenty that had needed taking care of. He was so pleased that he actually felt full of energy as he stood looking at the old Raptor, and Hamid had hosed it down to finish things off.

'She looks good, sahib?'

'You were a great help,' Slay told him.

Wali Hussein came down the steps and paused, gazing in awe at the helicopter. 'My God, what have you done?'

'A complete overhaul, which is what was required. You look a mess, so go and stand under a shower for half an hour. That's an order. We may need your brain working.'

The van swung into the hangar and braked to a halt. Colonel Hamza got out of the front, Ferguson leading Miller and Dillon out of the back, followed by Holley and Sara.

They all stood staring at the helicopter, the

muzzle of the machine gun poking out of the side door, which had been rolled back, Slay and Hamid standing beside it.

Dillon said, 'I thought it was supposed to be some kind of wreck.'

'Well, it looks pretty damn good to me,' Sara said.

'And to me.' Ferguson held out his hand. 'Captain Slay? I can only congratulate you on a job well done. If it flies as well as it looks, our problems are over.'

'Oh, I think she might surprise you, General,' Slay told him. 'She's surprised me already.'

'That's good to hear, so let's all sit down, talk things over, and discuss our next move.'

The rear of the hangar was still the departure hall from the old days of the airport, with chairs and tables in profusion, toilets that still worked, and kitchen facilities. They put some tables together, and Sergeant Hamid went to make coffee and tea while the plan of action was considered.

'It could all be very simple,' Ferguson said. 'Ali Selim is in Amira and waiting, probably contacting his people in London to try and find out what's gone wrong. No news from his niece or Jemal, no big bang at Westminster.'

'The important thing is who's waiting with him in Amira,' Slay said.

He went and got into the Raptor, and Hamza, who had noticed Wali Hussein hanging around on the fringe of things, said, 'Here's a man who must have a point of view. He owns three of these Raptors and does a brisk business running guns and drugs to the Taliban.'

Slay leaned out the door of the Raptor, one hand on the machine gun. 'You're wasting your time. He's half-American and can't even speak Pashtu.'

'It's true,' Wali Hussein said. 'Just leave me out of it,' and he turned, moved away to the back, and disappeared into the kitchen area.

Ferguson and Miller had their heads together with Dillon and Hamza, and Holley approached Sara. 'Are you all right?'

'I was impressed with what Slay had to say. I could do with another cup of coffee. Let's see what Hamid's got going in the kitchen.'

There was no sign of him, only a pot bubbling on the electric stove. She switched it off and was suddenly aware of a low voice coming from the next room. Holley started to speak, and she held up her hand and shook her head.

'Someone's speaking in Pashtu,' she said, and eased the waist-high screen door gently open to reveal Wali Hussein talking softly into a mobile phone. She turned to Holley. 'He said he couldn't speak Pashtu.'

'We'll see about that.' Holley darted out of the door, appeared in seconds on the other side, a Colt in his hand, and rammed the barrel into Hussein's neck. 'Now then, you little bastard, let's have some truth.'

★　★　★

Everybody watched as Colonel Hamza questioned Hussein, who stood before him handcuffed, Sergeant Hamid at his side.

'I have no time to waste in this matter,' the colonel said. 'You will answer my questions or it will be the worse for you.'

'They will cut me to pieces,' Hussein told him.

'Who, the Taliban or Al Qaeda?'

'I dare not say.'

Hamza turned to Sergeant Hamid. 'Take him down to the military prison. Don't book him, turn him loose in the general cell, lose him. We'll see how he likes that. Twenty-four hours and he won't be able to walk.'

Sara, horrified, said to Hussein in Pashtu, 'Don't be stupid. He means it. Tell him what he wants to know.'

He raged at her in fluent Pashtu. 'All right! The Taliban rule in Amira, but on behalf of Al Qaeda. Ali Selim arrived from London in a gold Hawker jet, with two prominent businessmen with him as cover. I flew him to Amira myself in the Raptor that you didn't think was safe. He's waiting for you, whoever comes, but not to return to England. You are meat for the dogs, all of you, and a Jewish whore like you knows what to expect.'

She punched him in the mouth, knocking him back into Hamid, and Ferguson said, 'Tell me the worst, Captain Gideon.'

Which she did.

*　*　*

Hamid took Wali Hussein off to the kitchen, while the rest of them sat around the table and considered the situation.

Slay said, 'Can I ask a question of you, Major Miller? As there was always the chance that things would go sour when you met Ali Selim face-to-face, what did you intend to do if that happened?'

'Shoot him dead,' Miller said. 'That's why Dillon and Holley came along, to back me up.'

Dillon said, 'His importance stretches way beyond Europe. He's been responsible for more deaths than you could ever imagine, from Yemen to New York. If I could get close enough, I'd shoot him dead without a thought.'

'Are you saying you'd still like to go through with it?' Hamza said. 'Even though you know Ali Selim has got his own troops ready for whoever comes along?'

Slay said, 'On the other hand, what if we changed that some?'

'How could we do that?' Ferguson asked.

'Let's be a little inventive,' Slay told him. 'Say, Wali Hussein phones Ali Selim up to tell him that the whole mission's been aborted. That he's been told that the Prime Minister's got cold feet, decided he can't risk losing Miller, and has called them all home. You could order the Gulfstream to take off as if returning to London, put down at Islamabad perhaps.'

'What would be the point?'

'A considerable one, if Hussein could be

216

persuaded to tell Ali Selim he'd be dropping by in the Raptor to report in person, especially if he had us on board.'

'Good God, what a wonderful idea!' Ferguson exclaimed.

'It does have merit, though there would be no guarantee you could get close enough to guarantee killing Ali Selim.' That was Hamza, who was frowning but suddenly smiled. 'Of course, and so obvious. A mullah's blessing, the most precious gift a young woman contemplating marriage can have. If Wali Hussein begs for such a blessing, as if for a relative and his intended bride, such people would be privileged to meet Ali Selim face-to-face.'

It was Holley who said, 'Before we go any further, we'd need a woman—'

'We've got one, Daniel, don't be silly,' Sara told him. 'I could pass without comment in my black burka. One of you would have to go native and dress up. You could get away with a cotton head-cloth across the face, only the eyes showing.'

'Two would be better,' Dillon said. 'Men, I mean. I'm small enough to pass as Wali Hussein wrapped up. You could play the lover boy, Daniel.'

There was silence for a while, everyone considering it. Sara took Holley's hand under the table and squeezed it hard, and he knew that what she said was as much for him as anyone else.

'I'm a soldier and I take a soldier's risks. Ali Selim is as bad as it gets, so I say let's take him out.'

Greg Slay said, 'Well, you get full marks from me, Sara.'

Ferguson turned to Hamza. 'How do you feel about this, Colonel?'

'I'm in complete agreement with Captain Gideon. We're doing the world a favour by disposing of this wretched man. Let's have Wali Hussein in, and I'll make him an offer he can't refuse. You speak to your pilots, and I'll apply the right pressure to make sure the Gulfstream flies out within the next hour. I would also suggest trying to arrange the flight to Amira for as soon as possible. I see no reason why it should not be this afternoon.'

'Then by all means get Wali Hussein back, and let us do what has to be done.'

Hamid produced Hussein, still in his handcuffs. He looked a sorry sight and was obviously terrified. Hamza said, 'Do you remember what I said before? I could send you to the military prison, not even book you in, just allow it to swallow you up until you die from abuse.'

Hussein moaned, shaking his head. 'In the name of Allah, don't do this.'

'On the other hand, we could put you on a flight to Florida with your American passport in your hand, and a thousand dollars to tide you over, as long as you never come back.'

Which stopped Wali Hussein dead in his tracks. He stared at Hamza. 'What would you expect of me in return? Just tell me. I don't care what it is – I'll do it.'

'I thought you might say that, so now we will have the truth. When you were on the phone talking in Pashtu, was this to Ali Selim?'

'No, to Ibrahim, his bodyguard. Ali Selim prefers to speak to me in English. I was to call back. He was at his prayers.'

'Then you must try again, but first we must get your story straight.'

To Wali Hussein, deceit and low cunning were second nature, and he was actually smiling when Hamza finished planning what he had to do. 'That's really very clever,' he said. 'You've got it right about the value of a mullah's blessing. There are parents who'd pay through the nose for one of those, but from Ali Selim' – he shook his head – 'you couldn't put a price on it. Mind you, the things I've done for him, I could ask him this favour, but it would have to be for relatives. My mother's Italian American, so it'd have to be one of my father's cousins. Selim is an amazing guy, he knows everything about everybody who works for him. I'd have to use real names.'

'But that wouldn't matter,' Hamza said. 'If everything goes according to plan, Ali Selim would be dead.'

'You've got a point.' Wali Hussein smiled strangely. 'Or maybe we could be the ones to end up dead. But okay. I'll say my cousin Malik is marrying Zara Khan. The families have been arguing about it for years.'

'Excellent. What happens now?' Ferguson demanded.

Hamza said to Hamid, 'We'll need suitable clothing for Mr Holley, Sergeant. You go and see to that.' He turned to Ferguson. 'Come into the office with me, and we'll arrange for the Gulfstream to take off for a simulated trip to Islamabad.'

'Of course,' Ferguson said, and followed him to the office, leaving a disconsolate Wali Hussein sitting with his wrists still handcuffed.

Sara and the three men sat talking about the situation at one of the tables, and Dillon glanced across.

'Are you all right there, Wali, me ould son?'

'What do you bloody think?' Wali Hussein replied.

Dillon peered out to the rain falling outside and wet snow-flakes drifting in it. 'Just look at that weather and think how lucky you are to be returning to the place where you were born. Good ould Florida – oranges, blondes on the beach, and tourists to fleece. You've got it made. Remember that, so be a good boy and don't cock it up.'

The clothing Hamid returned with was what you'd expect in winter: boots, long shirts, baggy trousers, a three-quarter-length sheepskin coat, and a choice of headcloths in various colours and with loose ends to wrap around the neck and face against the bitter mountain cold. Every so often there was the sound of a plane landing or taking off, and suddenly, Ferguson's Codex sounded.

He answered, listened for a moment, then said, 'Excellent, Squadron Leader, let's hope everything goes to plan.'

'Was that Lacey?' Greg Slay leaned out of the Raptor.

'Yes, on their way, but with any luck, they might be able to turn back without landing at Islamabad, so let's get this show on the road.'

Hamid unlocked Wali Hussein's handcuffs, and Ferguson said, 'Everybody stay well back, please, and keep absolutely quiet. He's going to make this call using my Codex on speaker. Sara, you stand close.' He handed the Codex to Wali Hussein. 'Get on with it.'

'I've been expecting to hear from you. Tell me what Ferguson and company are up to.'

The voice was dry and precise, the English perfect. Wali Hussein said, 'Good news, master, they've gone.'

There was a pause, and then Ali Selim said, 'Gone where?'

'Back to London. The Gulfstream has just left.'

'You're absolutely sure about this?'

'Of course. You may confirm it at the airport. There were many phone calls, which led to a great deal of talk among Ferguson's people. It seems the British Prime Minister has changed his mind about the whole thing and ordered they return.'

'How amazing,' Ali Selim said. 'What else do you recall?'

'Many things, master, but I'm not sure what is important and what is not. Perhaps I could come and see you. I'd like to try the Raptor out. The pilot they brought with them has given the engine an overhaul. I was going to give it a test flight anyway.'

'An excellent idea. Come, by all means.'

'I would beg a favour,' Wali Hussein said. 'My cousin Malik and Zara Khan are to be finally wed. A mullah's blessing is the most precious gift, but one from you would give them a lifetime's happiness. Forgive my impertinence.'

'No need to beg,' Ali Selim said. 'You have served me well. Bring them with you, by all means. Come as soon as you like.'

Amira was a typical frontier village on the edge of a plain at the foot of soaring mountains that were invisible behind a curtain of grey mist. It was raining here, too, the same mixture of large wet snowflakes. There was an air of poverty and decay to everything – the crumbling flat-roofed houses, the water streaming down the centre of the streets. No sign of people, no sign of life, not even a dog, but there was smoke drifting out of the stovepipe poking up from the largest house.

Ali Selim sat at a table by the window to catch the light, and the wood-burning stove produced a certain amount of heat. In spite of that, he wore a large sheepskin against the cold as he sat there, still holding his mobile phone in his right hand.

His bodyguard, Ibrahim, a fearsome creature in black robes and over six feet tall, stood impassively at the door, an AK-47 automatic rifle slung across his chest.

Ali Selim said, 'That was Wali Hussein to tell me the English are returning to London. He comes to see me bringing his cousin Malik and his intended bride, Zara Khan. What would you say to that, old friend?'

'That Allah is merciful if he allows the dead to walk, master, for Malik Hussein and Zara Khan were killed in the Raga bombing six months ago.' Ibrahim spoke excellent English. Ali Selim nodded. 'Wali is a clever young fox to fool them like that. He is obviously under duress. We must be prepared.'

'I'll go and see to it, master.' Ibrahim went out.

Ali Selim sat there, thinking about it, then tapped a long number into his phone. In bed at his Park Lane flat, Owen Rashid groped for his mobile in the dark.

Ali Selim said, 'Ah, there you are, Owen. This is Abu.'

'I was asleep. It's the middle of the night.'

'Ah, pardon me, I'm in a different time zone. I just wondered how the reception went at Parliament.'

'Rather crowded, and it rained. They had to put the canopies out.'

'Did Jean Talbot enjoy herself?'

'She certainly did. The President had a word with her.'

'Was he in good form?'

'He seemed so, though his day was busy. He's gone now, off to Berlin.'

'So there were no problems, then, no disturbances?'

'No, nothing at all. Why do you ask?'

'Oh, no reason, just curious. Sorry I bothered you, Owen. Go back to sleep.'

Selim nodded to himself and switched off his mobile, thinking about his niece and Jemal, wondering what had gone wrong. But that would have to wait. He had enough on his plate right now.

At the aircraft hangar, Sara said, 'Ali Selim's voice on the phone was so different from when he delivered that speech in Hyde Park. He sounded so benign.'

'I wouldn't count on that,' Holley said.

Wali Hussein said, 'Did I do well?'

'Yes, I have to admit you did,' Ferguson said. 'Now you'd better get changed, all of you, so we can be on our way.'

Sara went off with her bag, and Ferguson, Hamza, and Dillon watched as Holley picked up his clothes and went, followed by Miller. Greg Slay had been leaning out of the Raptor, watching, no need for him to change. Only Wali Hussein was left.

'Can I get my flying gear?' asked Hussein.

Dillon said, 'I'll go with him. Whatever he puts

on, I'll have to do the same, if I'm going to have any chance of looking like him,' and he followed Wali Hussein upstairs.

Ferguson said to Colonel Hamza, 'You don't trust Hussein, do you?'

'Not even a little bit, which is why I've decided to go along for the ride,' Hamza told him.

'My dear chap,' Ferguson said. 'You've been absolutely splendid, but I really don't think that's necessary.'

'He's my responsibility, General, so there's no argument here. I'll stay in the helicopter when we get there and keep an eye on him. I'll leave Hamid here with you, of course. Use him in any way you see fit.'

Miller came in wearing combat fatigues, his head and face wrapped in black-and-white chequered cotton, and Holley moved in after him. The costume was perfect, and as Sara had suggested, he had wound a cotton headcloth about his head, its folds falling to his shoulders.

'They'd love you in the bazaar,' Miller told him.

Wali Hussein came down the stairs with a baseball cap pulled down over his eyes, a blue cotton scarf wound around his neck. He wore a black flying jacket and a khaki shirt and trousers. Dillon was wearing identical khaki.

'I'll fly like this and steal his flying jacket and the baseball cap when we get there.'

'My spare shirt and trousers,' Wali said.

'You should be honoured,' Dillon told him.

All conversation died at that moment, as Sara drifted in, moving out of the gloomy shadows like some dark ghost in her black robes.

'Will I do?' she asked.

'Most certainly,' Colonel Hamza told her. 'You fit the part perfectly.'

'Then let's get going.' She went to the Raptor and reached for the helping hand that Gregory Slay offered her.

CHAPTER 11

Wali Hussein had discussed the flight with Greg Slay before they left. Short flights to towns and villages by his three Raptors were commonly accepted by air traffic control at Peshawar. The one he had filed for a twenty-mile run to Dimla aroused no comment; nor did the fact that at five hundred feet and ten miles south, it swung west across the border with Afghanistan. Greg Slay at the controls, they set course for Amira.

The weather was atrocious, heavy rain mixed with those large wet snowflakes, the mountains in the distance shrouded in mist. The landscape below, in the heat of summer arid and barren, stretched to a grey and miserable infinity, patchy with snow. Here and there, what had once been fissures in the ground were now swollen with water.

They passed the occasional mud house, sometimes four or five such dwellings huddled together. Occasionally two or three people would appear and stand together, staring up, although, muffled as they were in winter garments, it was impossible to tell if they were male or female.

Harry Miller, who was wearing an old sheepskin robe over his uniform, stood by the machine gun, peering out. 'What a bloody awful place. The backside of the world.'

'That's why they call it the Wilderness,' Hamza shouted. 'Tribal laws alone apply here. They can do what they want.'

Miller crouched beside him. 'I'm trying to imagine Ali Selim fitting in here. In London a couple of days ago, now here in some mud hut, living a primitive life.'

'But with a mobile phone, don't forget – that's all he really needs,' Hamza reminded him.

'Why is it so important for him to be here, of all places?' Miller asked.

'Al Qaeda reigns supreme in areas like this. The tribesmen from these mountains are warlike by tradition and easily recruited for the training camps in Waziristan. To them, Osama bin Laden was the next best thing to the Prophet himself. A great man who made them proud to be Muslim, proud to see Americans and British humiliated by what the West calls terrorism, but they regard as a holy struggle.'

'So when Ali Selim appears in their midst, it's like the Second Coming?' Miller asked.

'A Christian concept, that, and quite different,' Hamza said. 'But he has enormous power and respect.'

Miller shook his head. 'I still think religious differences are a poor reason to kill someone. I'm sure most people would agree if pressed, whatever their religion.'

Wali Hussein turned and scrambled down, leaving Greg Slay on his own, and said to Miller, 'Not long now. You and the colonel will stay well back out of sight, and Slay must join you. They will expect to see only me at the controls, and my cousin and the woman.'

Hamza said, 'All right, we're not fools. Raise your arms.'

'Not again,' Wali Hussein said, but did as he was told.

Hamza searched him, running his hands everywhere, and found nothing. Wali Hussein said, 'Can I go now?'

'Just get on with it.' Hamza turned to Miller. 'He's such a devious little bastard, I always expect him to try to pull a fast one, because so often he has.'

A few moments later and a mile away, they saw Amira nestling at the edge of the plain, a great sloping snow-covered hillock rearing a couple of hundred feet above it, the mountains swallowed by the mist behind.

'We're starting our approach,' Wali Hussein called, and Slay dropped down from his seat and found Miller and Hamza at the rear of the cabin. He peered out a porthole with binoculars he'd brought from the flight deck.

The Raptor went straight on, turning at the last moment, flying parallel to the village, finding no sign of people, turning in again and starting to descend thirty or forty yards away from the edge of the village, for the streets between the mud houses were extremely narrow.

Inside the crude porch of his house, Ali Selim peered out at the heavy rain, watching the helicopter descend.

He was holding a mobile in his left hand and said in English, 'Stay online, Omar, but tell the crew of the second Raptor to take off when I call. Hold the other in reserve and fly that yourself if needed.'

'As you order, master,' came the reply.

Ibrahim said, 'They come, lambs to the slaughter, and the Jewish woman in a burka.'

'I have plans for her, a very valuable young woman. Once she's in your charge, it will be your responsibility to see that no harm comes to her. Now step outside so that they can see you, beckon to them and tell them to come here,' Ali Selim told him.

Ibrahim obeyed and stood in the rain, watching them approach, a formidable figure in black headcloth and plaited dreadlocks, black robes, a bandolero about his waist, and holding an AK-47.

They stopped dead, looking at him, and at that moment, shots rang out inside the helicopter.

Wali Hussein was responsible for everything that followed. As he landed the Raptor and switched off, he instantly removed his flying jacket and baseball cap and threw them across the cabin to Dillon.

'There you are, then. Let's see how you get on being me.'

Dillon put them on, reached up and yanked the scarf from around Wali Hussein's neck, and put it on. 'Will I do?'

The resemblance was remarkable, and he picked up a bag. Wali Hussein frowned and said, 'What's in the bag?'

'You wouldn't want to know.' Dillon jumped down to the ground, reached up to help Sara, who was followed by Holley, who had found a large black umbrella in the helicopter and opened it, pulling Sara close to him in the pouring rain as they walked.

Inside the Raptor, Slay, Hamza, and Miller were still holding back, and Wali Hussein said, 'What's he got in the bag, Colonel?'

Hamza ignored him and focused on Ibrahim further up the street. 'A very nasty-looking piece of work has just appeared, black robes, armed to the teeth. He probably doesn't kill anyone, just scares them to death.'

Wali raised his voice. 'I'm not interested in that. I asked you what's in the bag.'

Greg said, 'What do you think? A special thank-you present for Ali Selim.'

For a moment, Wali sat there staring down at them, his face working, and then he shook his head. 'I don't know what's going on, but I'm not having it.'

He felt under the centre of the instrument panel, pressed, and a flap fell down with a .38 snub-nosed Colt held by a clip. He turned, and Hamza tried to pull his Browning out of his holster. Wali fired wildly, hand shaking, missed Hamza but shot Miller in the shoulder, knocking him off his feet.

At the same moment, Greg Slay drew the .25 Belgian Leon from his ankle holster and shot Wali Hussein between the eyes, killing him instantly. He reached up, caught him by the belt, heaved him down, and rolled the body out under the machine gun to fall to the ground.

Hamza turned from examining Miller. 'What now?'

'God knows what effect the sound of shooting will have on this place, but you've got the machine gun, and I'll fly this damn thing, so be ready for anything,' Slay said.

Dillon, Holley, and Sara paused in the middle of the street at the sound of the shots, and ahead of them doors opened, and tribesmen, with AK-47s at the ready, emerged. Holley dropped the open umbrella to the ground, obscuring them for a moment. Sara reached inside Dillon's bag, grabbed a pineapple grenade in each hand, pulled out the pins with her teeth, then held them up, holding each release bar tightly.

'See the gift I bring you,' she called in Pashtu.

'I'll kill myself and my friends, but also every man in a fifteen-metre radius.'

She released the bars, and there were cries of dismay. They turned and fled as she lobbed the grenades, chasing them. The effect was catastrophic, men blown from their feet. Dillon had her by the arm and across the street, kicking the nearest door open, Holley following them.

There was no one at home, although a fire smouldered on a stone hearth. Dillon and Holley had taken Uzi machine pistols from the bag and passed another to Sara. They all went down to floor level as a storm of bullets flew in, splintering the wooden shutters at the windows.

'I'll check the back,' Dillon said.

He reached the kitchen as the outside door opened and a man appeared, whom he knocked backwards into the yard with a quick burst of fire, then closed and barred the door. He returned to the others, crawling as bullets reduced the shutters to matchwood. Firing stopped for a moment, and Holley peered out cautiously.

'I can see at least twenty out there. I think they'll try to rush us at any moment.'

Indeed, there was the chatter of the Raptor's machine gun, and in that instant, Holley saw seven or eight men go down in the street. He looked the other way at the Raptor.

'It's Colonel Hamza doing the firing. Maybe we could make a run for it.'

There was the unmistakable rattle of a helicopter

approaching, and Holley peered out to see another Raptor swoop in, a machine gun poking out of it, a man standing behind it, ready to fire, just too late, as Greg Slay boosted engine power to lift off with extraordinary rapidity, causing the other Raptor to take immediate evasive action to avoid a mid-air collision, exactly what Slay had intended.

The other Raptor needed to fly parallel to be able to bring its machine gun to bear, but Greg Slay, his skills honed by years of flying in combat zones, put the Raptor through a dazzling sequence of avoidance turns, during which Hamza's attempts to bring the machine gun to bear on the other craft proved as fruitless as his opponent's.

Slay half-cursed, aware of Miller in the far corner, clutching a bloody shoulder, and shouted to Hamza, 'This is getting us nowhere. Try an RPG. I'll increase speed and look as if we're fleeing while you get ready, then we'll turn and take him head-on. Don't forget your safety harness.'

Hamza took it down from a peg, slipped it on and buckled it, the webbing strap with the hook hanging. He dropped to his knees beside Miller and the box of grenades beside him.

As he opened it, he shouted above the cacophony, 'How bad are you?'

Miller had his scarf tucked inside his tunic. 'I'll survive, don't worry about me. Just blow these bastards away.'

'That's exactly what I intend to do.'

He had the launcher out, inserted a grenade,

then hooked himself on by the machine gun and waited. They curved round and went head-first for the approaching Raptor, whose pilot panicked, turning away and exposing his blind side so that Hamza, trusting his restraining strap to hold him, was able to lean out to fire.

The hit was a direct one. There was a colossal explosion, the other Raptor a great ball of fire as it mushroomed in the rain, pieces of the wreckage flying all over the place and then descending through a pall of smoke.

Slay half turned again and laughed harshly. 'Bloody good show, Colonel. That's given Ali Selim something to think about.' Hamza stepped back, unhooked his safety belt, and Slay added, 'If you look in that locker above Major Miller, you'll find a pretty comprehensive medical kit. While you're attending to him, I'll take us back to Amira, and we'll see what the situation is there.'

Ali Selim had stayed in the porch to watch the air battle far out over the plain, recognized the undoubted superiority of Greg Slay's flying skills, and knew defeat when he saw it, the situation hardly helped by fifteen or so dead or wounded tribesmen sprawled in the street in the rain.

He said into his mobile, 'You must have seen what happened, Omar. Stay where you are. Be prepared for a quick exit.' He turned to Ibrahim. 'Bring the jeep out of the barn. We'll leave at once.'

He stayed on the porch, watching the Raptor

approaching in the distance, the remains of the other one sending a towering column of black smoke into the sky, and smiled slightly. Defeat was for this occasion only. There would be other times.

He turned inside the house, found his briefcase and laptop, put them into a bag, and went out to the back yard, where Ibrahim had already driven the jeep out of the barn and was waiting behind the wheel. Ali Selim climbed in and they drove away.

As they bumped along a track, scattering sheep to one side, Ibrahim said, 'A bad business, master.'

'Life often is – you should have learned that by now. I'm not finished with Ferguson and his people. There will be other days.'

'So where next?' Ibrahim asked as slush that the windscreen wipers were unable to clear obscured his vision.

'A place where the sun shines on a regular basis would be a change. Arabia, or Oman – or, I know, Rubat, where our good friend Owen Rashid's uncle is Sultan. Would you like that?'

Ibrahim, who was driving one-handed and reaching out through an open window in an attempt to clear the slush with his hand, said, 'I would prefer it to this, master.'

'Excellent. That's where we shall go. It fits into my plans perfectly,' Selim told him, and they topped the hill and started their descent to the Raptor waiting in the hollow below.

★   ★   ★

Greg Slay flew over the rooftops a couple of times, Hamza loosing off a machine-gun burst or two into the air to show that they still meant business, but only Dillon, Holley, and Sara appeared, waving up at them. Slay put the Raptor down and Hamza stood behind the machine gun, an intimidating figure, as Dillon and Holley walked backwards, one on each side of Sara, weapons ready for trouble.

Slay sat in his seat at the controls, waiting for them to arrive, decided to switch off, which he did. The silence was eerie, only the rush of the rain, and nothing stirred until there was the blast of engines breaking into life, the inimitable clatter that could only be from a helicopter. Slay hurriedly switched on again, and Sara picked up her skirt and started for the Raptor, Holley and Dillon running with her. She slowed, limping badly. It was very pronounced now, and there was pain on her face.

'God dammit,' she said when they got to the Raptor, where Hamza was reaching out to her.

Behind her, the third Raptor rose into view on the other side of the hill, but immediately swung away to the left. She watched with the others. The engine note deepened as it flew away to the west as fast as possible and was swallowed up by the mist.

'Are you okay?' Holley asked with concern.

'Just the damn leg, love.' She managed a smile. 'It could be a lot worse. That firefight – I thought

237

we were finished.' She reached up and grasped Hamza's hand. 'Until you decided to intervene. What happened here, and where's Wali Hussein?'

'His body's somewhere close by. We're in a different spot than when you left. You'll notice Major Miller feeling sorry for himself in the corner. Wali shot him, so Slay shot Wali dead and threw him out.'

She turned to look up at Slay in the pilot's seat. He shrugged. 'I didn't have much choice. He suddenly turned angry with all of us and produced a shooter from up here somewhere. That was what started heating things up.'

Harry Miller said, 'Sara, would you mind checking the medical unit for morphine? After all, I *have* been shot in the shoulder.' He winced with pain. 'And may I suggest to you, Captain Slay, that we get the hell out of here?'

Hamza said, 'I suspect Ferguson is the kind of man who prefers bad news sooner rather than later.'

'You're quite right.'

Miller pulled out his Codex with a bloodstained left hand and called Ferguson, who responded immediately.

'Harry, where are you? How did it go?'

'Wali Hussein turned out to be completely untrustworthy, so we found ourselves juggling with three Raptors, not one. There was a brisk firefight, but we've come through, thanks to some brilliant flying by Gregory Slay and some good work from Colonel Hamza, who shot down a Raptor for us with an RPG. And I mustn't forget Sara, who started playing bowls with a couple of pineapple grenades.'

'And Ali Selim?'

'Flown off to God knows where in the worst weather imaginable. Can we leave this dreadful place as soon as possible and come home?'

Sara grabbed the Codex and said, 'He has a bullet in his shoulder, General, which I'm trying to do something about, so I'll pass you to Colonel Hamza.'

Which she did, cutting Miller's shirt open, the medical kit at her side. She took out a couple of morphine ampoules and jabbed them in his left arm and then explored the wound.

'There appears to be an exit hole, which is lucky, but you'll need a doctor to confirm it.'

'Thanks, Sara, you're an angel.' He managed a smile, waiting for the morphine to take effect.

Hamza was still talking to Ferguson. 'I'll call in and arrange for Major Miller to be patched up at the military hospital, but then I think it would be better for all of us if you got back in that Gulfstream and returned to London as soon as possible.'

'And how will this affect you?'

'Why should it affect me at all? Wali Hussein, a man who has long been suspected of making illegal flights over the border, filed a flight plan to Dimla and has gone missing. There is no sign of his helicopter in Pakistan territory, crashed or

239

otherwise, so the inescapable conclusion must be that he's finally met with a bad end out there in the Wilderness.'

'How unfortunate,' Ferguson said.

'Not my jurisdiction. It's tribal territory and in another country,' Hamza told him. 'I'll have an ambulance waiting for Miller, and we'll have a surgeon see to him discreetly. No need to make a fuss. Bullet wounds are common enough in these parts. I'll also have a word with your pilots and suggest they make ready for a quick departure.'

'And Captain Slay will need a return to Hazar.'

'No problem. He can go back to Hazar the way he came in. I'll see you soon.'

Ferguson sat there in the hangar trying to come to terms with his disappointment. Hamid came in from the kitchen with a tray. 'Would you care for a cup of *char*, General?'

'To be frank, after the news I've just had I'd have preferred something stronger, but in the circumstances tea will be just fine.' He called Roper and gave him a summary of events.

Roper said, 'So where's he off to now, that's the thing.'

'I think Colonel Hamza might be helpful there.'

'He's certainly come up trumps so far,' Roper said.

'The Prime Minister's going to be furious, especially about Harry being shot,' Ferguson said.

'As long as it doesn't kill you, there's always a

slightly heroic thing about taking a bullet,' Roper told him. 'I've been there, remember, before the bomb? On top of that, the PM will enjoy being able to say I told you so.'

'Which I don't look forward to at all.'

'So what happens now? Will you call him personally, or do you want me to speak to Henry Frankel at the Cabinet Office?'

'Well, at least that would be following protocol, and it would give me time to get my act together here for the return home. You don't mind?'

'Why should I? It will quite make his day. Henry loves being the bearer of bad news.'

Not long after leaving Amira in the Raptor, Ali Selim spoke to the chief pilot of the Hawker that had delivered him to Peshawar after his flight from London. It had been waiting at Peshawar Airport while he considered his next move.

Having discussed where the Raptor should meet the Hawker, he stood and leaned up to the flight deck, where the pilot, Omar, sat alone. He gave him a destination and flight instructions, then sat down again.

Thirty minutes later, they came to a village in ruins named Herat, a crumbling runway beside it, a concrete control tower and some flat-roofed buildings. It was a relic of the Russian occupation, totally uninviting, no signs of life, brooding in the rain as if waiting for something.

The Raptor was different from the other two in

that there was no machine gun and only the one pilot. Omar was a young and energetic man in his twenties, in a brown flying jacket and jeans. He was obviously overawed by Ali Selim, who told him to land by the tower and switch off.

Ibrahim stayed impassive, a sinister figure in dark robes, an AK-47 beside him, a bulging bag at his feet. Ali Selim took a book from his briefcase and read, and Omar, on the flight deck, stirred uneasily.

Finally, Ali Selim looked up and said, 'If you want to smoke, do it outside. Go now, I can't abide your twitching.'

'Yes, master.' Omar scrambled down, slid back the door, dropped to the runway, then ran through the rain to stand in the doorway of the control tower, where he lit a cigarette.

There was the sound of an engine approaching, and the gold Hawker dropped in below grey clouds, descending through the heavy rain, rolling to the end of the runway, turning and taxiing toward them, and stopping some little distance away. Omar hurried back to the Raptor, the airstair door opened on the Hawker, and a uniformed pilot came down, opening a large umbrella.

A handsome, bronzed-faced Arab, he smiled and inclined his head. 'It is an honour to see you again,' he said to Ali Selim.

'Good to see you, Abdul, but get me inside, this rain bothers me.' He ignored Omar but nodded to Ibrahim, went off with Abdul to the Hawker, and followed him up the steps.

Omar said, 'Where do I go now?'

'Inside, and I'll tell you,' Ibrahim said.

Omar pulled himself into the Raptor, turned, and Ibrahim, already holding a Beretta in his right hand, shot him in the head, knocking him back into the hold. He opened the bag, took out a magnesium night flare, pulled the toggle, and tossed it inside. As the flames took hold, he turned and hurried to the Hawker, went up the steps where Abdul waited, and ducked inside. He sat down on the opposite side of the cabin from his master and waited.

Ali Selim looked up from his book. 'Captain Feisal has had a word. We can forget winter in northern Afghanistan. In Rubat it's hot, with enough sun to satisfy even you.'

Ibrahim made no reply, simply nodded, clicked his seat belt into place, leaned back, and closed his eyes.

In London, Owen Rashid, unable to sleep, was sitting by the terrace window in his dressing gown, a glass of red wine by his hand, as he worked his way through a report on the current finances of Rashid Oil.

When he answered the phone, Ali Selim said, 'This is Abu. Were you asleep?'

'A touch of insomnia. What can I do for you?'

'I'm just letting you know the game is afoot again – isn't that the English phrase? Ferguson and his people are on their way back to London. This Sara

Gideon has become very important, not only to me but to Ali Selim and to Al Qaeda.'

'So what do you want from me?'

'Warn the Frenchman and Kelly that I'm particularly interested in Gideon. I want them on her case.'

'Can I ask why?'

'Not at the moment. One of my assets has left you a package in the glove compartment of your Mercedes. It contains several ampoules of Seconal.'

'What on earth would I need that stuff for?'

'All in good time, Owen. Put Legrande and Kelly to work, and I'll be back in touch very soon.'

So he was gone, leaving Owen Rashid more frustrated than he had ever felt before.

When the Raptor landed at Peshawar in front of the Hussein Air hangar, Hamid was waiting beside a military ambulance for Miller, who was stretchered and put in the back and taken away, accompanied by Ferguson and Hamza.

At the hospital, the two of them sat in the waiting room, drinking tea and discussing what had happened. 'One thing is certain, if you'll allow me to make a point,' Hamza said. 'Ali Selim must have an agenda.'

'I couldn't agree more,' Ferguson said, but before he could carry on, a grey-haired and rather distinguished-looking man in green scrubs came in.

'Well, my boy, how are you?'

'Very well, sir.' Hamza turned to Ferguson.

'Brigadier Mahmud is my uncle. This is Major General Ferguson.'

Mahmud shook his hand. 'How interesting all this becomes, General. But I am just a simple surgeon who knows his place, so I ask no questions. Major Miller has been patched up for the moment, pumped full of drugs and sedated. He should survive a flight by private jet, but will need the best of treatment at the earliest possible moment.'

'I promise he'll get it. We're very grateful.' Ferguson shook his hand.

'Happy to help,' Mahmud said. 'And you, Nephew, remember where we live. Your aunt thinks you've forgotten.'

At that moment a comatose Miller was wheeled out, and they followed him down the corridor and outside to the ambulance, where he was lifted inside by two male nurses. Hamza and Ferguson joined him and the ambulance drove away.

The Gulfstream was waiting outside the hangar, and Lacey and Parry supervised the careful loading of Miller into the cabin. They were all there now.

Ferguson said, 'Time to go, people, but not before thanking Colonel Hamza for conduct far above the call of duty, and Captain Slay for some extraordinary flying.' He gave Slay a package. 'It's a bit late in the day, but here's one of our nylon-and-titanium vests with our appreciation.'

Slay smiled and took it. 'One never knows.'

Ferguson shook his hand. 'So Hamza's arranged a lift back to Hazar for you?'

'Yes, all taken care of. All I can say is it's been an amazing couple of days and I wouldn't have missed them for anything,' Slay said. 'Watch your backs, you lot.'

He walked across to where Hamid waited and was driven away. The others said their goodbyes to Hamza and boarded, leaving him and Ferguson alone.

'Our governments may sometimes disagree,' Ferguson said. 'But in the world we inhabit today, it's vital for us to keep in touch. What we've just been through together proves that. It was good working with you, Colonel.'

'And you, General. And I have one last piece of information. Ali Selim's plane left an hour and a half ago with a flight plan for Bahrain. Only the two pilots on board.'

'I'm sure Roper will find that useful.' Ferguson shook hands. 'Take care, my friend.'

He turned, went up the steps to where Parry waited, and went inside. As Hamza turned away, the Gulfstream started to move.

It rose to 30,000 feet and turned north-west, still climbing into a darkening sky. Ferguson sat on his own at one end of the cabin and talked to Roper by Skype. He told him of his final conversation with Hamza.

'I'll put a trace on that jet and I'll try and do something about the Raptor helicopter Ali Selim cleared off in,' Roper said. 'How's Harry?'

'Out for the count, thanks to the medication Brigadier Mahmud gave him. It's all a bit subdued on the plane at the moment, but, then, night flights usually are. Walking on eggshells around a wounded man makes it even more so. Any word from Downing Street?'

'I believe the Prime Minister was speaking in the House today. Maybe Henry's not been able to give him the bad news yet.'

'Damn Frankel,' Ferguson said. 'He's enjoying my humiliation.'

'Don't be so silly,' Roper told him. 'If he was, it would mean he was treating Harry's being wounded as unimportant, which is rubbish. This damn operation was a complete failure. We couldn't lay hands on Ali Selim, and every one of our people had to kill to survive. It was like a bad day in Afghanistan. You're lucky we got away with just one wounded man.'

'Good God, Giles,' Ferguson said. 'You're angry with me?'

'You're damn right I am,' Roper said. 'So go and get yourself a large Scotch and shut up.'

He logged off, the screen cleared, and Ferguson sat there, completely deflated. 'God help me, I'm getting old,' he said softly, turned to get up, and found Sara holding out a glass of whiskey.

'I heard,' she said. 'Try not to take it to heart. But he was right, you know. A lot of people died so we could be here. If it weren't for Greg Slay and Hamza – well, they saved the day.'

'The way I heard it, you, Daniel, and Dillon were into it up to your necks, too. But there you are.' He toasted her. 'My sincere thanks.'

She turned and went back to Harry Miller, tucked in his blanket, then sat beside Holley, who lay back, eyes closed.

An hour later, a signal beeped and the screen flickered into life again, bringing Ferguson awake from his doze to find Henry Frankel on his screen.

'Ah, there you are, Charles.'

'So what do *you* want?' Ferguson asked.

'The Prime Minister would like a word.' Frankel smiled. 'If you can spare him one.'

He was replaced by the PM sitting at his desk, who said, 'A bad business, Charles.'

It was impossible to argue with that, and Ferguson said, 'I'm afraid so.'

'How we play this with the newspapers is beyond me,' the Prime Minister said. 'They'll be wanting a statement in the House. I can see the headlines now. "Where Is Ali Selim?" Lots more juicy publicity for Al Qaeda. So what's your next move?'

'It's difficult to say. He's being protected by important people in Arab circles. Almost anything we do could be made to look like harassment of a holy man.'

'And he's certain to play that card. He could even surface in London again, for all I know, and defy us to do anything about him. One would have hoped, Charles, that during this little battle of yours, a stray bullet might have gone his way, or was that expecting too much?'

To which there could be no answer. Ferguson took a deep breath and tried to be honest. 'Right now, we're in his hands, Prime Minister. We have no idea where he is, what his intentions are, or what he plans next.'

'Which is no use to me at all. Find him, Charles. Put everything else to one side and find him, and that's an order. I'll leave you to get on with it.'

His image faded, the screen went dark, and Ferguson contacted Roper and found him, as usual, in the computer room at Holland Park. He relayed what the Prime Minister had said.

'My head's on the block here, Giles.'

'Nothing new in that,' Roper said cheerfully.

'Is there anything you can do to trace the sod?'

'I'm doing everything I can, Charles. There's no instant response possible here. You'll just have to sit it out and hope. The moment I've got any news at all, you'll be the first to know.'

So the screen went dark again, leaving Charles Ferguson more embattled than he had been in years.

CHAPTER 12

About two hours later, Harry Miller came back to life to a certain extent, groaning and trying to sit up. Sara was with him instantly, and Dillon and Holley scrambled up to see if there was anything to be done.

Harry was hot and feverish. 'Where am I? What's going on?'

Dillon got an arm round him, and Sara said, 'The instructions the brigadier left with him say more morphine and penicillin if an episode like this occurs. Just hold him while I take care of it.'

After a while, he slipped back into troubled sleep, and Parry, who had come in to see what was happening, said, 'Another four hours before we land, I'm afraid.'

'We'll just have to make him as comfortable as possible,' Ferguson said. 'Rosedene has been notified, and Charles Bellamy will be available for advice, Sara, if Harry's condition gives you cause for concern.'

Roper came on screen again. 'Bad news, I'm afraid. That jet for Bahrain altered destination twice, then vanished.'

'How can that be?' Ferguson demanded.

'It happens all the time. I shouldn't need to remind you, Charles, how often we've done the same thing in our line of work. All the pilot has to do is stop calling in, and in this case, Arab pilots flying in Arab aircraft in Arab airspace can usually do anything they want.'

'So what now?' Ferguson asked in despair.

'Hang on, there's more,' Roper said. 'That Raptor helicopter that cleared off from Amira carrying Ali Selim?'

'What about it?'

'Its wreckage has been discovered by a Canadian special forces patrol on an old Russian airfield in a place called Herat, about fifty miles west of Amira. There was a badly burned corpse in it.'

'Are you suggesting Selim was picked up?'

'I've looked up Russian Army records for that place. It has a concrete runway and was originally constructed to take large fixed-wing transport planes. Selim's Hawker, even though it's a jet, would have had no trouble landing,' Roper said. 'In fact, the only problem would be an inconvenient Raptor helicopter and its pilot. I think it's obvious what happened there. It is a cliché, but dead men tell no tales.'

'Fascinating stuff,' Dillon put in. 'But it still doesn't tell us where Selim is at this precise moment in time and, even more important, what his intentions are.'

'You're absolutely right,' Ferguson said. 'I think

251

the next thing we might hear is another of Ali Selim's anti-West diatribes in the interest of self-advertisement for his glorious cause.'

'The newspapers will love that,' Holley said.

'Which is exactly why he says that kind of thing,' Sara put in. 'It makes sense, doesn't it? Just like Adolf Hitler, when you think of it. The villain who is so outrageous that you can laugh at him becomes tolerated by the public.'

'Which is when he becomes most dangerous,' Holley observed. 'Because he takes himself seriously.'

'A fascinating theory,' Ferguson said to Sara, 'but also a depressing one. The most important thing is that the Prime Minister is not a happy man. His orders are to find Ali Selim and to put everything to one side until we do. Let's get going on that, shall we?'

Sara checked out Harry Miller, then sat down beside Holley again as her Codex sounded. It was Sadie. 'Where are you?' the housekeeper demanded. 'I tried the house last night. No one was home, and I got worried.'

'I've been on a training course,' Sara told her. 'We're on our way back. A night flight. How are things?'

'The baby is doing well, but my niece isn't so good. I need to give her another week to see how things work out.' A smile crept into her voice. 'Have you been seeing any more of that Mr Holley?'

252

Sara rolled her eyes. 'Yes, Sadie, I have.'

'Oh, well, at least you're getting looked after.'

They talked for a minute more, then hung up.

'Sadie,' Sara said to Holley. 'Her niece needs her for longer than she thought.'

'I'm surprised she hasn't got in touch with you before this,' Holley said. 'If only she knew what you've been up to, she'd have a fit. What about your granddad?'

'I haven't exactly had time on my hands,' she said. 'But you're right to remind me. It's a little early. I'll have some coffee and call him in an hour.'

'I'll get it for you,' Holley said, and left her there for a few moments, thinking about what had happened in an astonishingly short period of time and wondering how she would manage to appear normal and collected when she spoke to her grandfather. In fact, he took care of the situation for her.

He sounded very cheerful. 'You must have wondered what happened to me. I'm sorry I haven't been in touch. I've never been so busy. Where are you, by the way, not at home? I called you there.'

'In an airplane,' Sara told him. 'London-bound. I've been away on a training trip for a couple of days. How are things going?'

'That's what I'm calling you about. Such good news! St Andrews University wants me to hold a seminar on comparative religion for doctoral students. It's a great honour.'

'When do you start?'

'I'm already there! Two weeks, my love, I hope you don't mind. I know Sadie is away.'

'Nonsense. Why should I mind?' She'd put her Codex on speaker.

He said, 'Is Daniel with you?'

'Yes, he is.'

'Excellent. I'm not a fool, and I'm sure you're up to all sorts of devious things which occasion danger now and then. I'm glad he's around to keep an eye on you.'

'I'm sure he'll be glad to hear that,' she said, deciding not to tell him he was on speaker.

'He's almost biblical in a way, just like his name. A man who will always do the right thing, in spite of himself. That's very rare. I must go now – I've got an early meeting. Stay in touch.'

Holley couldn't think of a thing to say. She took his hand and held it tight. 'There we are, then, a good girl I am. I always believe everything my granddad tells me.'

Every aspect of Rubat society was so touched by Al Qaeda that Colonel Abdul Khazid, the chief of police, had long since learned to go with the flow like everyone else and do as he was told. When the Hawker put down to refuel, he knew who was on board and exactly what was expected of him. He drove out personally in an airport security van to make an apparent courtesy call on the pilots, but returned with Ali Selim and Ibrahim concealed in the back.

The Hawker was already taking off as the security van left the airport, and Khazid said, 'It's good to see you again. They've been giving you problems in London, it seems.'

'They always are,' Ali Selim said. 'Which is why I try to give *them* problems.'

Khazid, ever the diplomat, said, 'That was a great speech in Hyde Park. Al Jazeera had it on television.'

'Unfortunately, such popularity also brings some inconvenience, which is why I've dropped in here incognito. I stopped off in northern Afghanistan with British agents on my tail, intent on killing me. I'm lucky to be here, out of sight while I consider the future.'

'Naturally, I will do everything in my power to assist in this unwelcome situation,' Khazid said. 'My police force is small but well trained.'

'And capable of recognizing strangers when they see them, or those asking the wrong sort of questions?'

'Are you suggesting that the British know you are here?'

'They'll just look everywhere, and the CIA will help them. Tell me, is anything different from the last time I was here? Does Captain Ahmed still command the ship?'

'He likes to think he does, but only when it suits, which is seldom.'

'And Fatima Karim?'

'Is still administrator, which means she runs

everything, including Ahmed, who lusts after her helplessly.'

He had breached the hill with the view of the port below, a jumble of white terraces and flat roofs tumbling down to the harbour crowded with boats. Anchored in the centre was the *Monsoon*, a three-masted traditional Arab dhow, lovingly restored by the same Gulf sheikh who owned the Hawker.

'Why have we stopped?' Ali Selim demanded.

'You usually like the view.'

'Damn the view. And as far as Ahmed is concerned, that big oaf may be able to handle a ship in a storm, but it beats me how he can let a woman like Fatima walk all over him.' He sighed. 'Just drive.'

At the main jetty, Ali Selim and Ibrahim parted from Khazid and boarded a motor boat crewed by two sailors from the *Monsoon*. They reached the boat in fifteen minutes and found Captain Ahmed waiting at the rail to greet them. A gaunt and anxious-looking man with an iron-grey beard, he wore traditional robes plus a dark blue naval blazer with brass buttons and a cap with gold braid.

He spoke in Arabic. 'Welcome, master, it is good to see you.'

'You look ridiculous,' Ali Selim told him. 'Where is Fatima?'

'She waits for you in the owner's quarters.'

'Then go about your business. When I need you,

256

I'll send for you. Go with him, Ibrahim. Get something to eat.'

The owner's quarters were in the stern of the ship and very fine indeed, with polished and restored wooden floors, Persian and Indian carpets everywhere. Shuttered doors stood open in the stateroom, revealing the study behind, beautifully panelled in finest walnut and oak. Fatima Karim stood at the side of a wide Victorian desk.

She wore a black jumpsuit of raw silk and a chador in the same material. She was handsome rather than beautiful, with olive skin and violet eyes that made her extremely attractive. Her degree from the London School of Economics also made her attractive, but for different reasons.

Ali Selim spoke first and used English, reaching for her hands. 'It is good to see you.'

She responded warmly, her English faultless. 'So good to have you here safely. Things haven't gone well, from what I heard. Can I serve you coffee? It's all ready.'

'That would be wonderful.'

A section of panelling opened into a thoroughly modern kitchen, the coffee smell heavy on the air. He sat at a small table, and she served coffee for both of them, sitting opposite. The coffee was Yemeni and excellent.

'I needed that.' He pushed his cup over and she refilled it.

'It was bad, then?'

She was totally dedicated to Al Qaeda and completely trustworthy, so he told her everything, and she listened intently, taking it all in.

He was rather sombre when he finished. 'So death for death was my aim with Ferguson and his people, and we've failed miserably.'

'You must not talk so. It's not you who has failed, but those who were supposed to serve you.'

'How is the Sultan?'

'Dr Hassan does his best. He has an excellent set-up at the palace, top staff and equipment.' She shrugged. 'But what do you do with strokes, heart attacks, and age?'

'Aptly put. Do you think the Council of Elders would favour Owen for Sultan?'

'I wouldn't bank on that. A majority of them are traditionalists who don't care for him at all. They also don't like that he's not even married, and a known womanizer.' She poured him more coffee. 'What do you think?'

'I've only met him once,' Ali Selim told her. 'The first time I visited the *Monsoon* when the sheikh brought it down to Rubat and gave a party. You hadn't joined then. Owen was a guest, and so was I.'

'So you've never met again.'

'Well, to be honest, I've haunted his life in a way.'

'What do you mean?'

'I've been a ghost in his machine.' He took off

his glasses and polished them with his handkerchief. 'A ghost called Abu.'

'What an amazing story,' Fatima said when he was finished.

Ali Selim said, 'Owen Rashid is not the only one who made the mistake of responding to Al Qaeda advances for corrupt reasons. He believed it would give him an advantage in the oil business, some extra muscle when wheeler-dealing in the marketplace. But like others, he discovered there was a price to pay. He had to obey orders. Osama bin Laden made that clear. There can be no difference between rich and poor in this matter.'

'And so it should be,' she said. 'But where does that leave Rashid? I suppose if the Elders do choose him as Sultan, that would at least be good from Al Qaeda's point of view.'

'But Al Qaeda is already powerful in Rubat,' Ali Selim told her. 'Powerful in its effect on ordinary people, most of whom work in the oil industry. You know this is true, I've seen the reports you've collated. However, as you say, such people are not the majority of the Council of Elders. They may well say no to Owen.'

There was silence for a moment between them, and she frowned uncertainly. 'Are you suggesting something else? If so, what is it?'

So he told her.

She was unable to speak for a few moments

when he had finished, staring at him in awe. 'Oh, my God,' she whispered.

Ali Selim said, 'In a newsroom, this is what a reporter would describe as a hell of a story.'

'In *any* newsroom,' Fatima said. 'It could run for weeks.'

'Thanks for the input,' Ali Selim told her. 'Now go and find Ibrahim for me and bring him here. I know he looks frightening, but he has a highly developed sense of low cunning – and that's just what we need.'

Owen Rashid was running in Hyde Park when his mobile sounded. Ali Selim said, 'Good morning, Owen. Starting the day as usual with a run?'

'God help me, what do you want now?' Owen demanded. 'It's breakfast time, Abu, though since I've no idea where you are, I don't know what you're up to.'

'Looking out the stern window of the *Monsoon* in Rubat Harbour.'

'What bloody nonsense are you giving me now?'

'No nonsense, Owen, I'm calling you from the *Monsoon*. I'm here on Al Qaeda business. By the way, it isn't Abu. You must excuse my little subterfuge.'

Owen said, 'So who the hell are you?'

'Mullah Ali Selim.'

Owen laughed wildly. 'I've never heard such rubbish in my life.'

'What a shame. I never pegged you for a stupid

man. I'm just calling you to tell you I'm going to phone Henri Legrande in twenty minutes. He's utterly failed me, and I thought I'd let him know his shop could burn down one night this week – unless he does what I say. I've got a job for you all. If you leave now, you should be able to get there in time for me to talk to the three of you.'

He switched off his mobile and turned as Fatima and Ibrahim entered. 'We'll have to wait for approximately twenty minutes or so.' He smiled at Fatima. 'I've stirred things up. If I'm right, Owen's running across Park Lane through heavy morning traffic to get to his Foreign Legion friend. In the meantime, I'd love another cup of that Yemeni mocha coffee.'

Owen, behaving exactly as Ali Selim had predicted, had crossed Park Lane and was running so fast down Curzon Street that he missed Jean Talbot emerging on the other side of the road, bound for the park. Intrigued, she crossed the road and ran after Owen, noting him turn into Shepherd Market. A final burst of speed brought her there in time to see him hammering at the door of Mary's Bower. She stepped into a doorway, waited, saw Henri Legrande open the door, Kelly at his shoulder. The alley was quiet at that time in the morning, and she heard what they said.

Henri Legrande: 'What the hell is it?'

Owen: 'I've just had a call from Abu. Only it appears he's really Ali Selim.'

Kelly: 'Come off it, Owen.'

Owen pushed past them, went inside, and the door closed. *Mystery piled on mystery here.* Jean conquered an insane impulse to go knock on the door herself, turned, and jogged away.

In the sitting room, Kelly said, 'It can't be for real.'

'Oh yes it is, and he wants to speak to us.' His mobile sounded. 'I think this is him now,' and he put it on speaker. 'So what do you want?' he demanded.

'Listen to me carefully,' said Selim. 'After the riot in Hyde Park, friends spirited me away, but Ferguson's gang tried to assassinate me and nearly succeeded. So now they are going to pay, and you're going to help me. Or else you're all going to see the inside of a British prison.'

Henri laughed out loud. 'Why should we? You can't get us into trouble. We haven't done anything.'

'Is that so?' Ali Selim said. 'Within a three-day period, Daniel Holley's Alfa was sabotaged and almost went into the Thames. And hired thugs waited outside the Gideon girl's home, followed her down the street, attacked her, and would have raped her if not for Holley and her willingness to use a weapon without hesitation.'

There was a stunned silence, and Owen said lamely, 'Now, look here.'

'You told me none of these things. And we have still one more pearl in the oyster: the attempted

262

car bombing in the driveway of the Gideon girl's house. And the reason you did not tell me about any of this was because they were all failures.'

Henri said calmly, 'Okay, fair enough. How did you find out?'

'You and Kelly certainly talked about them enough.'

Kelly's head shot up, and he looked around the room.

'We've been bugged,' he said. 'In the shop.'

'But of course, all three of you were. Four, as we had to include Jean Talbot, you being in the habit of visiting her so frequently, Owen.'

'Damn you,' Owen said bitterly.

'The technicians must have been good, whoever it was,' Henri said.

'Oh, they are. A Muslim organization we call the Brotherhood. They cover all trades and professions. For example, if I wanted Mary's Bower accidentally burned to the ground this week, it would be done. I could take my pick of brothers who would shoot you in the back on the street. As for your friend Jean Talbot, Owen, I would advise her not to try to walk home in the dark from now on, not even in Mayfair.'

The three men exchanged looks, and it was Owen who said, 'So what is it you want us to do this time?'

'Kidnap Sara Gideon. That's where the Seconal that one of my assets left in the glove compartment of your car comes in. One ampoule jabbed

263

in the arm, and it's goodnight, Vienna, for eight hours.'

'But to what purpose?' Henri demanded. 'What do we do with her?'

'You wrap her up carefully, so you can push her in one of those collapsible wheelchairs, drive to Frensham Aero Club, put her in one of Rashid Oil's jets, fly to Rubat, and deliver her to me at the *Monsoon*.'

'No way.' Owen was shaking his head. 'This has gone far enough.'

Henri patted him on the shoulder, trying to calm him. 'What will you do with the girl?' he asked Ali Selim.

'What do you care? You tried to drown her, left her in the hands of possible rapists, then attempted to car-bomb her.'

'I just want to know,' Henri said.

'You've heard of the Gideon Bank? Well, she *is* the Gideon Bank. What would you suggest for ransom? Fifty million, one hundred million? And why stop there?'

'So you wouldn't kill her?'

'Don't be stupid. She's far too valuable.'

Owen nodded. 'He's right, she is.'

'So that's it, then,' Henri said. 'We'll do it.'

'Nobody asked me. I don't agree,' Kelly said. 'I didn't sign up for this.'

'Don't worry,' Henri said, 'I'll sort him. When do you want us to do this?'

'As soon as you can. Their plane must have

landed by now. If she goes home to Highfield Court, she'll be on her own. Both the housekeeper and her grandfather are away.'

'But she could also be staying at the Dorchester with Holley.'

'That's your problem. I'd advise grabbing her as soon as possible. No more failures. If so, it'll be your last one. And no funny business. Osama may be gone, but Al Qaeda is everywhere, particularly in London. Put a foot wrong and I'll know about it. There's nowhere to run, gentlemen.'

Jack Kelly had the bar cupboard open and poured whiskey with a shaking hand. 'God damn him to hell,' he said. 'He'll be the death of us.'

He slopped more whiskey into his glass, and Henri took it from him and tossed the contents into the living-room fire. He shook Kelly hard.

'Pull yourself together. What's done is done. There is only one way out of this mess, and that's to do as he says. Go and have a shower. You look terrible.'

Kelly went out, and Owen said, 'A hell of a mess, but I don't see any choice for us except to play along.'

Henri said, 'Would we really be able to just load her into a jet at Frensham?'

'Yes, it's a circus for the rich there. Talbot International uses it. It's where Kelly landed when he flew over. Security really is slack. Their motto is: You mustn't offend the rich. Even with a wheel-chair, we'll be waved through.'

'As it happens, I've got a very nice one in the stockroom,' Henri said. 'Antique, of course. Will weaponry be a problem at the airfield?'

'Not for me. I've never been checked,' Owen said. 'Give me what's suitable in a bag, and I'll see it gets on board. Now I'll leave you to get on with it, and take a run down to Frensham to make sure the Learjet will be ready to go. At this hour of the morning, I can get there in forty minutes, so I'll be back in no time. I suggest you come with me now, and I'll give you this Seconal stuff while Jack's at his ablutions. But wait for me before you attempt anything.'

'Kelly will be all right,' Henri said. 'A nervous touch, is all. I'll look after him.'

They went out. It was suddenly very quiet, and then Kelly came in, stripped to the waist, took the whiskey bottle from the cupboard, poured a huge one, and drank it down.

'Mother Mary, what am I going to do?' he murmured, and went back upstairs, a very unhappy man indeed.

At Rosedene, Ferguson, Holley, and Sara sat in the reception lounge with the matron, drinking coffee, waiting for news of Harry Miller, who had been in the operating room for an hour.

'He's been wounded before, I believe,' Sara said.

'I think this must be the fourth time,' Ferguson

said. 'Harry was supposed to be a Whitehall Warrior for many years, a desk-man in the Intelligence Corps. The truth is he was involved very much with one of the execution squads that brought the IRA to its knees and led directly to the peace process.'

Professor Charles Bellamy appeared at that moment in green scrubs, a mask hanging down from his neck, revealing his face. He looked a little weary, sat down, and accepted coffee gratefully from Maggie Duncan.

'Everything okay, Charles?' Ferguson asked.

'Not really.'

Sara said, 'I treated him first. My impression was that there was an exit wound.'

'True. But when I got there, I discovered bullet fragmentation. It wasn't immediately obvious.'

'It wasn't hollow-point, I hope?' Holley said.

'No, not as bad as that, but similar. I've removed all the detritus, but I really must say in my report that Harry Miller has taken the pitcher to the well too often. It's got to stop.'

'And the Prime Minister will see that report?'

'Of course.'

Ferguson sighed. 'That's all I need. Can we see him?'

'Certainly not. He's dead to the world. Tomorrow, perhaps.' He turned to Sara and smiled. 'You appear to have been through the mill again. You really must take care, Captain, accept what you are. There are limitations.'

'I'm fine,' she said. 'Any problems and you'll be the first to know.'

He and Maggie went off, talking in low voices. Ferguson's Codex sounded. 'Ah, Roper,' he said, and put it on speaker.

'What about Harry?' Roper asked.

'It was more complicated than they'd thought, but it's been taken care of.'

'Well, the Prime Minister will be relieved. Anyway, I've just had a call from Harry Salter. Dora's back from Holland and confirms that the photo Claude Duval took is definitely the same man who asked her for Pernod the night Holley's Alfa was interfered with. I've spoken to Claude, and now that it's a criminal matter, he's allowed to forward it to DGSE records in Paris. If there is a match, we should get it soon.'

'Many thanks, Giles,' Holley called, and put an arm around Sara. 'Home, or we could go to the Dorchester.'

'Home, I think,' she said. 'Check the mail, the answering machine, then I just want to go to bed.'

Ferguson joined them. 'You must be incredibly tired, Sara. We must take better care of you. This recent affair just exploded out of all proportion.'

'Well, as we used to say in Afghanistan, General, hope for the best and prepare for the worst. Goodnight.'

Jean Talbot, thinking things over, decided that the best way to solve the mystery of what she had seen at the shop in Shepherd Market was to act normally with Owen and see how he behaved. To that end, she left the house still and called him on her mobile as she walked along Curzon Street.

He answered, and she said, 'Hello, darling, are you up for a run in the park this morning?'

'Sorry, love,' he said. 'I had some overseas problems come up last night. I've had to come into the office at an unearthly hour.'

'That's a shame. I'd hoped we could finalize which day we're leaving on the Rubat trip.'

'Actually, I'm not too certain about that at the moment,' he said. 'All of a sudden, a hell of a lot's happening.'

'Well, that's a disappointment,' she said. 'Any particular reason?' She was still walking across to the Dorchester.

'Oh, oil prices again. The Arab Spring, trouble in so many oil-producing countries. Al Qaeda causing mayhem all over the place since the demise of Osama. Look, we'll get round to it, but just now I'm really pushed. I'll be in touch, but I've got to go.'

All of this was making her feel rather sorry for him. Then she turned into Park Lane just in time to see his Mercedes emerging from the underground garage of his apartment block. She dodged back out of sight as he joined the traffic and moved on.

She was surprised at how much it hurt her, the dishonesty. A kind of betrayal, really. She deserved better, and when she turned to walk back home, she had to fight to control hot, angry tears.

Henri Legrande and Kelly had arrived at Highfield Court to find the drive empty. They parked at the end of the street behind several vehicles that were already there.

'What do you think?' Kelly asked. 'Maybe she *has* gone to the Dorchester.'

Before Henri could answer him, the Alfa turned into the drive. Holley and Sara got out. She looked surprisingly fresh after such a long trip, had changed on the plane, wore a khaki shirt and slacks and a well-cut bush jacket. The cropped red hair looked magnificent.

Kelly said, 'The whole thing is ridiculous.'

Henri didn't bother replying, but leaned forward so he could catch what Sara was saying as she took the key from her shoulder bag. 'I've never felt so tired. I think I'll sleep for a week.'

'Then I suggest you do just that,' Holley said, and followed with her bag as she entered the house.

'Do you think he'll stay?' Kelly asked.

'Who knows, Jack. We must wait and see.'

In the hall, Holley said, 'Can I carry your bag up to your bedroom for you?'

'Just leave it there, love.' She moved in close, slipped her arms around his neck and smiled up at him. 'You're a really special man, Daniel Holley. I don't give a damn about you having twenty years on me, because I love you to bits and I don't care what anyone else thinks.' She kissed him deeply for a few long and satisfying moments, then pushed him away. 'So say it – say you love me.'

'I can't,' he said. 'It wouldn't be true. Would "I absolutely adore you" do instead?'

She reached up and rumpled his hair, a contented and tired smile on her face. 'Well, I suppose it will have to. I'll see you later.'

She had the door open, reached up to kiss him again, giving Henri and Kelly a perfect view, then closed the door as Holley went down the steps, got into the Alfa, and drove away.

'What do we do?' Kelly demanded.

'Wait, of course. Holley might come back, and Owen made it clear we don't try anything until he gets here. You go to that convenience store round the corner and get us some coffee, sandwiches, and newspapers. We may be in for a long wait.'

Which Kelly did, also purchasing a half-bottle of whiskey and having a good pull at it on the way back, while upstairs in her bedroom Sara Gideon kicked off her suede desert boots, fell on the bed, still in her clothes, and was instantly asleep.

Greg Slay had arrived back in good time, thanks to a lift in an RAF Hercules from Peshawar that was due to refuel at Hazar. He walked across the runway, whistling cheerfully, to the flat-roofed office and the two hangars that housed Slay Flying.

There was a new Scorpion helicopter, a Beech Baron, and an old Cessna 310, and Feisal, the mechanic, was working on the port engine. He was a handsome thirty-something Bedu of the Rashid tribe with one wife, whom he told Slay he truly loved, and a five-year-old son. When he'd arrived from the Empty Quarter to try town life, it had become immediately apparent that he had a genius for anything mechanical. From cars and trucks, he had moved up to aircraft.

There was significant history between him and Slay. Earlier that year, Slay had taken Feisal with him on a contract job to fly an old Dakota from Bahrain to Hazar. Five miles out, the starboard engine had caught fire, and the undercarriage had collapsed during the emergency landing on the edge of the airfield.

Feisal, his seat buckled, his safety belt so twisted that he couldn't break free, had thought that his time had come, as the fire started and Slay left him. And then Slay had returned with the fire axe, hacked him free, and they'd escaped together – and just in time. It was a debt of honour to be paid when the opportunity arose, the Bedu way.

'Happy to see you, sahib. We've missed you, with the oil well coming in nicely at Gila. Hakim's been flying back and forth, sometimes at night, only stopping to refuel, and the other Scorpion's been standing there doing nothing.'

'Is Hakim up at Gila now?'

'That's right.'

'Well, here I am, back in the saddle and raring to get started. Where's the schedule list? What have you got for me?'

Feisal consulted the noticeboard. 'Machine tool parts, grade-A priority and needed at Gila urgently.'

'I'll take care of that.'

'But they aren't here. They were off-loaded in Rubat yesterday.'

'So I drop in at Rubat. It's only another half-hour on the journey. Give me the consignment bill and I'm on my way.'

The Scorpion was an excellent helicopter, good to fly, a fine performer, and it would be even better when it was fully paid for. He told himself this as he drifted across the outer fringes of the Empty Quarter, the greatest desert in the world, then swung towards the sea and the white buildings that were Rubat. The old military airfield was on the edge of town, and he swung in towards the cargo hangars and settled gently.

A police sergeant in khaki was sitting in a canvas chair, smoking a cigarette, a man Slay had met many times, so he simply waved and went to the foreman on duty, gave him the consignment bill, and stood watching as his goods were loaded.

He had reasonable Arabic, and used it when offering the man a cigarette, which was accepted. 'Not so busy. It must get boring for you,' he said, offering a light.

In spite of the fact that Khazid had issued an

order that any mention of the Hawker would be a serious breach of airport security, the foreman, who had dealt with Slay many times, answered instinctively.

'Oh, one never knows what the day will bring us. For example, earlier we had a very beautiful jet plane land, gold in colour. One of the mechanics, Achmed, told me it was called a Hawker.'

'So where is this marvel of the skies?' Slay asked.

'It did not stay. The chief of police drove out to meet it in a security van to speak to the pilots, but came back alone. It refuelled and took off again.'

'To have seen such a thing must have been a wonder,' Greg Slay told him. 'I must go now. The cargo you loaded is needed urgently at Gila.'

'Take care,' the foreman said. 'I sense a wind coming, a sandstorm perhaps. May Allah guard you.'

'He always does,' Greg said, and took off.

Fifteen minutes out into the desert, he called Giles Roper, who answered at once. 'Slay, my man, good to hear from you. Where are you?'

'Straight back to work. There's a lot of pressure due to a big oil strike. I've just done a cargo pick-up at Rubat airfield and heard something strange.'

'I'm all ears.'

'A golden Hawker dropped in at Rubat earlier. The police chief drove out to greet it in a security van on his own, spoke to the pilots, then returned on his own, and the Hawker flew away after refuelling.'

'Are you sure no one was in the back of the van?'

'No idea. I'm just telling you what I've heard.'

'Well, I've got something strange for you.' He told Slay about the Canadian patrol finding the burned-out Raptor at Herat with a corpse in it.

'Curiouser and curiouser,' Slay said. 'I haven't the slightest idea what it all means, but if I find out, you'll be the first to know. I must press on. I could be flying into a sandstorm.'

The police sergeant at Rubat airfield noticed the lengthy conversation between the cargo foreman and Slay, after the gift of a cigarette, and questioned the man.

'You seemed to be getting friendly with the Englishman from Hazar. Enjoying a smoke and a chat? What were you talking about?'

'Oh, the usual things. The comings and goings,' the foreman said uneasily, wondering where this was heading. 'He's flying up to Gila to the new strike with urgent equipment. I warned him I thought a sandstorm was coming.'

'So the comings and goings did not include a mention of a certain golden jet plane landing here?'

The foreman could have said no and left it at that, but such was his fear of Khazid, he went into denial at once and, in a garbled panic, put all the blame on Slay.

'It was no doing of mine, but he did raise the

matter. He said he'd heard a mention of some such plane making a brief visit and asked me if anyone had got off.'

'And what did you say?'

'The truth, Sergeant, that nobody did. What else should I have said?'

The sergeant nodded. 'Good man. Get back to work.'

Ali Selim had been working on a speech at one end of the desk, Fatima at the other end working on accounts and taking phone calls on speaker so that he could listen if he wanted to.

Khazid finished his account of the incident involving Greg Slay at the airfield, and Fatima said to Ali Selim, 'I'm sure this is nothing. We know about this man. He retired from the British Army Air Corps last year, bought the air taxi firm Ben Carver had been running in Hazar for years. His partner is one of our own people in Hazar, Hakim Asan.'

'Would you be surprised to know that he attacked me in Amira flying a Raptor helicopter, acting under Charles Ferguson's orders?'

She looked bewildered. 'Are you certain it was the same man?'

'Get in touch with this partner of his and ask him where Slay has been for the past few days. I'm going out for a cigarette.'

He was standing at the rail when she joined him ten minutes later with two cups and a pot of coffee on a serving tray. She hung the tray up, poured and handed him a cup, and raised hers in a kind of salute.

'He got a lift from a plane refuelling at Hazar, to Peshawar, the day before yesterday. Was dropped off from an RAF Hercules on a run from Peshawar to London, refuelling at Hazar, no more than a couple or three hours ago. Is he a danger to your plans?'

'I don't know. It could be nothing. He returns to Hazar and goes about his business, flying to Rubat to pick up cargo for Gila, so it is only by chance that he is here not long after the Hawker landed. As far as he knows, I didn't get off and the plane had a legitimate reason to be here. You could argue that *perhaps* I was on board all the time, but that won't help people like Ferguson unless they know where the Hawker is going, and they don't.'

He took a sip of coffee. 'On the other hand, I don't trust people who ask nosy questions.' He turned to her. 'Contact his partner, this Hakim, at Gila. Tell him Gregory Slay is a threat to Al Qaeda and must be disposed of at once. Is he reliable?'

'A dedicated jihadist.'

'Then tell him that Allah is great and he is privileged to have been given this task. You will not say my name.' He smiled. 'I am not worthy of even being mentioned.'

'At your orders, master.'

The wind was coming in forcefully from the

desert beyond the town, stirring the sea into waves, the *Monsoon* pitching on its two great anchors, the one at the stern, the other forward. He stood there gripping the rail, looking out to sea, thinking of Slay flying in such weather. A good man, and there was much to admire in him, but this was war and he was on the wrong side.

Fatima appeared. 'It is taken care of. Hakim says he knows his duty.'

'Thank you, Fatima,' he said calmly.

A sudden fierce gust dashed sand in his face, and she grabbed his arm with surprising strength. 'You will come in now. You could damage your eyes. Such behaviour is foolishness when so many depend on you.'

His smile was unlooked for and unexpected. 'Why, Fatima, you are quite right. I stand corrected.'

He passed inside, and she closed the shutter.

CHAPTER 13

During the run from Rubat, the wind had increased considerably, picking up more and more sand, but it wasn't at the stage where it was giving Slay any serious trouble, although he thought it likely that might happen. His mobile sounded, and once more it was Roper.

'It's me again. Did you really mean that about the sandstorm?'

'It's shaping up to one now. This is the last place God made,' Slay told him. 'In other places, people go to market to buy food. Here down on the border with Yemen they go to market to buy arms. Anything from a general-purpose machine gun to a pistol for your pocket, and most things in between. It's a savage old world.'

'Are you regretting you ever went there?'

'I didn't have much choice, old son – the cutbacks in the military in the UK saw to that.' A violent wind rocked the Scorpion. Slay managed to control it. 'All of a sudden, it's getting interesting. I'll check in with you later.'

'I'm open at all hours.'

★   ★   ★

Slay tried going up above the storm and seemed to do better, so he increased speed and pushed on until in the distance he saw three or four derricks next to various trucks, cars, and prefabricated buildings. He dropped to where red and green lights marked the landing site, and he put down.

Sand was beginning to coat everything like a different kind of snow; he noticed that as three men manhandled a trolley towards him, the foreman leading. Slay got out of the pilot's seat, opened the side door, and jumped out.

'Help yourselves,' he shouted to the foreman in Arabic. 'Where is Hakim?'

The men were already transferring the cargo. 'He's gone,' the foreman shouted back. 'He said he thought it was going to get worse. I told him he should stay until it blows over, but apparently he needed to get back to base.'

'Damn fool,' Slay said.

'That's what I thought. You'll be staying, then?'

'No, I'm a damn fool, too.'

The men had finished their task, were driving the cargo away. The foreman said in English, 'It's your funeral – isn't this what you British say?'

He was laughing as he followed his men into the buildings. Slay closed the main door of the Scorpion, went back to the cockpit, and took off, sand devils dancing all around as the helicopter lifted.

★   ★   ★

Hakim had envied Gregory Slay from the start, although he had managed to conceal his feelings. There was more than one reason why. He had been taught to fly by Ben Carver, but hadn't been able to raise the money to buy it when Ben retired. Slay referred to Hakim as his partner, but he knew it was more to salve the man's pride than anything else, and Hakim's flying was only adequate, whereas Slay gave a master class in how to fly a helicopter every time he took off. Hakim, however, *was* totally dedicated to Al Qaeda, what Osama himself had described as the perfect *jihadist*, a man who gave no indication of being one.

He knew nothing of Fatima personally. To him, she was just a voice on the phone who occasionally passed on orders to him in Al Qaeda's name. Even more important, he had to keep her informed well in advance of flights to anywhere, such as Djibouti, Muscat, Bahrain, or Dubai, so that he could act as postman when required.

Fatima's first call, asking for details of Greg Slay's recent whereabouts, had excited his curiosity, but she had not explained the reason for her interest. Her second, just before he landed at Gila, certainly did.

Gregory Slay was a direct threat to Al Qaeda. He had been given the task of disposing of him, she told him, and by a famous man, Mullah Ali Selim – surely he had seen him recently on Al Jazeera? Hakim had. Fatima had disobeyed the master's

281

order not to reveal his name because she hadn't been able to stand his questioning his own worthiness. *Such nonsense.* She wanted to shout out his greatness to the whole world, but had to be content with just telling Hakim.

'I want to hear from you the instant Slay is disposed of,' she said. There was crackling on the line. 'What's wrong with the reception?'

'The wind will get worse before it gets better,' he told her. 'If a full sandstorm drives in from the Empty Quarter, it will probably kill any signals for mobile phones for some time. I will handle this matter as fast as possible, but may not be able to report a successful outcome for a while.'

'Then you must fly down to Rubat and make your report to us here on the *Monsoon*.'

'As you wish.'

He gripped the steering column tightly and laughed, head thrown back. So Al Qaeda wanted Greg Slay disposed of? How perfect an answer to all his problems. Change was coming; it was inevitable that Al Qaeda would fill the vacuum of power that would bring to Hazar. With Slay disposed of and the goodwill of Al Qaeda behind Hakim, there was nothing to stop him from taking over the company and its aircraft.

Gila loomed up in the distance, and he increased speed. He couldn't wait to land, discharge his cargo, and get back in the air and strike out for Hazar before Slay arrived.

★   ★   ★

It was pouring with rain in London as Henri waited in the Citroën. Owen Rashid had called him, saying he expected to be there in half an hour, but still hadn't arrived, probably because of some hold-up with the weather. Kelly had taken an old umbrella from the rear of the Citroën and gone off to the shop, ostensibly for more coffee, but in reality for whiskey, having emptied the half-bottle. He got two coffees and more whiskey, stopping in a doorway to drink some, then carried on, to find Owen's Mercedes parked just beside the entrance to Highfield Court. He and Henri were loading the collapsible wheelchair and a couple of bags into the luggage compartment.

Owen turned to face Kelly, disgust on his face. 'For God's sake, what are you playing at? You're drunk.' He knocked the two paper coffee cups on the cardboard tray from Kelly's hand and grabbed the umbrella. 'Go and wait in the Citroën.'

He pushed Kelly violently away. Henri said, 'What's your plan?'

'We'll break in from the back if we have to, but let's try the frontal approach. Did you bring the white coat and the stethoscope I suggested?'

'I'm wearing it under my raincoat, and the stethoscope's in my pocket.' He took his raincoat off and put it in the luggage compartment. 'Let's do it.'

Sprawled across her bed hugging a pillow and still fully dressed, Sara came awake to the insistent pealing of the front doorbell. Dazed and conscious only of her throbbing headache, she lay there waiting for the bell to stop ringing, but when it didn't, she got up wearily, pulled on her desert boots, and limped down the stairs to the hall, feeling decidedly shaky. She opened the door and found the two men confronting her, Owen holding the umbrella over their heads, a small wheelchair beside them.

'Captain Gideon. I had the pleasure of meeting you on the terrace of the luncheon for the President. Owen Rashid.'

'Oh yes,' she murmured, deeply tired, conscious only of that throbbing headache. 'What can I do for you?'

'General Ferguson asked me to look in on you and introduce Doctor Legrande here.'

He lowered the umbrella, took a step forward, and instinctively she moved back so that Henri followed her in. She was so tired, she felt no alarm at all, so that what happened was so very simple.

'What's it all about?' she asked wearily.

'You seem tired,' Henri said. 'Permit me to take your pulse,' and he reached for her left hand. The prick itself was of no account, but the Seconal was so instantly effective that Owen had to grab her as she started to slide to the floor.

Henri pulled the wheelchair inside and, leaving Owen to lower her into it, opened the cloakroom door, searched hurriedly, and came back with a black beret and a grey rug, with which he covered

Sara, adjusting the beret over the red hair. He went back to the cloakroom and returned with a khaki trench coat, which he draped over the back of the chair.

'So, my friend, let's go.'

They lifted the chair down the steps just in time to see Kelly drive away in the Citroën.

'The bloody fool's drunk out of his wits,' Owen said. 'He'll probably hit the first car he sees.'

'Nothing to be done about that.' Henri lifted Sara in strong arms. Owen opened the rear door for him, and the Frenchman placed her carefully inside and belted her in. 'I'll sit beside her, playing the doctor, and you will do the driving. Are you still convinced we can get away with this?'

'I told you, we'll be waved straight through the gates.'

He joined the traffic in Park Lane, moving towards Marble Arch, then Bayswater. Henri said, 'It sounds too good to be true, but I suppose we have no choice.'

'No, we don't,' Owen told him. 'We're not playing the game any more, it's playing us, so think positive and keep your fingers crossed.'

The rain was torrential as they drove in through the members' entrance at Frensham, and the security officer on duty simply peered out the half-open office window, recognizing him at once.

'Nice weather for ducks, Mr Rashid,' he called. 'I hope you're going somewhere better than this.'

He didn't bother coming out, simply raised the bar, and Owen drove in.

He threaded his way through an array of parked airplanes and helicopters, and pulled up under an overhang where cars were parked in bays that bore company logos. The Learjet was some little distance away. It took only two or three minutes to get out the wheelchair for Henri, who handed Sara into it. Owen raised the umbrella and walked with him toward the Lear, going ahead and opening the airstair door.

Henri carried Sara's limp body up the steps, ducking his head to pass inside, and Owen followed with her coat and the rug. He squeezed past them and lowered one of the rear seats into the reclining position. Henri passed her to him.

'Gently, now, she'll need the belt, and cover her well. The change in body temperature may not be helped by the Seconal.'

'Why, Henri, I didn't know you cared,' Owen said.

Henri's habitual smile vanished. 'But I do, my friend – this is a great lady. I respect her both as a woman and a soldier. See that you do. I'll see to the wheelchair.'

'Leave it, for God's sake.'

'Which would draw attention.' The slight smile was back on Henri's face. 'I would also remind you of the bags in the Mercedes.'

He went out, and Owen took the deepest of breaths, realizing the stress was beginning to get to him, which wouldn't do at all. He tucked Sara in, then went to the cockpit, took the right-hand seat, and started preparing for take-off.

Henri, holding the umbrella over his head with one hand, pushed the wheelchair with the other to the Mercedes under the overhang. He opened the trunk, took out the two bags, then closed the wheelchair and placed it inside.

Someone said, 'Can I help you, sir?'

Henri turned as a man moved out of an exit tunnel a few feet away, wearing a peaked cap, yellow oilskins streaming. He half-turned, looking towards the Lear, and Henri saw that he had 'Airport Police' on his back and he was holding a radio.

'And what exactly is going on here, sir?'

'Such a shame,' Henri said as if to himself.

'What is, sir?' the policeman asked.

'Oh, life,' Henri said. 'Everything going so smoothly one minute and a total fuck-up the next.'

He took a silenced Walther from his right-hand raincoat pocket and shot the policeman in the heart, hurling him back against the next vehicle, a Toyota service van. He'd dropped his radio to the ground, and Henri stamped on it, picked it up and threw it several cars away, then went round to the rear of the Toyota and found that the door was unlocked. He opened it, dragged the body round and heaved it inside, slamming the door shut, then he returned to the Mercedes, picked up the bags, and returned to the Learjet, where the engines were already rumbling.

Owen, headphones and mike on as he talked to control, glanced over his shoulder and, seeing him enter, closed the door. He received permission to move and felt a sudden elation as Henri eased into the left-hand seat.

They taxied to the end of the runway, paused, rain drumming against the fuselage, then, on the instruction from the control tower, took off, climbing fast to 30,000 feet, leaving the rain behind and levelling at forty, setting a general course south-west.

Henri had put on the co-pilot's headphones and mike. 'How far?'

'Four thousand miles, perhaps a little more.'

'How long would you say?'

'Depending on weather, particularly wind, eight hours.' Owen laughed. 'I told you we'd manage okay at Frensham. You worry too much.'

'Tell that to the policeman who turned up out of nowhere back there and wanted to know what we were getting up to.' His laugh was ugly, and he shook his head. 'No, I was forgetting. You *can't* speak to him.'

'Why not?' Owen's question was automatic.

'Because I double-tapped him in the heart.'

Owen shoved the Lear on autopilot and turned to him. 'You killed him?'

'He wanted to know what was going on, so what did you expect me to say? We're just kidnapping a British Army officer, so mind your own business and clear off?'

'What did you do with the body?'

'There was a Toyota service van parked next to the Mercedes. I put the body in the back.'

'Was that the best you could do?'

'Better than sticking it in the boot of the Mercedes. I stamped on his radio and threw it as far as I could along the line of parked cars. A number of the owners must be up there flying. No reason to connect us particularly. It could be anyone.' He got up. 'I'm going to go check the woman, then I'll find the brandy and make some coffee.'

Owen, filled with despair, said, 'Damn you, and damn that interfering cop.'

His mobile phone sounded. He took it out, sat there looking at it, and Henri said, 'Now, I wonder who that is. Probably your master's voice all the way from Rubat. Aren't you going to tell him the good news?'

Owen glared at him helplessly, then answered. Ali Selim said, 'There you are, Owen. I've been waiting to hear from you. Where are you? Do I hear aircraft noises? Are you flying?'

Owen took a deep breath. 'Yes, Henri and I have just left Frensham and are on our way in the Lear. Kelly decided he wanted no further part in the matter at hand and did a runner on us.'

'How unfortunate for him. Someone should have told him that there's no place to hide. So, what news of Captain Gideon?'

'We've got her. She's deep in a Seconal-induced sleep in the back of the cabin.'

Ali Selim said, 'How long before you get here?'

'Almost eight hours.' The Lear was still on auto-pilot, but he suddenly felt tired, his brain refusing to function. He could have told Ali Selim about the policeman in the Toyota, but he didn't. It could come later.

'You've done well, Owen – I'm pleased with you. Al Qaeda will be right behind you when the Council of Elders decides on the succession. I regret to tell you that the Sultan seems close to the end.'

'Well, I hope he goes to a better place,' Owen told him. 'But as far as I'm concerned, Al Qaeda can go to hell. I'm signing off now.'

Henri clapped his hands. 'Excellent, my friend, there's hope for you yet. I'll go and see to that coffee now.'

On the *Monsoon*, there was unholy joy on Ali Selim's face as he turned to Fatima, who had been listening on speaker. 'So they have her. I am thrice blessed that I should see such a day.'

Holley and Dillon were enjoying a Turkish bath at Holland Park when Roper called through on the internal phone.

'I've got something very interesting for you lot on my screen.'

They put on terry-cloth robes and went to see him and found exactly what he was talking about when they went into the computer room. There were photos of Henri Legrande at various stages of his career, medals and all.

'Just in from Claude Duval. He was called to Paris on another matter, and DGSE records had these for him. Serious business, this man.'

'And living right here in Mayfair in this antiques shop in Shepherd Market,' Dillon said.

'Not for the first time, I dare say, that the French know more about someone in London than we do. Have a look at the text on Legrande.'

There was his military history, not only in the Foreign Legion but of the time he had spent training terrorists at the camp in Algeria. There were even lists of his pupils, including members of the Provisional IRA, particularly one Jack Kelly.

'This is particularly interesting, because when Legrande inherited the antiques shop in Shepherd Market he also started taking classes at London University, where he met student Mary Barry, a PIRA activist whose father was a friend of Kelly's, who put her in touch with Henri, who became her lover. You'll note the details of her unfortunate death at what would appear to be British hands.'

'All good stuff, but what's the connection with what happened to me and Sara, and where's this leading?' Holley asked.

'Well, the peace process wiped the slate clean for men like Kelly, who was released from prison. As no one knows better than you and Dillon, he's been at it again. We keep an eye on him. He came over from County Down the other day in a Talbot International plane.'

'So?' Holley said.

'We monitor Jean Talbot's comings and goings. Just look at this film of people visiting her home,' Roper said. 'There's Kelly more than once with Legrande outside the house. There are shots of her with Owen Rashid going into the house together.'

'What are you suggesting?' Dillon said.

'That they see a lot of each other,' Roper told him. 'But that isn't the point. Besides surveillance cameras, we have an asset who now and then observes her, sees where she goes, who she speaks to. She was being watched this morning when she emerged from Marley Court in a tracksuit, obviously bound for the park, when Owen Rashid appeared, running along the pavement, on the other side of Curzon Street.'

'So she followed him?' Dillon asked.

'So did our asset right to the antiques shop in Shepherd Market, where Rashid hammered on the door and was admitted by not only Henri Legrande but Jack Kelly. She watched from a doorway and then left, not looking very happy.'

'So what's it all add up to?' Dillon asked. 'These incidents involving Holley and Sara?'

'The way I see it, I would guess that Jean Talbot was shocked to see Owen Rashid and the other two together,' Holley said.

'So anything not kosher that they've been up to has nothing to do with her,' Dillon added. 'Does Ferguson know about this?'

'He isn't in London. The Prime Minister invited

Henry Frankel and him to join him at Chequers for the weekend.'

'Have you tried to pull Sara into the frame?'

'Good God, no,' Roper said. 'She's really been through it the last few days. She's sleeping the sleep of the just, I trust.'

'So we can go and lift Jack Kelly and Henri Legrande?'

'I don't see why not,' Roper said. 'You've got your SIS warrants. Technically, you should be accompanied by the police, but when did we let that stand in the way? I'd get on with it, if I were you.'

At Hazar, the wind was blowing curtains of sand every which way, but visibility wasn't so bad that Hakim couldn't see where he was going. He made a bad landing outside the hangars, rocking from side to side. Opening the door to get out was a struggle, the wind gusting, and Feisal had closed the great hangar door for obvious reasons. Hakim, holding the tail of his headcloth across his nose and mouth, lurched to the Judas gate, opened it, and stepped inside.

Feisal, working on the Cessna, turned to greet him, wrench in hand. He spoke in Arabic. 'I wasn't expecting you.'

'Well, I'm here.' Hakim crossed to the office, opened a corner cupboard, took out an AK-47, selected a magazine from several on offer, and returned to the hangar.

Feisal, wiping oil from his hands with a rag, frowned. 'What's happening? What's the AK for?'

'The execution of Gregory Slay. He should be arriving shortly from Gila.'

'What madness is this? Why would you wish to do such a thing?' Feisal demanded.

'He is not only an enemy of Islam but an enemy of Al Qaeda.'

'On whose authority?'

'Mullah Ali Selim, at this moment staying in Rubat on the *Monsoon*. I am privileged to have been given this task, just as you are privileged to have the opportunity to aid me.'

Feisal said, 'I am a Bedouin of the Rashid tribe, born in the Rub al Khali, the Empty Quarter, where a man's word is his bond and honour comes before everything. Slay risked his life to save mine. I won't let you do this thing.'

Hakim reversed the AK-47 and rammed the stock into the side of his face, Feisal collapsing sideways. He had just missed the Cessna wing as he fell, and lay there, blood on his face. Hakim pulled off his headcloth, using the folds to tie his wrists, then propped him up against a wheel, stuffing another loose fold into his mouth. The wind was rising out there, howling in from the desert, and Hakim opened the Judas, peered out, and immediately drew back quickly as sand blasted into his face.

He went over to Feisal, who had his eyes open

now. Hakim kicked him. 'Wake up. I'll let you watch the fun before I kill you.'

There was a genuine menace in the voice of the wind now, and then it grew louder unexpectedly and changed into the distinctive clatter of the helicopter, which rose to a crescendo outside, and then stopped. The wind howled as if trying to get in, rattling the hangar door, and then the Judas gate opened and Gregory Slay entered.

He stood there, shaking sand from his hair, wiping it from his face with the palms of his hands, and paused at the sight of the tableau before him. Outside, the wind had subsided a little, so that it seemed rather quieter in the hangar.

'What's going on?' he asked. 'Why is Feisal tied up?'

'Because he's a traitor to his own people,' Hakim said. 'He actually refused to help me kill you, even though it's in the name of Islam. It seems it's a matter of honour. Can you believe that?'

Feisal groaned, eyes desperate, but Slay smiled. 'Yes, I can.'

Hakim said, 'Take off your flying jacket. I know you always carry a .38 Smith & Wesson in the left-hand inside pocket. Toss it away and kneel.'

'Anything to oblige.'

Slay did as he was told, dropping to one knee, drawing the .25 Belgian Leon from his ankle holster very quickly as he went down, shooting Hakim in the forehead, the hollow-point cartridge blowing away the back of his skull.

He untied Feisal and heaved him up. 'He made a mess of your face.'

Feisal kicked the body. 'This dog tried to get me to help him kill you.'

'What was his reason?' Slay asked.

'He was under orders from Mullah Ali Selim, who is staying on a boat called the *Monsoon* in Rubat Harbour. It seems you are an enemy of Al Qaeda.'

Gregory Slay said in astonishment, 'Are you certain about this?'

'That's what Hakim told me.'

'Does it bother you that we've just killed an Al Qaeda follower?'

'Why should it? I'll probably take my family, travel far out into the Empty Quarter, and join up with my fellow tribesmen. They won't find me.'

'No need for that,' Slay said. 'We'll empty his pockets, take his watch and wallet, drive him into the outskirts of town, ditch the jeep, and leave his body beside it in an alley. Such robberies occur all the time. You take him in one jeep, I'll follow in the other to bring you back. If a story is needed, he left here to go home. He's living on his own these days anyway.'

'That is true. An excellent plan,' Feisal said.

'Then let's get on with it.'

Everything worked perfectly, they did what was necessary on the way into town, and were back in forty minutes. The drive through the increasingly bad weather had been difficult and truly frightening, the sandstorm raging at full blast.

They returned through the Judas gate into the comparative calm of the hangars, but the storm still raged outside.

'I'll make some coffee in the kitchen,' Feisal said. 'And there is a goat stew that may be heated up if you are hungry.'

'Excellent. You see to it, while I phone friends to reassure them of my safety.'

'In such a storm as this, I think not,' Feisal said. 'It makes the signal for the mobile phones impossible for a while. You have not experienced such a great storm as this during your time here, but it happens.'

Slay was already calling Roper, praying for a connection but without success. He tried several times, then went into the kitchen. The stew was heating on a bottle gas stove and smelled good as Feisal stirred.

'No luck, sahib?'

'I'm afraid not. How long will this last, would you say?'

'As Allah wills.' Feisal shrugged. 'I remember several years ago a storm of such anger that there was no connection for five hours. You could keep trying, though.'

'I hope we can do better than that,' Slay said. 'But what about some of that goat stew while we're waiting?'

★   ★   ★

297

Jack Kelly had made it back to Shepherd Market in the Citroën, had let himself into the shop in despair at the situation into which he had got himself. His years in prison should have taught him a lesson.

He'd had it all, the chance of a new life, a good job as the estate manager at Talbot Place, his pub in the village. Why had he listened to the siren voices of dissidents who wanted Ulster to return to armed struggle? It had been total madness.

Suddenly the quiet of the place was too much for him. What he needed was people and more whiskey, so he went out through the shop and started along the street to an Irish bar he knew.

As he was about to enter, he glanced back and saw a red Mini pull up in front of the shop. To his horror, Sean Dillon and Daniel Holley got out and moved to the entrance. Kelly panicked on the instant, and dashed into another narrow alley that brought him into Curzon Street.

He paused at a boarded-up house with a builder's sign and was violently sick, then moved out into Curzon Street, wiping his face with a handkerchief. The drizzle he'd been walking in suddenly increased into a downpour. He stood there in total despair, then realized there was only one place he could go, so he crossed the road and made for Jean Talbot's house in Marley Court.

She opened the door, hair tied back. 'Good God, Jack, you *are* in a mess,' she said.

'I'm in trouble.' He was half-sobbing. 'Deep trouble. Can I come in?'

'Of course you can.' He staggered past so close that he bumped into her and made for the sitting room. She frowned then, some inner caution making her leave the front door slightly ajar, and went after him.

He was helping himself to a whiskey from the sideboard. She said, 'I'd say you'd had strong drink in abundance, from the state of you. What's this all about?'

'Well, your good friend Owen Rashid could make a better story of it than I can. Not that he's available to tell you anything, as he's out there in the wild blue yonder flying to Rubat in his Learjet.'

'He's what?' She was not pleased, and it showed. 'I think you'd better explain what you're talking about, or Talbot Place will be needing a new estate manager.'

Kelly was helping himself to another whiskey. 'You wouldn't want to know what lover boy got us all into.'

She was furiously angry now. 'Tell me what all this is about, damn you.'

'Why not?' He held his glass high. 'To Owen Rashid, the Real IRA, and Ali Selim and Al Qaeda, may they all rot in hell. I was in over my head, I was so stupid, but I can't go to prison again. I'd rather die.'

So he took a deep breath, tried to pull himself together, and told her everything.

* * *

Five minutes was all it took and her life changed totally. She sat there, looking at him gravely and rather sadly.

'So you've told me the truth, Jack? They've flown off with the young woman and are on their way to Rubat right now?'

'Absolutely, Jean, you've hit the nail right on the head.'

'If you'll excuse me for a minute, I've just got something to do. Have another drink if you want.'

She walked out, crossed the hall into the study. There was no way she could leave Sara Gideon to her fate. How strange then that the man she needed to do the right thing now was the man she had threatened to have killed. She had put Sean Dillon's mobile number into her phone from the card he'd given her at the luncheon, called him now, and he answered at once.

'Who is this?'

'Jean Talbot. I believe you might still be in the vicinity of Shepherd Market?'

'How the hell did you know that?'

'I think you should know that Henri Legrande and Owen Rashid have kidnapped and drugged your friend Sara Gideon and are en route to Rubat with her, acting under the orders of Ali Selim. Jack Kelly's at my house now, drunk out of his wits, and has confessed everything to me.'

Kelly appeared in the doorway of her study in time to hear, and pulled a Colt .38 semi-automatic from his pocket and aimed at her, hand shaking.

'Stop that,' he bellowed.

'You can go to hell,' she replied.

He fired, bouncing her back against the wall. He stood there staring at her, shocked at what he had done. There was the roar of the Mini Cooper arriving outside, and Holley, first out, came through the front door, already ajar, and flung himself down, firing blindly. Kelly appeared from the study, gun raised, and it was Sean Dillon who shot him twice in the heart.

He stepped across Kelly as Holley picked himself up. Jean Talbot was trying to stand, blood seeping from her sleeve and soaking her blouse.

'Oh, dear,' she said, as he raised her, then eased her into a chair. 'I'm stuck with having to thank you for saving my life instead of making plans to end yours.'

'I'll expect you learn to live with it,' he said, as Holley came in with some kitchen towels. 'Good man, Daniel. I'll see to Jean, you call Roper, tell him what's happened and what she said about Sara. Also, a disposal team will be needed for Kelly. We'll leave the front door unlocked.'

'A disposal team?' Jean enquired, as Dillon padded a towel and slipped it inside her blouse.

'We have our own funeral people. They'll clean the place up, take the body away and deal with it.'

'And what happens to me?'

'We're going to take you to Rosedene, our own private hospital.'

'How kind.' She smiled, but winced. 'It's beginning to hurt.'

'Don't worry, they're the best in London for gunshot wounds. They also do a great cup of tea.'

'That's comforting,' she told him and fainted. He caught her, held her close, and called Holley, who had been in the hall, talking to Roper, then trying to contact Sara.

Holley's face was hard and set. Dillon said, 'You look like the devil himself, Daniel.'

'I feel like him. Roper said we must get Talbot to Rosedene as soon as possible. Professor Bellamy's been notified and is on his way over from Guy's Hospital to receive her. I've been trying to reach Sara on her Codex. Only got her recorded message. Roper has sent Tony Doyle straight round to Highfield Court to do a proper search.'

'Bring Talbot, put her in the back seat, and let's get moving. We have to pass Sara's place on the way. Tony is bound to be there. He'll do the full police search, he's very methodical.'

Holley carried Jean Talbot out, Dillon put the front door on the latch so that the disposal team would get entry, and a few moments later, the Mini Cooper was on its way.

Doyle's van was in the drive of Highfield Court, so Dillon dropped Holley off and carried on, with Jean Talbot still unconscious in the back. Holley tried the doorbell, and Doyle appeared, his face sombre.

He held up a Codex. 'This is Sara's. I found it beside the bed, and from the state of that, I'd say she'd not been between the sheets. But it did look as if it had been slept on.'

'She was absolutely exhausted when I left her,' Holley said. 'I think she probably flung herself on the bed fully dressed and just crashed.'

'No sign of a struggle. Whatever happened must have been slick and quick.'

'According to Kelly, she was to be drugged with Seconal.'

'Now that would really put you to sleep,' Tony said. 'Anyway, there's nothing more that we can do here, so let's get back to Holland Park.'

They left, Doyle locking the door, and as they went down the steps, Holley's Codex sounded. Roper said, 'Are you still at Sara's?'

'Just leaving.'

'Well, get here fast. I've just had confirmation of where Ali Selim may be from Greg Slay. Quick as you can, Daniel. I think time is of the essence now. I'll contact Sean.'

'Anything interesting?' Doyle asked.

'Oh yes,' Holley said as he got into the van. 'I'll explain as we go. Holland Park and fast as you can.'

At Rosedene, Dillon walked behind the wheeled stretcher on which Jean Talbot lay, all prepped up for her operation, drowsy from drugs already. They paused at the entrance to the operating room, where Charles Bellamy and his team waited. Dillon stood to one side, gazing down at her.

'You know, I used to be an actor before the IRA got its hands on me, and actors never say good luck.'

'So what do they say?'

'Break a leg.'

'There's an old Irish saying: When you've sinned, a devil is waiting.' She smiled faintly and touched his hand with some difficulty. 'God knows, I've sinned enough in my time, so you must be my devil. May I say break a leg to you?'

'And why would I need that?'

'Oh, I think you know, my friend. Another performance, I'm sure. You'll never leave that woman in such dire straits. It's not in your nature. Give them hell. They deserve it, all of them.'

Her eyes closed, and the nurse pushed her through into the operating room. Bellamy nodded, and Dillon nodded back and went out to reception, where he found Maggie Duncan.

'A lovely lady,' she said.

'She's certainly that,' Dillon said. 'Can I see Harry Miller?'

'I wouldn't suggest it. The operation was fine, but he's had a secondary infection. Lots of penicillin will make it right, but at this moment in time he has a fever.'

'Well, tell him I was asking for him.'

'Try again tomorrow,' she said.

'I've a strong suspicion I'm needed elsewhere right now, so I won't be here tomorrow.'

She sighed and shook her head. 'How many times have we patched you up, Sean? You'll never stop until—'

He cut in. 'They bring me in inside a body bag.'

She crossed herself. 'God forgive you for saying such a wicked thing.'

As he went out, his Codex sounded, and Roper said, 'Things are hotting up, Sean. I've just heard from Greg Slay that Ali Selim is definitely in Rubat on this boat, the *Monsoon*. You'd better get there fast.'

'On my way,' Dillon told him, and ran to his Mini Cooper.

At Hazar, Greg Slay had tried innumerable times to connect with Roper, but the sandstorm blew fiercely, and it was well over an hour since his first attempt when he finally heard Roper's voice.

'How are you?' Roper demanded. 'What about the sandstorm?' He'd phoned Slay again so the others could hear him.

Slay said, 'To go through it once more, the Hawker *was* delivering Ali Selim to Rubat. He's down there now, staying on a luxury dhow owned by the sheikh who loaned him the Hawker that got him out of England.'

'Have you had any dealings with him?'

'Only second-hand. My partner, Hakim, turned out to be Al Qaeda, and Ali Selim ordered him to kill me.'

'Why would he do that?'

305

'I can only imagine he'd discovered I was the Raptor pilot who'd been giving him problems in Afghanistan.'

'So what happened?'

'Hakim beat up my mechanic, Feisal, because he refused to help him, and was about to blow my head off with an AK-47 when I shot him dead. We dumped the body, but Ali Selim remains a problem. The Sultan is extremely sick, with only a medical man keeping him alive. The Council of Elders are old fogies who get no respect from the lower orders. Most of them work for Rashid Oil, so they enjoy a good standard of living, but Al Qaeda has a strong following.'

'What about the military?' Holley asked.

'There's only Rubat town and port to bother about, so a sort of police militia is in charge, run by a Colonel Khazid. He and his men are totally controlled by Al Qaeda. What are we talking about here?'

'Well, I don't know what anyone else wants to do,' said Holley, 'but I intend to fly down there as soon as possible to retrieve Sara Gideon.'

'You think you can do that?'

'If it's going to be done, now is the time. Sara is in the air on her way, fast asleep, not knowing what's happening. Now Roper tells me Ali Selim hasn't been crowing about this, hasn't phoned in to say he's got her, and she's destined to be the most valuable kidnap victim of all time. He's got her, in the sense that Owen Rashid and Legrande have her on the Lear, but they won't arrive in Rubat for a while. My Falcon is one of the fastest planes around. I'll have the advantage of surprise. Ali Selim's keeping quiet about where he is, but doesn't realize that we know. That should count for a lot.'

'Well, I wouldn't land at Rubat if I were you. Hazar would be much more sensible.'

'Then we'd drive down to Rubat?'

'Good God, no, it would take forever, and the roads are hell. We'll use one of my Scorpions. It's only half an hour in one of those, and we do it so regularly, we're not even checked. So when are you coming?'

Holley turned to Roper. 'You didn't tell Ferguson that we were going to lift Legrande and Kelly. Have you told him about these developments?'

'No, I haven't, because it would mean Henry Frankel and the Cabinet Office and the Prime Minister all getting their political knickers in a twist. And the newspapers, who don't give a damn about anything except their front pages, would all spew the story worldwide. Then the government would tell the Gideon Bank that they can't pay to get her back because it would set a precedent, and that would be the ministerial cherry on the cake.'

He swung his chair round to look up at his screens, and Holley said, 'We'd better check that my plane is fuelled.'

Roper turned. 'Good God, are you still here? I ordered your Falcon filled up at Farley Field within ten minutes of hearing she'd been taken. I asked the armourer to sort out the weaponry you're likely to need – Semtex, timers, all the usual toys.'

'You're a gem,' Dillon told him. 'I always said it.'

'Just one thing more, since we're circumventing every avenue of government. I'd just like to say, as a crippled veteran who's seen it all, that I don't give a stuff for Owen Rashid and Henri Legrande, and my opinion of Ali Selim is even lower. Blow them away, and let's get rid of these people once and for all. I want to see Sara Gideon back here in this computer room, bright and cheerful and unsullied. That's what it's all about.'

'And that's what you're going to get.' Holley turned to Dillon. 'Let's get moving, Sean.' And they hurried out.

CHAPTER 14

Roper called in to Greg Slay to tell him of the Falcon's departure. After that, he left Dillon and Holley alone for the long flight. It was five hours later that he called them and discovered Dillon was doing the flying.

'What's Daniel up to?' he asked.

'Checking the weaponry.'

'He's taking it hard, I think.'

'Wouldn't you?' Dillon shook his head. 'He adores Sara Gideon. I've never seen such a change in a man.'

'How are you doing?'

'Wonderfully well. This latest Falcon is a fantastic plane with phenomenal speed, so we're catching up enough to say we could be landing at Hazar around an hour after they've landed at Rubat.'

Holley had come in, wearing desert fatigues, moved into the co-pilot's seat and put on the headphones. 'How are things, Giles?'

'Not as good as they are for you. Dillon tells me that you're eating up the miles.'

'That's what we need, but our greatest strength will be the total surprise when we come knocking on the door. It will be close to midnight,' Holley told him.

Dillon cut in, 'Any word from Ferguson?'

'Not a one. They'll be too busy putting the world to rights and having a good dinner. I've checked at Rosedene on Harry. His fever is improving, so the penicillin is doing its work.'

'And Jean Talbot?'

'She's post-operative, but Bellamy's pleased with her and says the operation was a success.'

'Give her my best,' Dillon said.

'You can do that yourself, Sean, when you two get back with Sara.'

'You think that's a given, do you?'

'It always has been. I can't see you coming back without her. I'll do my best to keep Ferguson off your back. I gave him a call, reported on Harry, and said he was best left alone.'

'Take care,' Holley called and turned to Dillon. 'Have yourself a break, and I'll take over again. Have a cup of tea and a sandwich or something. Have a look at the weaponry the armourer selected for us and check them out. There's enough for Greg Slay if he wants to come to the party, too.'

'Not much doubt of that, as he's flying us into Rubat. He'll play his part in the rest of it, I'm sure.'

Holley said, 'It's like going back into the past, to what happened to Rosaleen in Belfast when I killed the four men who'd raped her.' His face was bleak and hard. 'If anything bad has happened to

Sara, I'll have Ali Selim's life if it's the last thing I do on earth.'

'We're getting close now and you're feeling stressed.' Dillon patted him on the shoulder. 'Just take it easy, Daniel, relax. Put the plane on autopilot, let it fly itself for a while, and watch the stars come out. We're going to pull this off, I promise you.'

The Learjet was passing through considerable turbulence, Owen Rashid at the controls. He eased the column forward and went down 3,000 feet, finding things calmer, and Henri Legrande joined him on the flight deck.

'How is Sara Gideon?' Owen asked.

Henri sat down in the co-pilot's seat. 'Sleeping very peacefully. I've looked Seconal up on the laptop in the cabin. What I read confirms that the effect lasts eight hours. It seems that when the subjects come back to life, as it were, they're in good shape and able to operate physically and so on, but they've no memory of what's happened. They need to be told it's eight hours on.'

'That must be hard to grasp,' Owen said.

'I would think so,' Henri said. 'No news from our lord and master? I wonder what he's up to?'

Owen's mobile sounded. He put the plane on autopilot, turned his mobile to speaker, and answered.

'How are things?' Ali Selim said. 'I left you alone so long because I thought you had enough to think of with such a difficult flight.'

'We'll be with you quite soon now,' Owen said.

'And the woman?'

'Out cold.'

'Excellent. We've had extremely bad weather here. The most ferocious sandstorm in years, with a fury seldom witnessed. It has seriously interfered with mobile phone signals, but I think things will improve.'

'Yes, I know all about that from the weather reports,' Owen said. 'Have you been in touch with anyone in London about the woman?'

'Of course not. Today is Sunday, a day of rest to any true Englishman, and my information is that Ferguson is spending the weekend at Chequers, the Prime Minister's country retreat, with the French foreign minister.' He laughed harshly. 'Ah, if only we had the opportunity. A bomb would wreak havoc. We could change history. Ferguson must feel he's finally arrived, so close to the Prime Minister and the seat of power, his advice sought by international politicians. Just think what's waiting for him tomorrow when I call to break the news about Sara Gideon.'

Owen said, 'How's my uncle?'

'Just the same. When he goes, it will be like the snap of a finger, for everything will change, and for you also, is it not so?'

'Sorry, the weather's turning turbulent again,' Owen said. 'I've got to turn off the autopilot and get back to flying this plane.'

He switched off his mobile and took control,

breathing deeply, his hands firm on the column. 'God, but I hate that bastard.'

'Join the club,' Henri said. 'But as it isn't an option, settle for a cup of coffee, which I'll get for you now.'

Slay was speaking to Holley, Dillon listening. 'I checked with the control tower. I told them an Algerian Falcon was arriving carrying a diplomatic envoy booked through to Bahrain. It'd only be on the ground for an hour or two. Just passing through, that's your story. So you'll be in an hour after the Lear lands at Rubat. Round about midnight.'

'And how long in the Scorpion from Hazar?'

'Half an hour, and since the sandstorm has caused major disruption, we are allowed to land anywhere. The port area, for example.'

'And getting to the *Monsoon*. How would that be done?'

'I've seen the police launch going out there from time to time. That could be a possibility for men of enterprise.'

'Which includes you?'

'Wouldn't miss it, old son.'

'And how have you been surviving the sandstorm?'

'I keep myself hidden. A policeman turned up a couple of hours ago to ask where I was, but Feisal, my mechanic, told him that if I wasn't at my house, he had no idea, and he said the same about Hakim Asan. It's not surprising someone's not found his body yet what with all the disruption. Feisal asked the policeman what it was all about, and he told him there had been an inquiry from the Rubat police.'

'Ali Selim seeking information about his Al Qaeda brother,' Holley said. 'We'll have to deliver it personally. See you soon.'

The wind blowing out of the desert in Rubat was not as bad as it had been, but still carried sand, enough to keep the streets clear.

On the *Monsoon*, Captain Ahmed stood at the rail, watching Colonel Khazid in a motor launch crewed by three of his officers wearing yellow oilskins with *Police* emblazoned on their backs. They stayed unhappily in the launch while Khazid pulled himself up on the deck, nodded to Ahmed, who was tying the line, and went to report.

Ali Selim sat at one end of the table, Fatima at the other. 'There you are, and none too soon,' Selim said. 'Since Hakim is not with you, I assume there's obviously no sign of a Scorpion helicopter at the airport.'

'But there is at Hazar,' Khazid said eagerly, glad to have some sort of news at last. 'After repeated attempts, I finally managed to get through to a colleague on the airport police. It's chaos up there because of the weather. Lots of planes coming in, queuing up to refuel, then passing on.'

'I haven't got the slightest interest in any of that,' Ali Selim told him. 'What about Hakim and this man Slay?'

'The mechanic Feisal said that Hakim returned from a flight to Gila, and then took one of the jeeps and went home. If he isn't there, he has no idea where he is.'

Fatima said, 'And Slay?'

'He flew in from Gila some time after Hakim, when the weather was quite bad. He also took a jeep and left for a small hotel in town where he stays. My colleague checked there, only to find that they haven't seen him.'

Ali Selim got up and paced around, frowning. 'A mystery here, compounded by such extreme weather. Anything could have happened, don't you think?'

He had turned to Fatima, who nodded. 'There are more important things to consider now.' She glanced at her watch. 'The Lear will be landing in forty-five minutes. I'll meet it and bring Sara Gideon to you.'

'Of course. Wait for Fatima on deck, Colonel.'

Khazid retreated and Ali Selim said, 'Take Ibrahim with you. Make sure she's treated with all respect, whatever state she is in.'

'Of course, master, a great day.' She hurried out.

Owen passed over the harbour, Henri standing beside him looking down. Most of the town was in darkness, but there were mooring lights on the

315

Monsoon. There had been no lights at the airport, but they suddenly appeared, lighting up the runway.

'From the state of the rest of the town, I'd say they've had problems with the power supply,' Owen said. 'I suspect the airport's come on by royal command.'

From behind them, there was a clattering noise of something falling over and then Sara Gideon's voice was heard. 'What is this? Where in the hell am I?'

'Get us landed, and quickly,' Henri said and returned to the cabin.

She had tossed away the cover and was trying to unbuckle the seat belt. She paused and looked up at him angrily. Her voice was normal, yet she was furiously angry.

'Who are you and where am I?' She managed to free herself and swing her legs to the floor.

'Calm yourself,' he told her. 'You are about to land in Rubat, which is next door to Yemen. You've just enjoyed an eight-hour sleep from England on this Learjet.'

She didn't even seem bewildered, although that could have been the drug. She simply frowned and said, 'Do I know you?'

'You would have liked to get your hands on me, yes. I tried to blow up your friend Holley's Alfa and almost got shot.'

'So you were responsible for that?'

'And a couple of other things.'

'But not for you, for someone else? Am I right?'

'Completely. In a way, you may consider yourself to be a prisoner of war.'

'And who might be my captor?'

'Mullah Ali Selim.'

Throughout their conversation, the Lear had been descending, and now it landed, so that both of them went staggering, grabbing at seats as the plane braked, turning from the runway towards Fatima, Ibrahim, Khazid and several policemen who were waiting.

On the Lear, the engines were switched off, and as Sara pulled herself up, Owen Rashid moved in to the cabin from the flight deck. He didn't know what to say, a kind of desperation on his face.

'What on earth are *you* playing at?' she demanded. 'Does Jean Talbot know about this?'

'Of course not.'

'Ali Selim?' she said. 'What's *that* all about? You're a friend of the Prime Minister, for God's sake.'

'And not only half-Arab but nephew of the Sultan of Rubat, who could die any day now.'

'What's that got to do with anything?'

'Al Qaeda has got me by the throat, it's that simple. They want me to inherit.'

She turned to Henri. 'What's your excuse?'

'We don't make excuses in the Foreign Legion. If I didn't do what Ali Selim wanted, I'd be a marked man. Alas, I was looking out for a friend

317

who had enough sense to run away from this party.'

She nodded as Owen opened the airstair door. 'So what comes now?'

'Ali Selim is waiting to meet you on a dhow called *Monsoon*, moored in the harbour,' Owen said. 'Meet the welcoming committee. The fat man in uniform is Colonel Khazid, the chief of police, and it would be useless to seek his help. He's Al Qaeda to the hilt – they all are in this town. The woman is Fatima Karim, who handles administration for Selim. The big man in black is Ali Selim's bodyguard, Ibrahim.'

'We've met before,' Sara said. 'But at a distance, I'm happy to say.'

She went down the steps, as they moved towards her, and it was Fatima who took charge. 'Captain Gideon, you will come with me. Mullah Ali Selim is most anxious to meet you.'

'A great honour, I'm sure, which I could do without, but I don't appear to have much choice in the matter.' She followed Fatima, Ibrahim leading the way. When he opened the rear door of the car and turned to face her, she said, 'Why, Ibrahim, it's you. Last time I saw you was in Amira, with fifteen or sixteen dead men in the street.' His stare was frightening, but Sara smiled. 'Oh, dear, were they friends of yours?'

She got in the car, and Fatima joined her. 'Be careful, Captain, Ibrahim is a dangerous man.'

He got in the front beside a police driver, and

Sara said, 'Not to me, because his boss wouldn't like it. In any case, if this thing is going the way I suspect, then I'm far too valuable.'

'I'd take care, Captain, I really would.'

'I'm a serving soldier in the British Army, shot in combat in Afghanistan, a permanent limp in the right leg. I've killed many Taliban, which means many Muslims. What can Ibrahim do to me that has not been done? Ravish me? But what kind of dog does that? Not a real man, certainly.'

All this was delivered in perfect Arabic. Ibrahim reached up to angle the driving mirror, and she looked into eyes filled with hate.

He said, 'A time will come when you beg me for mercy.'

'I'm frightened to death,' Sara said, as the small procession of vehicles drew up on the jetty. Khazid and six of his men led the way to a police launch followed by Ibrahim, Fatima and Sara, Owen Rashid and Henri Legrande behind. They boarded, only the police remaining on deck in their uniforms, the others under cover. Henri's chest had been hurting for some time, probably as the result of flying at a great height for so long. He coughed, reaching for a handkerchief, coughed again. When he examined it, he found fresh blood. So it was finally beginning.

He looked at Sara Gideon in the corner and then to Ibrahim, evil personified, and thought of her in the hands of such a man, thought of Mary, the love of his life, and knew what she would have wanted him to do now that he was close to the end. He carried a Beretta in a shoulder holster. He also carried a folded flick-knife in his left trouser pocket.

When the launch reached the landing platform for them to go up the steps, and there was a momentary crush, he murmured, *'Excusez-moi, Capitaine,'* and slipped the knife into her hand. Her fingers closed over it, she gave him not even the briefest of glances, and went after Fatima, who had followed Ibrahim out.

Several sailors had appeared, and Ahmed was talking to them. Ibrahim carried on, leading the way through to where Ali Selim waited, sitting behind the table in his usual place.

'As you ordered, master.'

Ali Selim examined Sara gravely. 'You are a remarkable woman, Captain.'

'Why am I here?' Sara asked calmly.

'I'm sure you can answer that for yourself, Sara Gideon. You are the largest stockholder in the Gideon Bank, where your grandfather keeps the chairman's seat warm for you while you serve Queen and Country. How much would the bank pay to get you back in one piece? A hundred million sterling, to start with?'

'Oh, a lot more than that. After all, it's mostly *my* money, isn't it?'

'You know, you are absolutely right.' He smiled. 'But what a poor host I am. Sit down, all of you, at the dining table. I gave orders to the chef to provide something, in spite of the lateness of the hour.'

He nodded to Ibrahim, who went and opened the double door at the far end, and four waiters pushed in trolleys and started transferring a range of rice dishes, salads, and baked fish, working fast to lay it all out.

On the other side of the world in Britain, three hours behind Rubat, Charles Ferguson, after a first-class dinner at Chequers with the great and the good, was enjoying a cigar on the garden terrace with Henry Frankel, when the French foreign minister came out, elegant in his black velvet dinner jacket.

'There you are. The Prime Minister sends his apologies. He'll join us when he can. He's speaking to someone at the UN in New York. I've just been talking to my chief secretary in Paris. I'm glad to hear Claude Duval's been able to help you with the Frenchman you were after, Charles.'

'Claude Duval?' Ferguson asked.

'Colonel Duval, DGSE. They've managed a match on some mysterious Frenchman you had a photo of. It seems he is an ex-Foreign Legionnaire, one Henri Legrande, who used to train the IRA, and others of a like persuasion, in a camp in the Algerian desert.'

Henry Frankel murmured, 'You didn't tell me, Charles.'

'More like, someone didn't tell me.' The Prime

Minister looked out, called them in for drinks, and Ferguson whispered to Frankel, 'Make my excuses, I've got a phone call to make.'

He said to Roper, 'So it would appear that the anonymous Frenchman was very real indeed and up to no good?'

'Absolutely, *mea culpa*,' Roper said. 'You had other things on your mind, Cabinet stuff, keeping the politicians happy. That's what it's all about these days. Mind you, it might get you a knighthood.'

'That's damn unfair, Giles. What about this Henri Legrande? Who is he?'

'Has an antiques shop in Shepherd Market. Had Jack Kelly staying with him for a few days. They were responsible for the bomb under Holley's car, among other things.'

'What are you doing about it? Have you pulled him in?'

'I can't do that. Kelly's dead and taken care of by the disposal unit, killed by Dillon after he shot Jean Talbot. Henri Legrande is in Rubat. The unfortunate news is that Sara has been kidnapped at the behest of Ali Selim, who we've traced to Rubat. Holley and Dillon have flown out to Greg Slay in Hazar. Right about now, they're going to descend on Rubat in one of Greg's Scorpion helicopters and try to get her back.'

'Dear God,' Ferguson said. 'They're going in now, you say, and I've just been called in for drinks by the Prime Minister?'

'You do lead a rough old life, Charles. However, to cut to the chase, I wouldn't say a word about this. Just keep your fingers crossed that our gallant lads triumph and bring the girl home safe. That way, you might still have a job.'

'What a comfort you are, Giles. I'll go back in and try to keep smiling.'

When Ferguson returned, everyone was enjoying their drink and listening to the French foreign minister playing Cole Porter numbers on the grand piano. He was doing it rather well, and people joined in with the chorus of 'Night and Day.'

Ferguson pulled Henry Frankel into a corner, who said, 'What on earth is this, Charles?'

'Henry, you've got the biggest mouth on you in Downing Street, perhaps even the House of Commons.'

'Why, Charles, how unkind.'

'Henry, I beg you. No mention of a Foreign Legionnaire who trained the IRA in the Algerian desert, no mention of what a good job Colonel Claude Duval and the DGSE have done for us.'

'You're getting quite intense. Wouldn't it be a good idea to tell me exactly what's going on?'

'While we're living it up, Dillon and Daniel Holley are flying into Rubat to try and save Sara Gideon, who's been kidnapped by Ali Selim's people. That's where the bastard is – Rubat – and guess who's been working with him all along? Owen Rashid, the Sultan's nephew.'

Henry said, 'Is that so?' His smile had no warmth to it at all. 'You know, I never cared for Owen. When you reach my age, it's comforting to know you're right occasionally. However, thank you for the confidence. I realize of course that you are hoping I'll agree not to mention this to the Prime Minister.'

'That was the general idea.'

'Like Sara said, hope for the best and prepare for the worst. Just imagine, we could be both out of a job.'

'Or claiming all the success, as politicians do, if everything succeeds.'

'Exactly.' Henry smiled. 'It's going to be a long night, Charles. Brandy and bridge is my suggestion.'

The Falcon landed, taxied up to Slay's hangar, and parked. He immediately ordered priority refuelling, reminding the tower that it was an Algerian plane on diplomatic business.

In the hangar, they met Feisal, got him to find a blanket, and laid out the weapons. Each of them was wearing a bullet-proof vest, and the personal weapons were the same for each: a Walther and a .25 Colt, an Uzi sub-machine gun – all silent versions – a useful flick-knife for the left boot, a couple of pineapple grenades, Semtex with five-minute pencil timers.

Feisal had gone off to check with the tower, and returned as the refuelling truck finished its work and drove away. The wind was beginning to pick up again, and one could feel the sand.

He came into the comparative warmth of the hangar and found the three men pulling on desert fatigue tunics and loading up the capacious pockets.

'They landed at Rubat just under an hour ago. I have reminded my friend on night dispatch that the Falcon is on an important Algerian diplomatic mission and must be allowed a priority departure when you are ready to leave.'

Greg went out to his office and returned with a small leather purse, which he handed to Feisal. 'If something goes wrong, you must flee at once with your wife and child into the Empty Quarter. In the bag are fifty gold sovereigns, worth a couple of thousand pounds sterling in today's market. You have been a good friend.'

Feisal embraced him. 'My wife is already waiting for me fifteen miles out at the Shaba Oasis with her extended family to protect her, all Rashid Bedu warriors who have no fear where Al Qaeda is concerned.' He smiled. 'So I can take my chances here and wait for you. I have told my friend on night dispatch that you go to Rubat on a medical emergency with drugs.'

'Good man, yourself,' Dillon told him, and turned to the others. 'Here we go, then.'

They went out through the Judas gate, it slammed shut, and the wind rattled the roof, making a strange moaning sound. Then there was the unmistakable clatter of a helicopter starting to move, the sound very powerful, but then fading into the distance as the Scorpion moved away into the night.

Ali Selim sat at the end of the table, Fatima on one side, Sara the other. Owen Rashid and Henri faced each other, and Captain Ahmed and Colonel Khazid were at the far end, Khazid stuffing himself. Five of his men were at a table in the far corner, a waiter ladling some sort of stew to them, and three other waiters stood ready to handle any of the main table's requirements.

So long had it been since she had eaten at all that Sara had accepted what was offered to her, baked fish with rice. Ali Selim said, 'I can't ask if you enjoyed your flight, since you weren't aware that it was happening. It must have been an alarming experience. Tell me about it?'

'Do you really want to know?' she said.

'I do indeed. It's certainly to be preferred to watching two fat swine gorging themselves like pigs at the far end of the table.'

'I'll tell you, then. I believe that what I experienced was very much how death is going to be. I was alive one second when Legrande gave me the needle and then I didn't exist until I came back to life as the plane descended.'

Owen looked uncomfortable, and Henri sat there, face set, as Ali Selim said, 'So you experienced resurrection, which ordinary people don't after they die.'

Fatima's mobile phone sounded. She answered, her look immediately grave, and leaned over and whispered to him. He listened, face expressionless, then raised his hand and called for silence.

He turned to Owen. 'Do you believe in the resurrection, my friend?'

There was total silence. 'I've never given the matter much thought,' Owen said.

'Not even your Christian half, where the Gospels tell us that Christ died and rose again after three days?'

Ibrahim, who had been standing against the wall, eased forward, as if at a signal, and stood behind Owen. Ali Selim said, 'What if I told you the Sultan is dead? Would you be pleased or sad at the prospect of replacing him?'

Owen looked pale and desperate. 'I don't know what you mean.'

Ali Selim nodded. Ibrahim pulled the leather whip from his belt, flung it around Owen's neck, and proceeded to throttle him, jerking his head over the back of the chair.

Sara shouted, 'Stop it, damn you. I don't know what your game is, but it's gone far enough.'

'Quite simple, really,' Ali Selim said, watching Owen coughing and choking as he fought his way back to normality as Ibrahim released him. 'I have provided your resurrection, Owen, so that you may occupy your uncle's place. I'll make your decision, of course, on behalf of Al Qaeda. You'll need to marry, people will expect it. Fatima will make a perfect bride – no problem there, Fatima?'

She was obviously troubled, glanced at Owen for only a moment, then said, 'As you command, master.'

Before he could reply, there was a disturbance down at the far door, as a sailor came in, leaned down, and spoke to Ahmed and Khazid.

Ali Selim called, 'What is it?'

Khazid said, 'There seems to be a helicopter landing somewhere in the town.'

Selim glanced at Fatima. 'Hakim turning up at last, perhaps?' He nodded to Khazid. 'Well, do something useful for once, Colonel, go and investigate.'

'Of course, master,' Khazid gestured to his men, who followed him out, followed by Ahmed. They stood at the rail, listening, but the only sound was the moaning of the wind.

'Maybe it was a mistake,' Ahmed said.

'Perhaps, but the last time I saw him in this kind of mood, Ibrahim strangled the man concerned, then threw him overboard. I prefer to go and check. I'll take one man to pilot the launch and leave the others with you. With sailors, that will give you a dozen men. Tell them to stay alert. I'll be back soon.'

As the Scorpion drifted down over the town, the wind started to blow again. Slay said, 'I was looking this sandstorm business up on screen. It seems there can sometimes be a resurgence pattern where

328

the second shock can be worse than the first, just like an earthquake.'

'Then let's get on with it,' Dillon said. 'Where are we landing?'

Greg Slay said, 'By the cargo hangars at the east end of the pier. I've used it often to pick up stuff that's come in by boat. There's a small police station near it, and the police launches tie up at the steps.'

'How many police?'

'I've never seen more than a handful.'

Dillon pulled a ski mask from his pocket and pulled it on, just the eyes and the gash of the mouth showing. 'Put us down, Greg, and let's get on with it. Maybe we can frighten them to death.'

Holley said, 'Very funny, Sean, but remember where you are. The kind of country where leg irons are a permanent fixture. Torture of every kind is on the menu, and the sexual varieties don't bear thinking about. I'm here to get Sara. I'll kill anyone who gets in my way.'

'All right,' Dillon said, 'we get the point. So let's do it.'

They skimmed flat roofs, noticing that in most places where there was a light it was quickly turned off, dropped in beside the cargo building, hovered and descended. Slay switched off, pulled on a ski mask, pulled an Uzi out of the capacious pocket of his desert fatigues, turned and followed the other two out.

A uniformed policeman with an AK-47 moved out

from behind a container and called out in Arabic, 'Stay where you are and identify yourselves.'

Holley turned, pulled out his silenced Walther, and fired on the instant, knocking the policeman over the edge of the pier and into the water.

'Give the man a coconut,' Dillon said softly, and they paused at the sound of the launch approaching from the *Monsoon*.

'What now?' Slay asked, as they crouched, watching the launch come in, the pilot jump to the pier to the step. Khazid joined him, paused to light a cigarette, then walked towards the police post, the pilot following, opened the front door and entered.

'That was Khazid, the chief of police,' Slay said.

'Excellent,' Holley said. 'And as he's just over from the dhow, he'll be able to tell us exactly what's going on out there.'

He ran towards the police post, flung open the front door, and rushed inside. Khazid was handing out cigarettes to his pilot and four others, and they all turned in alarm.

'Who are you? What is this?' Khazid demanded in Arabic.

Holley took a step towards him, pulled the Walther from his pocket, and struck him across the face. Khazid cried out and fell back across a desk.

'We've come for the English woman,' Holley said. 'She only arrived an hour or so ago, so tell me the truth or I'll kill you.' That his threat was delivered in Arabic made it even more impressive.

Khazid, fear of Ali Selim heavily on his mind, moaned and said, 'What are you talking about? This is madness. Captain Slay, why are you mixed up in this?'

One of the policemen at the back of the group made a move to draw his pistol from its holster, and Slay knocked him back against the wall with a blast from the Uzi. It was enough, and those unharmed put their hands on their heads.

'Tell him,' someone called.

So Khazid did. What was happening on the *Monsoon*, who was on board – everything. Someone passed him a towel, which he held to his broken face.

Holley said, 'This is how it goes. You and your pilot will take us to the dhow in the launch and we'll go on board to retrieve the woman. The slightest thing you do wrong, you die. Is this understood?'

'We will do as you say.'

'We'll have three of those police oilskins so we look right on the launch. You and the pilot will handcuff the others, put them in leg irons and then lock them in a cell. Anyone who causes trouble will be shot instantly.'

The pilot, a wild young man, looked angry, but Khazid put a hand on his arm. 'Do as you are told and help me, Abdul, that's an order.'

The pilot nodded reluctantly. 'If you say so, Colonel.'

⋆   ⋆   ⋆

331

The gunplay so far had been with silenced weapons, so there had been no cause for alarm for Captain Ahmed, the three sailors and four policemen standing at the rail, watching the launch come in.

One of the sailors said, 'The colonel appears to be bringing more police with him.'

'I don't see anyone I know,' Ahmed said. 'Who are they?'

It was at that moment that Abdul, the pilot, angry and dissatisfied with the turn of events in the launch, grabbed for the very light signalling pistol that hung by the open starboard window. He reached out, raised the pistol and fired, the flare soaring into the night sky, illuminating everything in harsh white light.

He shouted at the top of his voice, 'They come for the English woman! Slay and his friends!'

Captain Ahmed ran away along the deck, and Holley clubbed Abdul across the side of his head, and, as he went down, Slay grabbed the wheel. There was still some way to go, and shots rang out, and a bullet punched through the windshield.

'Keep down,' he said to the others. 'I'll go in fast, then swerve up close. A couple of grenades might give them something to think about.'

'You're on,' Dillon said.

They all crouched, Dillon pulling Khazid down, and Slay pushed the launch as hard as it would go, aiming for the landing platform, turning at the last moment so Dillon and Holley could lob over two pineapple grenades. There were cries of dismay, men running to get away from the carnage. Slay brought the launch in again, bouncing against the landing platform. Dillon and Holley jumped to the deck, guns blazing, cutting some of the police and crew down, while others, shocked by the ferocity of the attack, turned and fled. Slay leapt on to the platform, the painter in one hand, and looped it over a hook to hold the launch ready against their departure.

He turned to see Khazid cowering back in the boat and shouted to him, 'Get up here – now!'

Suddenly Khazid was knocked out of the way by Abdul, the pilot, blood on his face and the signalling pistol in his right hand. As he raised it, Dillon, above him at the rail, fired a long burst with his Uzi that knocked him back over the side of the launch, the pistol discharging so that the flare glowed white hot under dark water for a moment before being extinguished.

Slay grabbed Khazid by the front of his tunic and said again, 'Get up here.'

Khazid was half-sobbing, and Dillon reached down and pulled him up. Someone was firing from along the deck, AK-47 shots that you *could* hear. 'Together,' he said, as he scrambled up with Holley and Slay, and they loosed off long bursts, sweeping the decks clear toward the prow.

There was only silence up there now and Holley pushed Khazid in the direction of the stern. 'You know where we want to be, so just take us there, if you want to live, that is.'

The sound of shooting had everyone at the dining table jumping to their feet, and Ahmed burst in through the door from the deck.

'Captain Slay is here – Slay from Hazar – with others. They say they have come for the English woman.'

A burst from Dillon's Uzi drove him headlong to his knees at the end of the table, and the police there fired back with their AK-47s. One of them fell sideways to the floor close to Henri Legrande, who drew his Beretta.

He said to Owen, 'I shouldn't imagine we'd get anywhere shouting, "I surrender" to these people. Are you armed?'

'I've never had to be.'

Henri leaned down and pulled a Makarov from the dead policeman's holster. He passed it across. 'Nine shots, make them count.'

At that moment, Slay, on the deck outside, fired through a porthole window, a sustained burst that hurled both men back across the table, killing them instantly.

Ibrahim was at the deck entrance with his AK-47, Ali Selim firing a pistol he had produced from under his robe. Seeing what had happened to Owen and Henri, he turned to Ibrahim, taking another magazine from his pocket and reloading.

'The women, Ibrahim, into the owner's quarters.

I'll follow you. We can get away from this mess in the stern launch.'

Fatima hurried ahead, pulling Sara behind her, and when she tried to struggle, Ibrahim gave her a heavy slap across the side of her head. Fatima got the wide mahogany door open to the bedrooms and pulled Sara in, Ibrahim at their heels.

The police and crew at the far end of the dining table had taken heavy casualties, and now Greg Slay, Dillon, and Holley rushed in low, sweeping the room, the men who were still standing dropping their weapons and raising their hands. Only one man was still on his feet with a weapon in his hand, and it was Ali Selim.

He levelled his pistol at Dillon and shot him twice in the chest, which because of the nylon-and-titanium vest Dillon was wearing only succeeded in knocking him down. Holley, in turn, emptied the magazine of his Uzi into him, throwing Selim backwards and close to the open door to the owner's quarters, where Ibrahim, Sara, and Fatima could see him as he fell.

'He's dead,' Ibrahim said, kicking the door shut, as Holley and Slay pulled Dillon to his feet.

Fatima cried out as Ibrahim locked the door. 'No, you can't leave him like that,' she cried in Arabic.

He knocked her down with a punch to the face. She rolled over, then got to her feet, a small pistol in her hand. Without the slightest hesitation, he pulled a Makarov out of his sash and shot her dead.

He turned, a figure of total menace, and spoke to Sara in English. 'The small door in the corner opens to steps leading down to the stern. A launch is moored there, which is how we shall depart.' He went and opened it. 'Lead the way.'

There was a kick on the other door. She said, 'Like hell I will.'

Ibrahim slapped her face, his fingers tightened on the hair, and he pulled her close. 'You will obey me by the time I finish with you.' He laughed, his head back, as a thunderous knocking sounded.

'I don't think so.' Her right hand found the knife that Henri Legrande had given her. She pressed the button, springing the razor-sharp blade, and stabbed Ibrahim under the chin, the blade shearing up through the roof of the mouth into the brain. His eyes burned into her, he started to fold, his hands clutching at her, the door crashed open, and Holley and Slay rushed in. Sara pushed, and he went down.

She stood there, looking at her hands, which were covered in blood, and Holley and Slay pulled off their ski masks. She gazed at them wildly. 'God knows how you managed it. I really *was* facing the prospect of a fate worse than death with this animal.'

She stirred Ibrahim with her foot, and Holley pulled his camouflage scarf off and wiped the blood from her hands. 'You don't need to worry about anything now.'

'Neither does she.' She looked down at Fatima. 'Poor girl, she really believed in it all, and in the end this is where it got her.' Holley led her out to where Dillon was taking photos of Ali Selim. 'What's the point of that?' she asked.

'Proof that it's him and that he's dead,' Dillon said. 'Otherwise, no one will believe it.'

'Are you okay, Sean?' Holley asked, and said to Sara, 'Ali Selim shot him twice.'

'Which I've survived, thanks to my titanium vest, and not for the first time. But I think we'd better get moving. Wouldn't you agree, Greg?'

'Absolutely,' Slay said. 'Back to Hazar as fast as possible.'

There were bodies aplenty, but those who had surrendered had disappeared. They closed around Sara and proceeded cautiously, and just before they reached the launch someone fired a rifle from up ahead. Dillon and Holley immediately sprayed the area, while Slay escorted Sara down to the boat and turned on the engine.

Holley still fired short bursts into the darkness, and Dillon heaved open a hatch cover, revealing steps down into some sort of hold. He produced a Semtex block from his tunic pocket, stuck in a five-minute pencil timer, primed it, and dropped the block into darkness.

'Let's get out of here,' he said, and as Holley went down, hurried after him, unhooking the painter, the launch surging ahead as it picked up speed and made for the pier.

As they turned alongside and disembarked, there was a low, deep rumble as the Semtex exploded in the depths of the dhow. They hurried to the Scorpion, embarked quickly and were taking off in minutes, Slay making a close pass over the *Monsoon* as flames started to eat through the wooden decks. There were men down there, leaping into the sea in life jackets.

'Not that they deserve it, but they'll be fine,' Slay said. 'The sea is nice and warm and not renowned for sharks. The sheikh who owns *Monsoon* is a billionaire. All that oil, you see. He probably didn't even bother to insure it.'

He took the Scorpion round on a curve, climbing to a thousand feet and heading fast across the desert to Hazar.

EPILOGUE

They landed outside Slay's hangar thirty minutes later and found Feisal waiting. He was excited and greeted Slay, smiling. 'A big success, I think, when I see the lady.' He nodded to Sara. 'But my friend in the tower speaks of a big disturbance in Rubat, a dhow sinking in the harbour. As there is no traffic at the moment, he suggests you get out of here in the Falcon while you still can. After all, Hazar and Rubat have no air force to go after you.'

'I'd say that's sound advice,' Holley said.

'There is one more suggestion he has to make,' Feisal said. 'The presence of a Scorpion helicopter has been noted. Some individuals who have met violent ends are policemen. Better for you, Captain Slay, to be on the Falcon when it leaves.'

'Wonderful,' Slay said. 'When you think how much I've ploughed into this business. But I must admit it would be sensible to vacate the premises while I still can.'

Sara slipped a hand in his arm. 'When you think that Ali Selim was expecting to get at least a hundred million sterling for me, Greg, I would imagine the board of the Gideon Bank would consider financial compensation to you for your loss to be cheap at the price.'

'Well, that's a comfort,' Greg said.

So it was that the Falcon jet took off twenty minutes later, climbing very quickly. Feisal Rashid, a Bedu from deep in the Empty Quarter and, for a time, an aircraft mechanic, watched it go with some sadness, then packed anything he thought was worth taking, including some interesting weaponry, in the remaining jeep and left to join his beloved wife at Shaba Oasis.

With Greg Slay on the flight deck, Holley sat with Sara, having coffee and considering what had happened. The pieces all fitted for her like a jigsaw. Owen Rashid's Al Qaeda connection, the Henri Legrande and Jack Kelly affair so important. Without it, Sara Gideon would have been a prisoner of Al Qaeda now. And then there was Jean Talbot who had done the right, if dangerous, thing and taken a bullet doing it.

It was all rather moving, and she turned to Holley. 'Can I borrow your Codex? I think I'll make my usual false report to Sadie and Granddad.'

'Of course.' He gave it to her. 'How are you feeling?'

'It still hasn't sunk in properly that I wakened from a deep sleep and found myself living a nightmare. Then you lot just appearing from nowhere like you did.'

'Thank God we were able to.'

She smiled. 'I'll make the call from the loo. I'll see you soon.'

Holley sat there in the dim light, half-dozing. It was half an hour before she returned. 'Everything okay?' he asked.

'Sadie was in bed, having an early night. The baby is good; the mother still under the weather, and Granddad was marking papers. He seems to be really enjoying the academic life. I have not been honest with them, Daniel, but on the other hand, the life I've been living would be totally incomprehensible to them, and I wouldn't want them to know anyway. The continual stress would be too much of a problem.'

'But not for you, I think,' Holley said. 'Just look at you. Fully in control, in spite of what you've been through. Heavy-duty stuff, Sara.'

'Do you find that hard to take?'

'I'd have killed Ibrahim myself without a moment's hesitation. It's interesting that you can do the same, that's all, and leave it behind.'

'Well, I can,' she said. 'Although it helps when the opposition are bad people.'

Holley said, 'I remember that Dillon told me once that there are two kinds of actor. The majority take the role home with them, and a minority can switch it on, then off again, no problem.'

'So what are we?' she demanded.

He smiled. 'Probably people who think that life is just like a movie.'

'What a good idea,' she said, and Dillon raised his voice. 'I'm going to call Roper and report in. I'll put my Codex on speaker so if anyone wants to listen, feel free.'

He went through everything that had happened. When he finished, Roper said, 'A triumph from our point of view, not least that we got Sara back in one piece. It's also good to know that the Gideon Bank will do right by Gregory Slay, whose sterling service, by the way, has earned him a recall to the Army Air Corps in the rank of Major. We've dealt Al Qaeda's London operations a crushing blow. Ali Selim dead. His unwilling accomplice, Owen Rashid, also dead. Henri Legrande, Jack Kelly. Our thanks to Professor Jean Talbot. I think we may have made a friend there—'

Holley cut in, 'What's the story that's being given out on Ali Selim's death?'

'Al Qaeda is huge in Yemen, as the world knows, and there is constant feuding between dissident groups, especially since the death of Osama bin Laden. The fighting on this occasion has obviously spilled over into Rubat, and Ali Selim seems to have been a victim.'

'I like it,' Dillon said. 'A convincing explanation. That's all the newspapers want, to say nothing of television.'

'Which leaves us with just one other matter. In view of the exceptional stress experienced by Captain Sara Gideon recently, the Prime Minister raised the question with General Ferguson if she was fit for purpose militarily.'

'Fit for purpose?' Sara frowned. 'Of course I am.'

'I'm sure the Prime Minister will be glad to hear that. General Ferguson even more so, since he wishes you to continue your posting to his unit for the full two years.'

'I thought that was the idea!' She was beginning to get angry.

Roper said, 'We are, in effect, the Prime Minister's private army, which makes working at Holland Park a security issue, that's all. But now that's settled. Just one more thing. The safety of you and your colleagues would be compromised by any kind of media coverage of your activities, so I'm afraid your Military Cross won't be listed. They'll send it to you, of course.'

'So I don't get it at Buckingham Palace?'

'Definitely not. This is Britain. Women aren't supposed to be war heroes,' Roper told her, with a certain irony.

'Tell that to those girls driving trucks in night convoys in Afghanistan at eighteen or nineteen. They all deserve a medal. General Charles Ferguson and the PM can go to hell. But I'll be at my desk in the morning.'

'I will, Sara,' Roper told her, and went.

Holley said, 'At least another six hours to London, if not more.'

'Then let's try and sleep through it. Dim the lights, Daniel. Do you mind?'

343

'Of course not.'

He did as she had asked; she snuggled against him, closing her eyes and yawning. 'I like having an older guy as a boyfriend.'

'And I like you liking it,' he replied, closing his eyes also, as the Falcon droned on into the night.

Roper sat in front of his screens drinking whiskey and thinking of what had happened. Everything fitted and it all made sense, except for the ending. His main screen rippled for a moment, then produced Ferguson sitting at a desk. When he spoke, his voice boomed out.

'How did she take it?'

'Badly, but she'll be at her desk tomorrow. You really can be a sod, Charles.'

'I just wanted to be sure that her heart was in the job, which it obviously is. So we can put my contingency plan into operation. At Clarence House on Tuesday morning, she'll receive her Military Cross in strictest secrecy from His Royal Highness, Prince Charles.'

Roper was astounded. 'Are you sure about this?'

'Of course I am. I spoke to him about Sara the moment we got back from New York. He told me it would give him enormous pleasure.'

'And you can do that?' Roper asked.

Charles Ferguson smiled wolfishly. 'My dear Giles, I would have thought you would have realized by now that I can do anything.'